P9-CFD-776

KINGS *of* COLORADO

David E. Hilton

SIMON & SCHUSTER
NEW YORK LONDON TORONTO SYDNEY

Simon & Schuster
1230 Avenue of the Americas
New York, NY 10020

This book is a work of fiction. Names, characters, places, and incidents either are products of the author's imagination or are used fictitiously. Any resemblance to actual events or locales or persons, living or dead, is entirely coincidental.

First Simon & Schuster hardcover edition January 2011

Designed by Akasha Archer

Manufactured in the United States of America

10 9 8 7 6 5 4 3 2 1

Library of Congress Cataloging-in-Publication Data

Hilton, David E.
Kings of Colorado : a novel / by David E. Hilton.
p. cm.
1. Teenage boys—Fiction. 2. Juvenile delinquents—Fiction. 3. Abused teenagers—Fiction. 4. Reformatories—Fiction. 5. Horses—Training—Fiction. 6. Human-animal relationships—Fiction. 7. Ranch life—Colorado—Fiction. 8. Colorado—Fiction. 9. Psychological fiction. 10. Bildungsromans. I. Title.
PS3608.I466K56 2011
813'.6—dc22 2010019691

ISBN 978-1-4391-8382-3
ISBN 978-1-4391-8384-7 (ebook)

for my boys, Drew and Cameron

KINGS *of* COLORADO

CHAPTER

one

In the summer of 1963, when I was thirteen, I stabbed my father in the chest with a Davy Crockett Explorers pocketknife. That was almost fifty years ago. I suppose I might as well be truthful with you and say that I only feel empty whenever I think back on it all.

It's a sad thing when a man keeps the most important things in his past locked tightly away, only to forget about how, for a time, they were all he cared about—all that shaped his life and made him who he was—but that's exactly what I did. I think sometimes a person even begins to forget what lies beyond that locked door of dead memories. And, sometimes, that door's been kicked in, and whether you want to or not, you do remember. That's what happened today.

The elevator doors parted to a hurricane of activity. There were gasps and shouting. People were running across the long marble floor of the lobby, eyes wide. Just outside the tall glass doors of the building's façade, a crowd gathered.

There had been an accident.

A pickup truck pulling a horse trailer had been sideswiped by a black Land Rover. The horse trailer, taking the brunt of the crash, lay flipped over. Inside was a beautiful white mare, struggling, dying. No police cars. No sirens. The driver of the mashed-in pickup sat on the street, holding his arm and looking dazed. A few people thumbed 911 on their phones, others just stared, not knowing what to do. The door of the trailer hung open, dangling, and the mare lay halfway out, its hindquarters in the trailer, its front on the smeared pavement. She tried to lift her head; the rest of her wouldn't budge. Her back was unnaturally twisted, but it was the sight of blood pooling onto the pavement below her mouth that stuck with me. The mare's large, frantic black eyes darted about the chaotic city center.

I ran to her, pushing through the crowd. "No," I whispered, dropping to my knees, moving my hand along her neck. She whinnied and more blood came. A moan, almost human, ripped from the animal's chest, and again she tried to raise her head. She was dying, and there was nothing in the world I could do about it except be there with her.

She tried a final time to force her body up, and she cried out again. Her deep and heavy breathing began to weaken. And then it stopped.

I hugged the animal as tightly as I could, and wept for her. Maybe I was making a spectacle of myself but I didn't care. In that moment, the people and places I'd long kept behind those locked doors resurfaced and I was flooded with the past.

CHAPTER

two

THE SKY BLOOMS, AND THUNDER ECHOES JUST BEHIND, STRETCHing out until I think it's not going to end. In the thick of the slicing rain and blasts of wind, the limbs of the oak outside my bedroom window rise and fall, and scratch at the glass with crooked fingers. It sounds like a bitch of a storm.

But it wasn't the storm that woke me. I'd been tormented by the vision of the dying mare all evening. Twisted, broken, struggling for breath. I think I was even dreaming about her. Her, and the secrets of my past.

I woke in a cold sweat and grasped my knee. I tried to remain still—to ignore the pain, and fall back asleep. Sometimes, I lie awake for hours this way. I could take something for the pain, but you should see how many pills I'm already on these days. I always wonder what would happen if I just stopped taking them. I can feel the pain in all my joints, but it's always sharpest behind my left shoulder. I can just reach it if I stretch backward enough and find the thick line of scar tissue.

My doctor says it's the onset of arthritis, and more than once he's suggested I move away from the cold Chicago climate. Somewhere dry, out west. That's easy for him to say; he's forty. I can't just leave and start over. Not at my age. Not alone.

There aren't new beginnings for men like me, but there are endings. Today, before the crowd and the blood and the horse, the insurance firm where I've worked for twenty-three years sent me a letter informing me I was part of their generic personnel reduction. It actually said that in the letter: "generic personnel reduction." I guess it was supposed to be more impersonal than indifferent, but it was both.

I suppose they didn't have to think too hard about whom to let go when it came time to downsize. I haven't exactly been an outstanding employee. Things have been hard for me the past couple of years; more and more, I found myself merely floating by, doing only what was necessary to keep from raising any eyebrows. Toward the end, I felt more like a ghost: lonely and invisible. Frankly, I'm surprised I made it this long.

This morning, as I cleaned out my desk, I received two visitors. The first was our receptionist, Wanda Bratcher. She's been at the firm almost as long as me. She stumbled through wishing me well, topping it off with an unexpected but heartfelt embrace. And when she squeezed her thin arms around me and whispered, "Good luck out there, William Sheppard," I felt like a prisoner being released back into the throes of society.

The second person was Ronald Perkins. He was perhaps the only coworker I could call a friend, though we really only spoke at the office. He, too, was serving out his last day. Ronald is a squat fellow who always relishes breaking bad news. It's really too bad he wasn't able to self-deliver his own termination.

"I've been thinking about time, man."

I lied, and told him I had not.

"Nev Lewis and Jeff Morgan thought about time, I'll bet you. Maybe it's better we didn't."

Each had retired the previous spring, and each had died shortly thereafter.

The rest of my day was mostly what I expected. A small group of coworkers took me to lunch and gave me a card with a bunch of signatures; some names I knew, others didn't trigger an honest clue. There were a lot of handshakes and slaps on the back. A lot of "good lucks," each one a reminder that I would sure as hell need it.

I was in the same sinking boat as Ronald Perkins. I could search up and down for another job, but I doubted there would be much opportunity for a sixty-two-year-old who could have already said uncle and retired. I'll admit it: I was afraid. I didn't want to become a feeble old man who sits on his couch all day watching countless loops of the Weather Channel.

Now, looking at the stark red numbers on the clock on my nightstand, I know this is not going to be a night I fall back asleep. This night is different. Tonight is for closure. Tonight it ends.

I fumble with the small lamp on the bedside table and long shadows reach across the room. There's a tin box on the nightstand. I take it, turn it over in my fingers, and listen to its contents slide and clink. Years ago, that little box lay tucked away on a shelf high in my bedroom closet, calling to me only on occasion. Now it is more of a night-light in my dark world, a comfort upon which I've grown quite dependent.

Too much has happened.

The sound of snapping bone comes from outside the window, and I feel a branch collapsing onto the house. I hear a ghost whisper, *"Go on, Lunch. Climb that bastard. Climb it, before I shoot you dead."*

Seeing the dying horse stirred the once locked and haunted memories of my past. Memories of those I once called my closest friends. And the one friend who still grips me.

MY SMALL CLAPBOARD HOUSE ON MAPLEWOOD AVENUE FEELS empty and cold. It didn't always feel this way, only since Mina died, four years ago. We tried for so long to have children, until the doctors told us it was my fault we couldn't conceive. Mina was strong, and never once said a negative word about it. She didn't have to; I saw the hurt in her eyes. Adoption? I don't know—we married late, on the verge of middle age. After years of trying the old-fashioned way, we felt we were just too old, and maybe it wasn't meant to be. Sounds silly, I guess, but it's the truth.

So we pressed on with our lives, enjoying every single minute. We never worried about all the small potatoes—mortgages, bills, gossip, so forth and so on. None of that meant shit. Sure there were bad times, and fights. But we also held hands, and we laughed. I played my Miles Davis albums on Saturday nights and we danced by candlelight. We did this for eighteen years, and it never got old. Never. She was my only family, and I miss her. But saying that doesn't really come close to describing a damn thing.

Tonight, I had the unmistakable feeling she was lying next to me in bed. I felt her warmth. I must have been dreaming of her, but then I heard a low voice from my past: *"Climb it, before I shoot you dead."*

I've known for some time what was coming, the decision I was going to make. And today, watching that beautiful horse suffering made me see what has held me back for all these years. For all my life.

I go to Mina's curio desk in the corner of the bedroom and take out a ream of notebook paper. The thought of putting my childhood down on paper scares the shit out of me. It will turn into something real, then. Something you can hold in your hands instead of dismissing as nothing but fiction. But it's the thought of an ending without closure that bothers me the most.

I don't care who might read these pages; I'm doing this for myself. Maybe if I get it all down right, I'll have executed some sort of justice, gotten some revenge, even. Not for myself, but for those I once called friends.

There's a quote I like. I copied it from a novel years ago. I don't remember who wrote it, but I scribbled the words on a napkin and tucked them away. It goes like this:

"Some stories are rooted in adventure, some in strife. Others are born of the heart, and the horrors and the joys locked therein are often immeasurable, and make us truly wonder what became of those children we once were."

When I was thirteen, I stabbed my father in the chest.

That's where I'll begin.

CHAPTER
three

I GREW UP IN IRISH CHICAGO; BRIDGEPORT, SPECIFICALLY. YOU learn a lot about life growing up on the South Side, and in the early sixties, I learned how to survive. I've tried hard to forget much of my early childhood, but I still remember the beatings. In fact, it's harder for me to recall the times my old man was sober than to remember him drunk. Or with a belt in his hand and the stink of liquor on his breath. Straight whiskey was his usual, and to this day my stomach churns at the smell of it.

He was a short man. Broad in the shoulders and thick across the chest. His eyes were so dark the pupils almost blended into the irises. He had thick, strong arms, and rough hands. Me—I mostly inherited my mother's features. Lean. Fair-skinned. I even had her wavy hair. My father always called me names like Sissy and Queer, which I never understood; I loved to play ball in the street with my friends, and I thought Carrie Francello, the girl who lived across the hall, was the prettiest thing I'd ever laid eyes on.

On most occasions, it took very little to provoke him—maybe I'd left a comic book on the floor, or spilled a glass of milk.

"Out, William!" he'd yell. "Out for your whippin'!" And Jesus,

Mary, and Joseph, you better believe if I didn't go out and face him, the hell would be ten times worse.

On my tenth birthday, he broke my arm. My mother was out picking up my birthday cake from Gillpatrick's, and Mrs. Francello found me crying under the stairs. She scooped me up in her arms and carried me four blocks to the doctor. It was an incredible act of kindness, but a socially bold move nonetheless. Back then, it was taboo for people in my neighborhood to interfere in other people's business.

My best friend was Jimmy Curio. We weren't blood brothers or anything stupid like that, but in all the vacant lot ball games, I played second and he played short, and most every time I found myself in deep shit, he was usually right there with me. Sometimes I slept over at his place, when his parents weren't fighting. He asked me one day how I could stand it, all the abuse from my old man. It's funny, because I was so used to things at home, I didn't know what he meant at first. He said if it were him, he'd have already run away. Or killed the bastard. He laughed when he said that, like maybe it was a joke or something. I got embarrassed and just changed the subject, asking him if he thought Carrie Francello would ever let me kiss her on the mouth. But what Jimmy said stuck in my head, kept me up most nights, wondering to God why I *hadn't* done anything.

I think now a lot of it has to do with my mom. That sounds absurd, but it's true. Back then, I could hardly swing a stick without wondering what she'd think. I know that makes it out like I was a momma's kid—and I don't know, maybe I was—but it was more than that. You see, without even meaning to, I'd fallen into a protective role with her. Often trying to save her from anything and everything, and to somehow salvage our family.

For me, the constant struggle of my youth revolved around which inner emotion won out: the instinct to protect my mother, or the absolute terror of my old man. Too many times, fear prevailed.

Christmas Eve, 1962. I came home to the sound of her sobbing, crying out in a subdued voice. It came from down the hall, from the bedroom, and from the assault of liquor in the air, I knew Dad had come home early. Her words were muffled, like she was face-first into a pillow, but the closer I crept down the hallway, the more I caught. I heard my name. And in between all the no's and the pleases, she cried something about me not seeing; something about waiting until I left. The door wasn't even shut all the way, and I gave in to temptation, wanting to go a little farther, to see what he was doing to her.

Another sound. He'd hit her, and she'd cried out. I inched closer to the crack in the doorway, and leaned to see what was happening, to see if I could help. I caught sight of his arm, coming down on her, striking once more. His other hand held a fistful of my mother's hair. She was bleeding, pleading for him to stop.

I was twelve, and felt as helpless as ever. I retreated to the family room, biting my lip and rubbing tears from my eyes. I went to the record player, set the needle on Mom's prized Bing Crosby holiday vinyl, and crouched to the floor beside the Christmas tree. The room was filled with the music of "Silent Night," but I could still hear my father grunting, and my mother sobbing. It was quieter now, and I knew she was crying into the mattress, not wanting me to hear. I tried to drive it all from my mind, and heard the words of Jimmy Curio instead. How he'd have already run away—or maybe done something else.

Later that night, my mother avoided me. I went to bed early, but just before I turned out the light, she knocked on my door. I tried not to look at her, at the way her lip had split, the way the bruise on her eye was both purple and yellow. She kissed me on the forehead, and must have seen the look on my face.

"He's a good man, William. It was . . . my fault."

I closed my eyes, and pretended she hadn't come in at all. I promised myself that night that I would protect her if she wouldn't do it herself.

THEN, THE NEXT SUMMER—JUST SEVERAL WEEKS BEFORE THE START of the new school year—it happened. One night in August, my father came home from Milligan's, down on Thirty-first, stumbled through the door, and started another row with Mom. Dinner, for which he was two hours late, lay cold on the table.

"The hell good are ya if ya can't keep the focking food warm?" he slurred, and enunciated the point with a backhand to her jaw. "Worken my ass off and I'm greeted with cold meals?" This time he open-handed her, bloodying her nose. She shrieked and dropped to the floor, shielding her face with her arms. In one trembling hand she clutched a long strand of rosary beads, and I can still see them jerking through the air with each frightened block. She cried out his name again and again, but he never backed off. His blurred mind was too far gone. When I peeked from my cracked-open bedroom door, I saw him kicking at her like she was nothing more than a mangy dog. There was such anger in his face. Then I saw my mother's panic-stricken eyes, wishing me away from behind the crisscrossed fingers of her shaking hands.

"Just have to teach you another lesson, won't I, love?" He picked up a pot of cold ravioli from the stovetop and slung the food at her. Then he swung the cast-iron pot against her arm. As soon as I heard the crack, my stomach tightened.

He held the pot in a clenched, shaking fist, ready for another go.

Acting purely on instinct, I took the first thing I saw from the top of my bureau. It was lying innocently enough next to my tattered pack of Bicycle cards. "Get away from her," I said.

The rim of that pot, so close to smashing into my mother's face, lowered. He stopped, blinked, and turned.

"Oh, you're next. And ya better pray to Jaysis I—"

"I do pray," I said in a small voice. I walked toward him. It was the first time I'd resisted him. He just stood there, holding that pot. I like to think he wasn't sure how to react. I moved my hand from behind my back and that's when he first saw the opened pocketknife. A color drawing of Davy Crockett wearing a coonskin cap was on each side of the knife's bone casing. Ironically, it had been a gift from my father, that very last Christmas.

He jerked his arm in self-defense, and the iron pot crashed to the floor. My mother screamed. Lashing in fury, I thrust out my arm. Then my father screamed. The blade penetrated his left side. I grabbed the knife and it slipped easily into my hand, almost as if his body had spit it out. The blood was immediate. I didn't hesitate to punch in the knife once more, just below his underarm. This time, it lodged. I continued my attack, now with only my fists.

"Don't ever touch me again! Don't ever touch my mother! We don't love you anymore so just leave! Oh, dammit, just *leave*!"

It felt like minutes had passed, but that couldn't be right. Much too quickly, a firm set of hands violently yanked me back.

"What have you done, boy? God's name have you done?"

It was Arnold Francello, Carrie's dad. My fury softened, replaced by the stinging reality of what I *had* done.

There on the floor before us, my father lay in a spreading dark pool of his own blood, still trying to clutch at the knife, and failing each time. My mother shrieked again, and hovered over him, cupping his face in her hands. She looked back at me just once, and the look in her eyes struck me to the core. It was brief, but I'll never forget the hatred that was there.

"How could you, William! Oh, *Jesus*! How could you!" She kissed my father on the forehead, just as she had kissed me last Christmas Eve after he'd raped her.

"Come with me, boy," Mr. Francello said, and pulled me away. I wanted to say something, to make her understand I was protecting her. Saving her. But nothing I could have said at that second would have mattered; nothing could have kept her from doting on him as though the most precious thing in her life were fading.

I didn't feel betrayed. It would have been easy to let that feeling creep into my heart, but what pressed into me instead was nothing more than pity for her. And that hurt even more.

CHAPTER *four*

On September 7, 1963, I left for Swope Ranch Boys' Reformatory in Colorado. I was put onto a long silver-sided bus with blue stripes at the Greyhound terminal over at Clark and Randolph. There hadn't been much of a send-off party—Jimmy was there, hands in pockets. My mother stood beside me on the verge of tears, fidgeting with my collar like I was about to leave for summer camp instead of juvy. I kept watching for Carrie Francello to appear, maybe to give me that kiss on the mouth I'd always dreamed about—but she never came.

There wasn't much to say. We all understood the more we talked, the more we'd probably just break down and start crying. Jimmy said, "You'll be fine. I'll keep your glove oiled." I guess he just didn't know what else to throw out. Who could blame him?

"Be strong," my mother said. It had been almost four weeks since everything happened, but I could still see the ghosts of bruises lining her face. The cast on her arm stood out in stark contrast to the navy dress she wore that day, and I wanted to tell her I'd done it for her. The way she'd looked at me that night, with the hate in her eyes—she never apologized for that. She never told me she was proud of me.

"And do your best," she said. It was something a guy might hear heading out the door on the first day of school. I hugged her, still seeking her approval. Always—seeking her approval. She began to cry then. With her good arm, she held me, and then pulled me tighter.

"Will you be okay?" I asked.

She never answered. She just held me close, sensing the time had come.

I'd been assigned an escort. An officer who would ride beside me the entire way. He wore an expensive-looking suit, and smelled like cedar shavings. He rapped his knuckles on the side of the bus. "It's time, ma'am."

Jimmy tipped his hat the way Mantle might, but my mother just stood there, staring at me as the officer led me onto the bus. She never said anything more. She just stared, as though she thought she might never see me again.

HIS NAME WAS RHYMES, BUT IN MY HEAD I SECRETLY NAMED HIM Pissed-Off; for the entirety of the trip, he acted as if he'd never been so inconvenienced in his life. He spoke to me only twice—once to tell me to stop leaning against him while I slept, and a second time simply to tell me to shut up. Other than that, there wasn't much else to remember of him.

I closed my eyes and leaned my head against the window. I thought about the whirlwind that had been the last four weeks.

It took the doctors two tries to finally set my mother's arm right; the bone had snapped completely in two. At the sentencing, she wept silently in the back of the courtroom. I stared at the rigid cast that ran the length of her arm. All her bruises were in full bloom, and it looked like Sonny Liston had done a number on both eyes. This pitiful creature surely wasn't my mother, but my broken heart told me otherwise.

My father suffered a punctured lung as a result of the pocketknife, but he didn't die—although I later found out he'd come as close as you can get. I think all of that anger helped him to stick it out. My mother said he was in surgery for more than four hours; apparently, the doctors had a hell of a time stopping the internal bleeding.

During my hearing, I stayed in a juvenile facility, which, all in all, I might as well just call jail. I had a cell with a single bunk and a wool blanket, an uncomfortable metal commode, and a door of heavy iron bars.

It wasn't until the nighttime that reality struck, and I struggled to hide my tears. It's funny how in a place like that I still had my dignity, but I did. It all felt wrong. I wasn't supposed to be there. I was a good kid. Just twenty-four hours earlier I had been listening to "The Phantom" on our family's AM radio and reading a *Batman* comic.

When the judge handed down my sentence, he might as well have punched me in the gut. That's exactly how it felt. There was no emotion in his voice when he said it; he didn't even look at me. I was to be sent to the Colorado reformatory for a period not to exceed twenty-four months. Two years of my life—gone. Just like that.

On the block were two brothers in cells across from mine. Their last name was Cofresi, and one looked old enough to buy drinks at Milligan's, with the other not far behind. Immediately after the judge's ruling, I learned two things from them. First, I could've been thrown a damn longer sentence. The older guy wore his hair slicked back, and according to him, a kid my age had just landed six years for holding up a Harold's Chicken Shack and shooting the manager in the leg. They said if I'd waited until sixteen to stab my old man, I'd have found my ass in Joliet Prison for five good ones, maybe longer.

The second thing was that Swope Ranch Boys' Reformatory was an honest-to-God nightmare. The younger brother went on and on about their cousin who'd spent eight months out there. He was never the same after coming back. Said the kid got kicked in the head while trying to saddle a horse, and from then on would often black out for minutes, having no idea what the hell just happened. Sometimes he even pissed himself, not being any the wiser. His parents just thanked God he made it back in one piece; there were rumors about guys trucking up to the joint and never coming back at all.

IT TOOK US TWO DAYS TO REACH THE RANCH IN GUNNISON COUNTY. The nighttime was the hardest. It was lonely to see the world outside my window cloaked in darkness; during the daylight hours, watching the land slip past was my only escape.

In my thirteen years, I had never ventured outside Chicago, so seeing the peaks of Colorado seemed about as foreign as seeing the jungles of Africa. I looked out the window as the bus weaved its way up through the Rocky Mountains, mere inches from the edge of the road, and saw nothing below. I was often glued to my window, overcome by the vastness of it all. Everything I saw was new, and it both excited and scared the hell out of me.

But the hailstorm. It's the one thing about that climb up into the mountains I can remember with absolute clarity. Just west of Denver, we twisted and turned and lurched for hours, and when I was finally sure I was going to vomit from the surging nausea, I jerked my window back and leaned as much as I could. When I'd finished, I unclenched my eyes just in time to see a posted sign that simply read: CONTINENTAL DIVIDE. On the ground beneath it were scattered patches of snow. Maybe my act was catching because right then a few other passengers hiked their windows back, too, letting the crisp air snake into the bus.

And even though it was midmorning, everything outside started to go dark. Just like that. The rain that started didn't last but a few moments before giving way to the ice. I never saw hail before, so I imagine I probably looked like a piss-scared baby, staring out the window with my mouth dropped open. Everything started out small at first. Weak. A shower of pebbles came and then slipped into a shower of golf balls, and then the storm choked what daylight there was out of the world. The bus slowed to nothing more than a creep when the road first started to disappear, and as the whine of the engine finally fell still, all we heard was the ice—pelting down on the roof like marbles spilling all over the sidewalk. I turned to Pissed-Off and asked in a whisper if he'd ever seen anything like it. All he told me was to shut my mouth.

I was paralyzed with both fear and wonder. In only a matter of minutes, the dark road we were crawling up and down had been carpeted in a blinding whiteout. And when it was over, the only things not underneath the ice were the ripped-open trees.

CHAPTER

five

After shifting down the western side of the pass, the blue-and-silver bus wound its way onto Highway 50 and into Gunnison. The sky began to lighten, and slim spokes of sunlight pierced the clouds.

The Greyhound slowed and jerked as the driver played the gears, and stopped at an intersection along Main Street. It was the first sign of civilization since leaving Denver the day before. There was Arthur's Barber Shop, complete with a candy cane pole out front. A faded sign in the window announced Tuesdays were half-off men's cuts. Then there was Simonton's Auto and a Sears, Roebuck. Down the sidewalk ahead of us was a radio station studio—KGUC—and beyond it, the Gunnison County bus terminal.

As the bus pulled into the station, Pissed-Off said (more to himself), "This is us." He reached down and collected his hat and the previous day's newspaper from the floor. Outside, I saw several parked cars and a few men in suits standing around, along with two men in cowboy hats.

I suddenly felt awkward, having no belongings. It was like remembering you forgot your schoolbag after the bus had already dumped you off at school. My only possession lay tucked inside my shirt's front pocket: a palm-sized black-and-white photo of my mother. I was self-conscious about what the other guys at the ranch might say about it, but was too terrified not to have it in the first place. I was thirteen, and I'd never been away from home, unless you count the handful of nights I'd spent at Jimmy Curio's, two buildings down.

The bus stopped, and a line of bodies crammed into the narrow aisle as we bumped and shuffled our way to the door. Outside, the air was chilled, and a strong wind bit into my face. Pissed-Off met with the cowboy hats while I stood in the shadow of the bus, feeling awkward and out of place. Pissed-Off turned, pointed to me, and the gaze of the cowboys followed. One of them had a thick mustache, and was the tallest man I'd ever seen. He caught my stare, smirked, and spit to the ground. It was the first time I had ever seen cowboys. They didn't look anything like the ones I'd seen on *The Roy Rogers Show.* They were the real deal. They had pistols holstered at their waists, wore dirty clothes, and had lined, leathery faces. Neither of them looked friendly. They looked more like a pair of hungry dogs.

Pissed-Off handed over a folder of papers, turned to give me a final, contemptuous look, and climbed back onto the bus. It was the last time I ever saw him, and I'm vaguely surprised I can still remember what he looked like.

The cowboy who resembled a skyscraper started toward me and unsnapped a small pouch from his belt. "Hands out in front."

I hesitated, confused.

"Hands out, goddammit! If you make me tell you again I'm going to put these ever-loving things behind your bony back."

The passengers on the bus glared out their windows, their curiosity piqued by the commotion. I didn't look away like the skyscraper must have expected. I held my gaze into his eyes, the eyes of a man who had already judged me, who had already made up his mind I was no good. I held out my hands.

The handcuffs were cold against my skin, and when I heard them click shut, a hard truth crashed down on me. I wasn't on vacation in the mountains—I wasn't heading down the road to camp. I was a prisoner and I was going to do hard time.

"Get your little ass in the backseat," he said. He gripped my shoulder and directed me toward an open door of a black, early-fifties-model Olds. "You belong to us now. For the next . . ." He glanced at the papers. His heavy moustache widened above the corners of his mouth. "Hell, this little shit's going to be staying with us for two."

I got into the car. A third cowboy sat in the back next to me. He was much older, and his skin wasn't as tanned as the others. He removed his wide hat, revealing curly white hair underneath. "A word of advice from an old man," he said. "Don't give that one"—he nodded out the window toward the tall cowboy—"a reason to hate you more than he already does. The others are mostly decent folk, but Frank Kroft has hate in all seven feet of him."

"Thanks," I said. And I meant it. He was the first person to really talk to me since I'd left Chicago.

"Frank Kroft. He's a mean son of a bitch. The other one, with the wide shoulders, that's Elmore Holling."

I was quiet. Elmore Holling was built like a Notre Dame linebacker. His thickness, under other circumstances, would have looked humorous against Frank Kroft's thin frame and shocking height. Holling's clean face made him look younger than his counterpart, but he looked every bit as coarse.

"I'm Grimsley," said the man next to me. "They call me Gus. Two years now? I hear right?"

"Yes, sir. I guess so."

"Seen worse. Guess I seen better, too."

I wanted to ask questions, but figured I was better off with my mouth shut. Better to not invite any unnecessary attention.

My nerves were a tangle of live wires, and I almost puked right there on the seat. Nearly a year before, as things grew progressively worse with my father, I took to smoking my first cigarettes. A couple guys on the block watched me, laughing as I lit up a Chesterfield. They laughed harder when I lurched, coughing uncontrollably. I stole the smokes from my dad's chest of drawers—not the whole pack, just enough to get me started. Pretty ironic for a kid who wanted to be the exact opposite of his father. Sitting there in the backseat of the

Olds, I'd have given anything for a smoke. Shit, I'd have even taken a Lucky Strike.

Gus Grimsley leaned back and stared through his window. The other two cowboys yanked open the front doors and climbed in. Even after removing his hat, Frank Kroft's head was just inches from brushing the roof of the car. The one Gus called Holling fell into the driver's seat. As the engine rumbled to life, the radio awoke and the Olds was filled with the sound of Buddy Knox's "Party Doll."

"Turn that shit off, Holling," Frank said. "You'd think this was a goddamned Sunday drive."

Holling rolled his eyes and killed the music. We started down a narrow road that wound south of town. Along the way, the talk was sparse. Frank Kroft said a western fence needed spot patching and that if someone named Addison hadn't brought two mares to the front pens he'd be sleeping in shit that night. No one talked to me, and that was just fine.

For an hour, we climbed and coasted up the steep two-lane roads of the Rockies. Off the shoulder, I saw a sign that we were entering into UNCOMPAHGRE FOREST. A few miles later, we turned onto a smaller road that, not long after, became nothing more than a bumpy dirt path. Then another sign. SWOPE RANCH BOYS' REFORMATORY—POSTED—PRIVATE PROPERTY. So this is it, I thought. This is where I'll spend the next two years of my life.

The car banked through dense collections of spruce pines, aspens, and mountain maples, and after that we traveled downhill for most of the way. I glanced toward Gus, whose eyes were closed. My heart raced, and I felt sick to my stomach again. I guessed this was how convicts felt punching their ticket and taking their ride to Joliet.

Is that what I am, a convict?

"Welcome to your new home, Sheppard," Frank Kroft said.

I digested the view through the front window.

Before us lay a wide valley as green as any fields of grass I ever saw, cradled between steep slopes and patches of dark pines. Its expanse seemed to stretch forever and, in the late afternoon light, was already in the shadow of the snowcapped peak to the west. We had just descended through the valley's only entrance, its single doorway to the outside world.

In the center of the basin were several primitive-looking structures and two long barns. Past these, split post fences adorned all of the outer pastures. There, in the pastures, were horses. Herds of them. Some were in groups, running fast and shifting direction like flocks of birds. Others just grazed. Until that day, I'd never even laid eyes on a real horse.

The ranch was a hive of activity and constant motion. Trucks carried bales of hay from the barns to the fields, boys lugged heavy sacks over their shoulders, or rode horses in the pastures. A few were painting a barn, just yards from where two others were digging fence postholes near a gate.

Not far from us was an incredibly large horse pen crawling with activity. Boys and men alike perched like vultures along the tall fence railing, screaming and shouting as if their lives depended on it. Inside, a figure sat atop an enormous bay-colored horse. It swung its head back and forth, grunting and whinnying. As we drove by, it kicked its hind legs into the air, sending the rider flying hard to the ground. The audience applauded and screamed even louder.

We came to a stop outside a large building with a deep porch that ran the width of its overhang. It was two stories, and two oversized windows looked out onto the entrance below. The front façade had an eerie, facelike quality, with a double entry serving as a gaping mouth.

"End of the line, sweetheart," Kroft said, craning his head from the front seat. His breath was sour and smelled like a combination of cigarettes and shit. He smiled, revealing a flash of brown and yellow teeth, and I wondered if he ever brushed them at all.

Stepping outside the Olds, I drew in a deep breath of fresh air. The smell of manure was everywhere, coupled with the sweet and sour odor of hay.

"Get used to it—the shit in the air," Frank said. He leaned over, eyes gleaming. "That's the smell of money for us. But for you, it's just the smell of shit." He slapped his hat onto his greasy head and turned to the building. "C'mon."

"You do, you know," Gus said.

"What?" I asked.

"Get used to it. You do, in time."

I watched him struggle to get out of the car, and I saw for the first time just how frail he seemed. He looked older than I'd first thought, and I suddenly thought of my Grandpa Jack, wearing a Roy Rogers hat. Gus walked slowly toward the two-story building, and I wondered just how long he'd been at the ranch.

I looked around, taking it all in. Something about the place didn't seem right, but I couldn't say what. I'd felt it as we drove into the valley and onto the ranch. Something out of place, or missing. I dismissed the feeling—told myself I was just being jumpy, and followed the men.

The wood slats creaked as I stepped onto the porch and followed Kroft and Holling through the doors. Inside, the smell of leather and wood stain permeated the room. On one end was a deeply varnished counter that ran the length of a wall, making the room look more like a historic hotel than a prison facility. We went behind the counter and into one of the numerous back rooms, and then into yet another, smaller room beyond.

"Sit down," Elmore Holling said, motioning toward the metal table and chairs. Gus Grimsley tipped his hat, and then the two of them left. Holling swung the heavy door shut, filling the room with a deep, metallic cry. After that, everything was quiet.

I sat. I waited. The room was cold and had no windows; the only light was stale and came from a lonely bulb that hung exposed from the tall ceiling. It cast colorless, empty glares onto everything beneath. On the opposite wall was a clock, protected by a crisscross nest of wires that ran the length of its face. Next to it was a painting of a crimson sunset stretched over an empty prairie. Otherwise, the walls were bare.

But the painting. It served as a window in its own way. Those on my side of the table had no doubt stared at the brushed landscape, wishing as I did that they could somehow crawl through the frame, into that narrow window, and escape to the peaceful world on the other side. Maybe begin a new life, leave the past behind.

The door opened.

Frank Kroft entered, ducking his head in order to clear the doorway. He held a large clipboard with a collection of pages wedged beneath its metal teeth. Behind him was a tall, heavyset man wearing crisp denim overalls. He was almost as tall as Frank, but with a giant stomach protruding from inside the overalls, and his face was masked under a thick, peppered beard. In his mouth was a long, wooden pipe, and I couldn't help but think of the time I approached Santa Claus in the Marshall Field's café. I'd stood in line and seen him four times that week already. Santa had been smoking a dark, polished pipe, and the deep woody smell of tobacco was both pleasant and nauseating. That smell still had the same effect on me.

The man in overalls shut the door and sat down across from me. Frank tossed the clipboard onto the table and pulled out a chair for himself.

The man pulled the pipe away. "Seems to me . . ."—his voice was deep and unrefined—"that you have your work cut out for you, Frank." He wore black horn-rimmed glasses, which he pushed higher onto his thick nose. With a sigh, he took the clipboard from the desk and thumbed through the first few pages.

"The next herd won't be coming for another month," Frank said. "I'll take care of it."

It made me feel small to sit before them and not be acknowledged.

"You will, Frank. You always do."

He flipped a few pages over the clipboard, then set it back on the table.

"Now, let's see what we have here." He glanced up, eyed me, said nothing. The silence in the room was uncomfortable; the clock's second hand was ticking, ticking, ticking.

He waited, as if I might say something. I didn't.

"Huh." He returned to the clipboard. "We'll break you, Mr. Sheppard. Just like we break each of the animals outside. One step at a time."

Kroft chuckled, all yellow-brown teeth and lips.

The other drew once more on his pipe, then said, "William Paul Sheppard. You are here for twenty-four months, son. Two years. You will spend those two years working for me. My name is Walter Barrow. But you will call me sir, Mr. Barrow, or even Warden, as I believe that somehow fits, doesn't it?"

I spoke softly, staring into his eyes. "Yes, sir."

"Very good. Now, let's get one thing out of the way before we move on. It is a luxury for you to be here, Mr. Sheppard. A privilege. Right this minute, you could be sitting in a state juvenile prison cell, seeing God's open sky only when you're told you can go and do so. Here on the ranch, you will be outside for the majority of the day. But believe me, those days will not be easy here, son. They will be *hard*. You will labor and you will sweat. And if you step one inch out of line, William, you will be dealt with."

"Mmm," Kroft agreed.

"You may have noticed as you drove up, Mr. Sheppard, that Swope Ranch Reformatory has no security gates, no iron or stone fences."

That was it. I knew something seemed off. No gates. Before he even began to explain why, I knew: there was no need.

"This ranch resides in a valley over thirteen thousand feet above sea level, in the shadow of one of the two fourteener peaks in the county. In the winters, the only accessible road out of the valley is covered under an average of three feet of snow. Even in summertime, the temperature at night falls to near freezing at this altitude. Without the luxury of a vehicle, we are many days' travel from any sort of civilization. If by some means of optimistic insanity a prisoner here does try to escape, there is a harsh policy we follow. You *will* be shot down with a rifle if found outside these boundaries, and without a second thought. In the twelve years this ranch has served as a reformatory, not one prisoner has tried to escape. The mountains aren't forgiving up here, that's the plain and simple truth."

I'm sure he could see in my eyes that I believed him.

"There are seventy-eight boys currently serving sentences on the ranch. You will make seventy-nine. We will provide you with two pairs of standard-issue blue jeans, a sweatshirt, coat, and two shirts. We'll throw in a pair of work boots, too.

"We have a military-style barrack for all the boys, complete with indoor plumbing, constructed just last year, so you don't have to shit outside."

He surveyed the papers. "Mr. Kroft will escort you to the commissary to get you sized for your new clothes, and then you will join the others."

He flipped the papers back over the clipboard and handed it to Frank. "Knifing your father. Almost to death."

I sat there, unsure what to say. "Guess I should have tried harder."

To my surprise, the two men laughed in unison and shared a knowing look.

Barrow turned back to me. "Oh, yes, Mr. Sheppard. We'll get you straightened right the fuck out."

CHAPTER

six

IN 1963, THERE WERE STILL VAST ACRES OF OPEN WILDERNESS IN the state of Colorado, especially outside the Grand Junction area, where herds of mustangs were often rounded up and trucked to various ranches across the region. And at Swope Reformatory, the horses were met and worked daily by a select group of inmates who were part of a special program to break them. They called themselves breakers.

After the horses were broken in and gentled, they were sold to various ranchers and landowners in Colorado, California, Arizona, and New Mexico. Sometimes farther away. And this was how the ranch made its cut. Call it what you want, but it was an institution more than anything, profiting from the use of free labor to generate revenue.

Horses came and went, delinquent boys came and went. The boys broke the horses, Swope Reformatory broke the boys.

"WHERE WE GOING?" WE'D FINISHED AT THE COMMISSARY, WHERE AN old man with a pockmarked face had peered down at me from behind a massive slab of varnished oak. With an eyeballed assessment, he nodded, and slurred that my clothes would be delivered to the bunks.

"Five o'clock. Time to eat. Mess hall opens quarter till." Kroft stopped and considered me. It felt almost like my own father standing before me, trying to intimidate, to threaten. "You don't get your ass inside the hall before five, you don't eat. Not until the next day, you don't eat a damned thing. Understand, asshole?" He leaned in to drive the point home; the dog-shit stink of his breath was hideous.

But I didn't want to give him the satisfaction of seeing me flinch. In some crazy way, I felt I had the advantage. What he didn't know was I'd been dealing with him my entire life. If I could take thirteen years of my old man, I could take two years of Frank Kroft.

"I'll set my watch. Understand?"

Man, he was fast. The left side of my face exploded in shards of white light and my ear started to whistle. My head hit the ground and even bounced a time or two before I realized he'd hit me. A sort of animal grunt rolled out of my mouth, but I didn't cry out. I wiped a hand across my head and it came away with blood. The whistling in my left ear turned into a clanging fire alarm, and throbbed to the beat of my pulse. I held my hand to it, half expecting the thing to maybe fall off at any second. It felt more like an overripe tomato than an ear.

"You watch that smart mouth of yours," he said. "It's liable to get you into some real trouble."

The clamorous dining room stilled when we walked through the doors, and seventy-eight boys looked up. A number of faces belonged to guys of no more than eleven, while others had tanned skin and budding moustaches. Some looked out of place—soft, pudgy. Others were rough-looking, and seemed experienced. But the eyes were all the same: curious. I moved to the serving line, wanting to shed their glances and avert the attention. Since I arrived late, I was told to take a seat at the one empty table at the back of the room. I sat and ate my first meal on the ranch feeling very much in a world of my own.

THE BUNKHOUSE WAS AN ENORMOUS QUONSET HUT, STRAIGHT OUT of World War II. The stretched building had two windows at each end, with a lone doorway centered between them. The walls were rounded from the ground up and met in an arch, the entire structure covered with corrugated metal. To this day, when I hear a storm, it is the sound of rain hitting the metallic roof of the bunkhouse that I hear.

The bunkhouse held exactly one hundred beds, all aligned in five long rows. An aisle divided each row of bunks, leading from an oversized island of a desk to the newly constructed bathroom wing. There were always supposed to be at least two guards on bunk duty. Sometimes there were more, and on rare occasions, less.

The narrow bunk assigned to me was directly next to the bathroom. Not the most sought-after real estate, but I didn't really care. The bathroom was something of a mismatch when compared to its adjoining structure. Militaristic and primitive, the bunkhouse featured smooth concrete floors and smelled of bleach. Iron-framed bunks, each covered with tightly pulled wool blankets, looked as inviting as one might suspect, and sitting squarely before each one was a cedar footlocker. In contrast, the bathroom was a lavish escape. Sleek, glossy-coated tiles crisscrossed the immaculate floor, and grand mirrors hunched over each of the fifteen porcelain washbasins. Stainless steel toilet stalls ran the opposite length of wall, though there were no privacy doors on any of them; Swope wasn't overly concerned with issues of privacy. I wondered why they had bothered with stalls in the first place.

Just like in the army, the bathroom was cleaned daily by a unit of two inmates. It was up to the bunkhouse guards to designate whom each unit comprised, and it was, as they now say, an equal opportunity work detail. I have stayed at only a few upscale hotels in my life, once on my honeymoon with Mina, another when my firm sent me to Raleigh for a conference. Neither had bathrooms that would pass inspection at Swope.

Waiting for me on my bunk was a neatly folded wardrobe. White cotton T-shirts, a sweater, and a few button-ups, each with the name SWOPE stenciled into the left breast. There were also two pressed pairs of blue jeans and a heavy coat, the color of a dreary and overcast sky. On top of my footlocker was a worn-looking pair of leather work boots, and atop my neatly folded clothes, innocently enough, was a small New Testament Bible. Standard issue.

A musky odor wafted upward as I lifted the lid of the footlocker, and I wondered who it belonged to before me. Who else slept in this bunk? How long was he here and where was he now?

"Hey, what's your name?"

I turned to see a short, husky guy with a stain on his shirt, no doubt from the evening's dinner. An abundant row of freckles spread across his nose and cheeks.

"Will," I said in a quiet voice, turning back to my things. I began placing my clothes in the creaky footlocker, and tucked the black-and-white of my mother underneath them all.

He stayed put, breathing heavy, like he'd just taken a run. Realizing he wasn't going to leave, I turned back. He smiled almost bashfully, and then mouthed something to the guys across the bunks.

"What's yours?" I asked.

The smile widened. "Eddie. Eddie Tokus." He laughed. It was an ignorant laugh that came from the back of his throat.

I stood there, silent.

"Yeah. Well, good meeting you, Will." He snapped his head, looking for someone in the back of the room, and smiled again. "Check it out, though, you're about to have a fight."

The room of boys erupted. My head spun and my ears filled with thunder from the screaming. Above me, yellow lightbulbs spun in my vision, and then the light was blotted out. Eddie Tokus pounced, straddled his fat legs around my waist, and began jabbing his fists into my ribs. His smile was gone, replaced by focused determination.

All around me, the shouts grew into amplified, nonsensical yells and whistles. It was like the Lincoln Park Zoo at feeding time. The noise bounced off the metal walls and buzzed inside my mind. Another blow rocked my head into the concrete beneath, sending shards of pain throughout my upper body. I could taste the blood running back into my throat, and I knew that if I didn't get up, I would choke.

"Stay still, dammit!" Eddie screamed.

I saw him reel his fist back a second time, ready for another punch. Still dazed, I rolled my head out of the way as he swung, just enough to avoid the brunt of the blow. His fist bounced off the side of my head and into the floor.

Eddie yelped in agony, drawing his hand up to his chest.

"Oooh! Dammit, my haaand! I think it's br—"

He didn't get to finish his sentence. I threw a punch as hard as my body allowed, directly into his throat. The result was immediate and highly gratifying.

"Gah!" He grabbed his throat with both hands. "You fuggin' nose-bleedin'—"

I took full advantage of the opportunity and punched him in the mouth. He had a sort of hurt look in his eyes, as if to say, "What'd you go and do that for?" Blood filled between his teeth, and the guy started to cry. He didn't get up. He just rolled over onto his back, ceding the victory to me. The room erupted in cheers.

Eddie held his busted hand half inside his mouth and swayed back and forth on the floor. Looking at him like that, I felt a surge of pity, the way you might feel sorry for a dog that's been kicked around.

Two guards came through the door; I recognized one of them as Elmore Holling.

The other, a middle-aged guard with a crew cut, reached down and grabbed Eddie by the shirt. "Come on."

Eddie recoiled, still clasping his throat. He said, "Leggo!" It came out raspy and wet.

"To the infirmary," Holling said. "Both of you. I said *move.*"

Eddie made it to his knees and almost stumbled again before finding his feet. The room went quiet as we made our way through the door. Everyone was already going about their business—the fight was already yesterday's news.

Outside, the air was even colder than before, and beside me, Eddie breathed harder than ever.

The nurse's station was just up the hill from the two-story office house. They'd called it the infirmary, but it wasn't much more than an oversized shack. There were three or four rooms, with a small waiting area at the front. We stood by the front desk and watched Doreen Little, the ranch's acting nurse, peer down another kid's throat with a flashlight. She didn't seem to mind that he was kicking his legs and on the verge of choking.

I looked at Eddie. "What'd you do that for anyway?" I asked. I wiped more blood from my face; it was beginning to dry inside my nose and the pain and the swelling made me sound like I had a lisp.

Eddie just breathed in and out, his nose whistling like my mother's old teapot.

"Some stupid prank you pull on the new guys?" I asked. "That it?"

He looked at me, then quickly shifted his gaze down to his gut.

"Forget it then," I said.

"It's just a rule. Older guys started it. The new guy comes, the fish before him starts the fight. Been going on since forever."

"Forever. And nobody has the balls to stop it?"

Eddie shrugged. "Don't wanna, I guess. Besides, if I hadn't fought, Silas would have raked me over for sure."

"Silas?"

"Silas Green. Runs the place. *No one* messes with Silas."

"I thought the guards ran this place."

Eddie rocked back and forth, cradling his hand. "You gotta lot to learn, man."

CHAPTER

seven

"STOP WHINING NOW, EDDIE. STOP IT!"

Her name was Doreen, but everyone called her Miss Little. And just like her last name, she seemed to have little patience for the local clientele. I later heard she'd been at Swope for almost nine years, hired not long after the ranch first underwent the conversion to a boys' reformatory.

She was a warm black woman with a crooked nose and a sweet Southern accent. And in contrast to her name, she was a rather tall woman. Tall, with pronounced shoulders and a narrow waist. Even though she spoke with a firm tongue, I found a softness in her eyes that made me feel comfortable. It was like a mother's toughness, for a child's own good.

I later found out that two years before my arrival, Miss Little was punched in the nose by a new addition to the ranch family. The delinquent? Silas Green. He spent the next day in the reformatory's version of solitary confinement.

"Oh, *Jeezis*!" Eddie whined.

He pulled away each time Miss Little reached for him. She finally succeeded in getting a good grip on his arm and held it still across the examining table. She felt meticulously along his hand with her long, slender fingers. Her hair was pulled back and tied off with a string. Not a ribbon, like my mother sometimes used, but simple packing twine.

"Now. I believe you've only broken one bone, Eddie. Not even a bad break at that." Miss Little turned and rummaged through several drawers in a nearby cabinet before she found what she was looking for. "Here we are. Don't suspect you need a cast put on that hand, but I'm going to set you up with the next best thing." She presented an odd glove with a long string of leather hanging from it.

"This here's a mending glove. Got a clip of metal running through the top and bottom of her that'll keep your hand from bending this way and that. We'll just wrap it around you here, and tie her on up."

Eddie inspected the glove. "I can't move my hand much, or my fingers."

"Well that's just the point, now isn't it?" Miss Little said.

"Guess so," Eddie muttered.

"Okay, Eddie. You're stuck with this for six whole weeks."

"Six weeks! You kiddin' me?"

"Six weeks. Take it off when you shower, if such an event ever does occur," Miss Little said, hands on hips. "And I'll talk with the warden and the rest of the men about your work detail."

"Six weeks." For the first time, Eddie looked content.

"Now off you go, back to the bunk with yourself."

Eddie slid off the table. He didn't so much as look in my direction.

"Now, I don't believe I've had the pleasure," Miss Little said, turning back to me. "What's your name, child?"

"Will." Then I added, "William Sheppard."

"Well, William Sheppard, on the table, and we'll have a look at that beaten-in nose of yours." I watched as she rummaged through drawers once more, and removed gauze and a glass bottle of alcohol.

She doused the gauze with alcohol and cleaned my face. She wasn't exactly gentle. My nose throbbed and had closed up completely. She dabbed it with the gauze, creating fresh needles of pain.

"This next is going to hurt a little, sweetheart."

As soon as the words were spoken, I felt fire shoot up into my nose.

The pain was worse than when Eddie had broken it. With one hand, Miss Little grabbed the back of my skull, while with the other she pressed my nose back into place.

"I don't know why I'm telling you this, Will. Guess I just have me a feeling about you. You're a good boy. I can tell about people sometimes. It's a gift I've had, ever since I was a little girl, weed high. I could just look at someone and see the evil, or the goodness, that lay inside them. Sometimes I see a little of both." My nose trickled its last offering of blood, and she wiped it once more, plugging each side with rolled-up tissue paper. "You have a good heart, son. Don't lose it in this place."

"Thanks." It came out muffled, hardly recognizable. She handed me my shirt, and with the greatest of caution, I pulled it over my head. "I'll keep my eyes open."

"Oh, you'll have to do better than that, little man." She put down the bloody gauze and placed her hands on my shoulders, leaning in close until, for a moment, I thought she was going to kiss me on the lips.

"There are certain people here you best avoid, Will. One most in particular is Silas Green. The boy is a damned soul walking this earth, child. Bullshit, that boy is an *evil* soul." Her voice was now low. "And you'll also pardon my French, if you please."

I didn't know what to say.

"Yes, sir. Got me a feeling about you."

CHAPTER
eight

I'd be lying if I said I wasn't on the verge of tears that first night. I would have given anything to be back home, even if it meant living with a piss-mean drunk for a father.

Lying in my bunk, in the darkness, I felt angry, and cheated. Angry that my mother never left the man who continued to abuse her, and cheated that I was wasting my life on a prison ranch when the bastard didn't even die.

Creaking filled the darkness from all areas of the bunkhouse. At first I couldn't place it, until I turned over on my side and heard the rusty springs that supported my own mattress. The squeaks and creaking only grew stronger, some coming from nearby, others farther away. A chill of disgust rolled through me as I realized it was the sound of masturbation. I attempted to push the sound out of my mind, to think of something else, but I couldn't stop hearing them in my head.

After a while, the sounds subsided, until finally I drifted off to sleep.

Elmore Holling was one of the usual bunk guards at Swope. Callahan Jenkins was the other. Jenkins was a guard in his thirties who came to Colorado from St. Louis a few odd years before me. Most of the guys just called him Cal. He took two nights off each week, but spent them, as most staff did on their days off, at the ranch's private quarters. When he was on guard in the bunkhouse, Cal sat at his desk and read *National Geographic* or the local paper. Every hour through the night, he and Holling walked down the aisles between the bunks to make sure each bed held a delinquent. His greatest satisfaction came in the morning. At promptly six o'clock, he flipped on the lights and yelled, "Rise and shine, ladies! God's given us another beautiful Rocky Mountain morning!" This was usually met with a series of murmured profanities. On Saturday mornings, he altered his routine, granting us something of a treat. After the wake-up call, Cal turned on his battery operated Philco AM to KGUC, the broadcast out of Gunnison, advertising itself as the place "Where Your Favorites Live." And so we would wake, shower, and dress to the sounds of Buddy Holly, Ricky Nelson, Jerry Lee Lewis—you get the idea.

Jenkins was easier to get along with than the other guards. I don't know, maybe it was because he hadn't been at the ranch long enough for it to harden him, or maybe he just had a decent enough heart. I think it was a little of both. He was the kind of guy that we could almost imagine being in custody right alongside us, if maybe just one or two things had gone differently in his own past. We all liked Cal.

The next morning after the fight was a Tuesday. No Jerry Lee. I pulled on a pair of jeans and the sneaks I wore on the bus. That was when a kid with buzzed hair, red as a sunset, shuffled over. The guy was a rail, complete with knobby bones sticking out under his tight skin. Acne scars lined his cheeks, and his ears stuck out like the doors of a Chevy. Hanging loosely over his nose were the thickest glasses I'd ever seen. I caught myself staring.

"Hey," he said, looking to the ground. "Cal wants to see you."

"What's your name?" I asked.

He'd already started to walk away, but paused. He looked almost surprised, or maybe even confused that I'd chosen to speak to him at all.

"I'm Will."

He regarded me, then finally said, "Coop."

I nodded. “My first full day. Can’t wait to get it over with.”

He smirked. “Yeah, I know. Heard you kicked that Eddie Tokus’s fat ass last night. I’m sorry I missed it; got stuck on KP duty after dinner.”

“You didn’t miss much. He broke my nose.”

“No, he’s a pussy. He coldcocked you, right? What I heard, anyway.” Coop stared past me, back to a group of guys heading out the door. “I remember my first day,” he said. “I had a fight, too. Didn’t really want to. Just happened. He was a little guy named Michael Moretti. Quick bastard. Turned out to be decent enough, though.”

“Yeah? He still around?”

“No. He got kicked in the head by a horse. Sort of a freak accident. Horse broke his jaw in three places. Spent a few weeks in a Denver hospital. After that, who knows?”

“Man.”

“Yeah.” He took off his glasses and rubbed them with his shirt. Without the magnifying lenses, his eyes were as ordinary as anyone else’s. “Anyway, Cal wants to see you.” He slid the army issues back over his acne-laced nose.

“MR. WILLIAM P. SHEPPARD.” CALLAHAN JENKINS OFFERED HIS hand. He wore jeans and a standard button-up with SWOPE stenciled over the breast. I noticed a pistol holstered on his left hip. It was an army-issue .45 semiautomatic. I’d seen my share of war movies, and recognized the classic M1911 handgun. I’d later discover that all the guards wore them.

Cal looked more like someone’s older brother than he did a guard. For one thing, his dark hair was long, touching the back of his collar. Most guards sported moustaches, or even beards, but Cal was clean-shaven.

“Yes, sir,” I replied.

“This will be your first full day as an inmate at Swope. Lots to do today, friend. After morning calisthenics, breakfast will be served in the mess hall. I believe you already know where that is.”

“Yes, sir.”

“After breakfast, everyone breaks up into their work detail groups.

You'll be on the stable line. I suggest you keep up with Mr. Benjamin Fritch." He motioned to a tall, blond-haired boy making up his cot.

"At noon, you'll break and eat lunch. Later, after more work detail, you'll have an hour back here before dinner at five. We mix it up sometimes. For instance, tomorrow you'll be bailing hay from the trailers coming in. Other times, you might work with some of the trail guards, learning how to mend fence rails or even just old-fashioned manual labor. It's hard work, but, it'll keep you busy."

"Will I get to help train the horses?"

He laughed, but it was a gentle laugh. "Slow down, William, slow down. This is only your first day, kiddo. And we don't train them like house dogs, we break them. When they come to the ranch, they are one hundred percent wild. Mustangs. We have a program made up of fifteen or so young men who work with the horses, to tame them. You'll get riding lessons, learn how to treat a horse and how to act around them, but if you're aspiring to be a breaker, you'll have to be patient. Each boy is handpicked. Usually, they've been here at least a year."

"A year, huh?"

"At least," he said. "Do a good job on the line, stay out of trouble, and maybe I'll see you there someday. Wouldn't surprise me a bit." He smiled. "Can I ask you something, William?"

"I guess."

"Do you regret what you did? What it was that sent you here?"

That cut me, the casual way he asked it. Why do people always feel they have the right to ask such things? "I bet most guys say yes, don't they?"

"Yeah, most of them do," he said.

I just looked away, and was quiet.

"That's your answer?" he asked. "Everyone tells lies here, William. Just make sure you're honest with yourself. That'll help you more than you'll ever know."

I was only thirteen, and didn't understand yet what that meant.

CHAPTER

nine

I'M NOT EXAGGERATING WHEN I SAY A ROUND OF VIGOROUS CALISthenics at 5:30 a.m. in the Colorado mountains is cruel and unusual punishment. The morning temperatures were just above freezing, and I would soon discover that the winter months to come would be nearly unbearable, sometimes forcing our rituals inside.

Regardless of the season, the exercise always left me feeling half dead and starved. Enough so that even the cafeteria's grimiest offerings seemed like heaven on a flimsy food tray. And on that first morning, I would have eaten anything slopped in front of me.

Elmore Holling pointed to a half-occupied table near the back of the room and said nothing more than "That's yours." I think I was more nervous walking to that table than I was meeting the warden the day before. When I sat at the end, the guys eyed me, appraised me as nothing special, and returned to their conversation.

I listened as best as I could, trying not to come off as too eager to join the discussion. Surprisingly, it was about me. It wasn't long before I discovered I had a new nickname: Fucking Nosebleed, or Nosebleed for short. My broken purple nose had but a small part in the matter, I suspect. My temporary deformity gave them a pretty good laugh, and I laughed softly along with them.

"Man, when he popped fat-ass Tokus in the throat—*jeez,* that was just the most," one of them said. He was the blond, moppy-haired guy Cal suggested I follow for work detail. Benjamin Fritch. But to everyone besides Cal he was just Benny.

Sitting across from Benny was Mickey Baines, the smallest guy at our table. Mickey put his hands around his neck, mimicking Eddie Tokus. "Gah! Fucking Nosebleed! Gah!" Although Mickey was the runt of the group, at fourteen he was one of the oldest. His face was wallpapered with freckles, and every time he laughed, his eyes seemed to disappear behind his cheeks. "Gah, my hand! It's berroke! It's berroke!"

More laughter.

As breakfast wore on, I began to feel more comfortable, and tried to make small talk. "So . . . what are you guys in here for?" I immediately wished I could take it back.

"JUST WHO THE FUCK DO YOU THINK YOU ARE?" Mickey yelled; my God, did he yell. Half the cafeteria turned to look at us. "Think you can just go around asking shit like that? Think you're special, now? That it?" He half rose from his seat.

"No," I said. "I just . . ." I felt my face rush with blood and turned back to my food.

Benny leaned over and elbowed me in the ribs, nearly knocking me out of my seat. "Don't mind him. He just got his period today."

"Lunch, you're a homo," Mickey said to Benny.

Benny went on. "He thinks because everyone gave him the treatment when he was a fish, he can do the same to you. Word of advice, though—guys don't ask each other why they're here."

He reached over and stabbed a piece of bacon from my tray. "Hey, you don't mind, right?"

"These juvenile delinquents owe you some gratitude, I hear," Coop Kingston said, slipping into an empty chair. Underneath one arm was a tattered book, which he let drop onto the table. "Especially you, Mr. Mickey Baines. I think the least you could do is show our guest a little appreciation." He wore just the hint of a stifled smile. "Seeing how you profited and all."

Mickey flushed and there went those squinty eyes. "My God, Coop, what a fucking wet rag you are! Sincerely!"

Benny let out a gust of laughter.

"I don't get it," I said. "What's the story?"

"The fights aren't just about who has the biggest balls," Benny said, reaching for a dinner roll off Coop's tray.

"All those guys surrounding you, watching, screaming . . ." Coop said. "That's all bullshit. None of that means anything. It's gambling. And it's not just these juvies who do the betting."

"Hey, Mr. Professor, you're no saint yourself," Mickey said, showing Coop a mouthful of chewed food while reaching for the tattered book. "How do you read this shit?"

Coop rolled his eyes. "Mickey, our miniature friend here, made out quite well. He bet on you, Will, and you paid off."

"How much?"

Mickey eyed me as though he couldn't hate me more.

"Come on, man," Benny said, shoving Mickey's head with his hand. "Cut the act. He's okay." He turned back to me. "You're okay, right? I mean, you don't seem like an asshole."

"No," I said. "I'm not an asshole."

Mickey gave Benny the finger, and said, "Whatever. But don't go thinking you're my fucking best friend, fish."

I asked Benny, "Come on, what was it?"

"Ooh, it was good," Benny said.

Mickey stuck his chest out and smiled. "A week of shit duty, three dollars twenty-five, and an honest-to-God six-inch cigar."

The thought of all that deal-slinging while I was getting the shit beat out of me was too much. "How'd you score the cigar?"

He smiled wider. "Aaron Gumm's older brother gave it to him. Snuck it past the office yin-yangs. Brought it all the way from San Francisco."

"Where he bought it in a five-and-dime Chinatown whorehouse," said Benny, laughing.

"No way, man. It's for reals. I think it's Cuban."

"If it's Cuban, then I'm the pope," Coop said.

Mickey threw out his arms. "Bless me, oh, eggsellency! Bless me!"

There went Benny, elbowing me in the ribs. I flashed a smile at Coop, who rolled his eyes.

"Cuban," he muttered, leaving the table.

It was weird. Here I was, eating at a table with a couple of pretty cool guys, joking back and forth, laughing it up. I could have been back in the lunchroom at school, not on a prison ranch full of juvies. It sure as hell beat sitting by myself.

Something about that took me back to when I was nine, and the haunted house that opened for Halloween. During the weeks before opening night, all the older guys told gruesome tales of how horrible and nasty the place was, getting us all worked up. When the day finally came, none of us wanted to go. We made excuses and agreed to stay home, but Jimmy Curio finally persuaded us to stop being pussies. So we went, and it turned out to be a cinch. Sure, it was scary, and sure, we jumped and screamed like a gaggle of five-year-old girls, but being together made it bearable, and fun.

Maybe that's what the ranch is, I thought. It's the same universal rule any kid faces: swim with the group or sink alone.

CHAPTER

ten

On my first morning at the ranch, I was sent to the east stable for morning work detail, where I was happy to see Benny's familiar face.

He held something in his hands, and turned it over and over. Each time he did, whatever was inside made a noise, like rocks knocking against each other. The thing was half hidden by Benny's palm, so it took me a while to see it was a tin Sucrets box—blue and silver and scratched. As soon as I recognized it, Benny shoved the tin deep into his pocket, and it was gone. He took a mashed piece of bread from his shirt pocket and stuck it inside his cheek.

"Cal wants me to show you the ropes, fill you in on all the exciting details," he said. I followed him to the far end of the building, where various tools and wheelbarrows were sorted against the wall. "There's really not much to it, right? We're just cleaning today. If we don't keep the stalls clean, all sorts of junk happens. Bugs, hoof problems, you know. Not to mention all the piss and shit. You don't want the horses standing around breathing it in all day."

I almost laughed; that's exactly what we would be doing ourselves. But instead, I just said, "Doesn't sound so bad."

Benny laughed. "Tell me how it sounds after you do it all morning." He showed me everything we needed for the job: gloves, rubber boots, pitchforks. "The other guys will put the horses out to pasture, then we'll go in. Nothing to it. Just fork out all the horse apples you see, shovel up the wet hay, throw in more dry hay. Damn, I guess that's about it."

I gave a shrug, dug my hands into my pockets, and imagined my friend Jimmy Curio there with me. How he would have laughed his ass off at the city kid cleaning up after horses!

"Someday, I won't have to haul shit all day. They're bound to make me a breaker, soon. I've always been good with animals, seriously!" Benny chewed on the bread that was still in his mouth. "Then I can hang out with Mickey and Coop over in the pens. I'm going to be the best breaker here. Hey, maybe you'll make it, too, you know?"

I kicked a clump of manure. "Yeah, hope so."

"Another thing," Benny said. "Don't go filling the wheelbarrow too high. Makes it harder to push out. You don't wanna scoop this stuff up twice, right?" He hee-hawed, reached into his pocket, and threw a handful of raisins into his mouth. I probably made some sort of face, thinking how he'd just touched practically every filthy thing in the stable.

THERE WAS ONE CONSTANT ON THE RANCH, I CAME TO FIND OUT: there was always a horse stall that needed cleaning. As long as I kept my mouth shut and turned a stall, the guards were happy. The routine varied here and there. Aside from cleaning up, I pitched in for odd jobs—sorting and hanging the horse tack, running feed to the empty troughs, watering, working on fences or roofs. And when I wasn't cleaning up after the horses, I was cleaning up after the juvies. Bathroom duty was always the worst, but I never minded helping out in the kitchen and mess hall.

The chores gave me time to think, and especially that first week, I thought of my mother. Mail at the ranch was a one-way street: only incoming. And occasionally I did receive letters from home. She never told me the important things, the story of her survival.

The second letter I received from home felt more like a confession; it was the first, and only, time she ever opened up to me. What she wrote wasn't as detailed as what I could put together on my own, which was all I really needed to know.

My father had spent seven weeks in the hospital, then finally returned home. She wrote that he broke down the night he came back, told her he was a changed man. A reformed man. No more booze, he said. No more late nights. No more violence. Lying there on the hospital bed had opened his eyes to a great deal of things that needed changing. He took her in his arms and hugged her, carefully minding the cast. He told her he loved her.

I think it was both the optimist and the realist in her that kept her from leaving. The overzealous optimist told her he was sincere, and he'd be true to his word. He'd be a changed man, and life would go on. In time, I would come home, a better person from my experience.

The pragmatic realist presented more sensible arguments: you could leave. But where will you go? How would you get by with no money? And really, do you think he'd just *let* you leave?

I'll bet you dollars to doughnuts she thought pretty hard about that one, next to him in bed each night.

My father was true to his word. He did treat her kindly. He did this for almost two weeks, until Horace McDaniels and the other guys from the warehouse slipped him a welcome-back gift: a silver flask filled with Kentucky's finest. Once he found the bottom of the flask, the search for more continued, and you know what the pisser is? It all started again.

I READ THE LETTER AT LEAST THREE TIMES, THEN TUCKED IT, ALONG with the other, carefully inside my footlocker, beneath all of my clothes and next to my mother's black-and-white. There were times later I'd pull them out and read the pages all over again.

CHAPTER
eleven

SOMETIMES, DURING THE MORNING WORK, I PAUSED TO WATCH THE horses. The most exciting times were arrival days. Mustangs were trucked onto the ranch in trailers, and then let loose in the fields. They were untamed, as nature intended, and the stallions were mammoth and lightning quick. I became increasingly drawn to the team of breakers who worked them, trying their damnedest to tame the untamable.

My second week there, I saw Coop get thrown into a fence post. He made a funny yelp and hit the post with an audible slap. He immediately began swiping his hands around in the dirt, and I realized he was looking for his glasses. Once he found them (amazingly, they weren't broken), he wobbled up, grinning. I laughed from across the yard, holding a wheelbarrow full of piss-soaked hay.

It was a tall white mare that threw him. She belonged to a herd that had been brought to the ranch a few months earlier. All the others from her pack were beginning to turn. All but her.

She was the wildest thing I ever saw. Her coat was completely white, except for her face, which was a deep caramel. Everyone called her Reaper. She was Coop's current project, and after each day of failure, he'd just point out that he was one day closer to breaking her. In

Coop's world, it seemed, books always came first, but after that, it was Reaper. He'd just finished with a mustang he aptly named Hemingway before tackling The Great White Bitch (as he began to refer to her as the days dragged on). He'd turned Hemingway in less than two months. Coop joked that he'd probably end up staying at the ranch just to finish off Reaper by the time they finally let him go.

"Honestly, she'll prove to be the ultimate testament to my skills," he said.

Mickey laughed and called him a douche bag. "She'll never break, you asshole. I know it. You know it. Sincerely, she's too mean!"

And she *was* mean, gladly taking any opportunity to kick, bite, or stomp anyone who came near. Benny said a boy named Duncan Embry got too close and she bit him hard on the neck. It was black and purple for a week.

If I close my eyes, I can still picture the first time I saw her at full gallop. There was a deep bellow from the east stable, followed by someone screaming. There was the sound of hoofs beating into the dirt, and then Reaper—busting through the half-open barn door. She pushed herself even faster once she hit the meadow, daring anyone to follow. At the fence, she didn't let up, but only shifted direction, running, running, trying to find a way out. She galloped across the pasture, charging one boundary, then another, before finally easing up. She circled in the center, making sure none of the onlookers—man or animal—approached.

"That's a pissed-off horse, right?" Benny asked, walking up to the fence with a gnawed apple core in one hand. His rubber boots were coated in soft green manure.

"You think she'll tame?"

Benny snorted. "Reaper? I'll tell you something." He tossed the apple core into the field and pulled off a pair of worn-looking gloves, stuffing them in the back pocket of his jeans. "Coop says he's gonna do it. But there's no way. That's what I think. Whoever does it ought to get a one-way pass out of this place."

"Yeah," I said. I wondered if I could ever do something so important.

"You see the way she's doing that, right? With her hoof there?"

The horse was stomping a hoof furiously into the ground, then digging back, the way a bull might before charging. Each time she did, there was a muffled *clomp* and thin clouds of dust drifted away.

"It's a challenge, you know? She's mad as hell, and just daring any of us to come near. We're the enemy; we've taken her off her land. Right now, there's nothing more she'd like than to stomp the ever-living shit out of us." He leaned on the fence and propped a foot on the lower railing just as easy as Roy Rogers. "But she'll cool it. They always do, right?"

"How do you know so much?" I asked.

He shrugged. "I don't know. It's like I said, I'm just good with animals, you know? Always have been. My dad worked a ranch once. Used to take me along and I watched. Sometimes the foreman there taught me things."

"Sounds like you're wasting your time teaching me how to fill up wheelbarrows," I said.

"Someday," Benny said. "Someday I'll show them."

Reaper circled. "So what's that under her eye? Blood?"

Benny turned back to the horse, still in the middle of the field. Benny started to say, "Nah—" but stopped. "Hey, it sure looks like it."

Just below Reaper's right eye socket was an open cut. Blood—from our distance it looked black—ran down her long face. She let out a piercing cry.

Benny stormed to the stable from which Reaper had emerged. I did my best to keep up, but as tall as he was, Benny's pace was unmatchable.

It was the first time I'd seen Benny angry, and I was glad to be on his side.

Only one of the pens was empty: Reaper's. A worn-looking trough bucket hung over the outer rail into the pen, along with a half-used salt lick. A tall, older guy was hanging a bridle and bit on the wall.

Another guy stepped aside as Benny barreled by. "What'd you do, Silas?" Benny asked.

Silas Green. Combed-back hair, the hint of stubble on his face. He just needed a toothpick in his mouth and a pack of smokes rolled up his shirtsleeve. Miss Little's words rang in my ears, telling me to stay away from Silas—*"That boy is a damned soul."*

Benny turned around, facing the other two. "What'd he do, Bobby? Aaron?"

There was no answer.

The bridle hanging on the wall was smeared with blood. Benny walked up and grabbed Silas by the shirt. "I said what did you do to her?"

In two moves, Benny was on the ground. "Don't you ever lay a hand on me! Ever!" Silas screamed.

I'd only been on the ranch for a couple weeks, and Benny was as close to a friend as I had. My instincts jerked my feet into motion. God knows what I planned to do once I reached Silas. Tackle him, kick him. Maybe a punch to the ear. I never got the chance, though. The other two—Bobby Pettigrew and Aaron Gumm—swooped in front of me like bodyguards, cutting me off.

Silas wasted no time. He rounded a kick into Benny's ribs, hard enough to crack them. Benny tried to catch his breath, wrapping his arms around his stomach like he was trying to give himself a bear hug.

He grabbed a bridle from the ground and slung the harness around Benny's head. He yanked the metal bit up into Benny's mouth. From where I stood, the metal against his teeth gave a gravelly sound, like his mouth was full of marbles.

Benny screamed.

Silas held the straps tight around Benny's head, and grabbed a fistful of hair. I'll never forget the way Benny's feet kicked at the ground, fitfully, with quick spasms, like Reaper stomping her hoof. Sometimes, in my dreams at night—the bad ones—I see Benny's worn-through workboots, stomping that way into the dirt. I never see his face, thank God, but I'm not so sure those kicking feet aren't worse.

"Okay, you little faggot. You want to fuck with me?" Silas said. "Want to be a big man and show off in front of your pussy friend?"

Benny mumbled something I couldn't make out.

"I swear to God, the next time you lay a fucking finger on me, I'll cut your balls off. You got that?"

Then, Silas looked at me. He pointed. "And you. You stay the hell outta my way. You dig me?"

I said nothing.

His grin didn't fade. "Yeah. You dig me. I can see it in your eyes. You're right to be scared. Don't let anybody tell you different." He made a deep sound in his throat that echoed in the still air. Silas Green turned back to Benny and spit a long, grayish yellow ball of snot into the side of his head. Silas let go of the bridle, and Benny's body went slack and fell to the dirt.

"Fuck it," Silas said, and walked out of the barn, Bobby and Aaron in tow.

"You okay?" I asked, creeping up to Benny. He knelt, holding his jaw. The yellow mass hung loosely from his hair. It dangled, then drooped, making its way down the side of his face.

Benny didn't speak. Only the sound of his heavy, uneven breathing filled the stable.

"Hey, man. Come on, you okay?"

"Yeah. Fine," he finally said. Benny spit on the dirt, most of it blood.

In all my years in Chicago, I'd never seen such a beating. It was over for Benny before it even started.

I tried to help him up. He was wiggling a tooth and I didn't particularly care to watch. He shrugged me off.

"Go away, Will."

"Come on, man."

"I said *GO AWAY,* dammit! Just . . . just go away." Benny was on his hands and knees. Blood ran down the side of his mouth, tears down his face.

It was the only time Benny ever raised his voice to me. It was the only time I ever saw him cry. I gave him a pat on the shoulder, stood up, and left. I stopped several times, turning back, feeling worse for him each time.

THAT NIGHT AT DINNER, IT WAS MOSTLY DEAD AT OUR TABLE, AND Benny wasn't talking at all. He was embarrassed and angry, and refused to go see Miss Little about the loose teeth. The fat, split lip and black eye couldn't be concealed, so he just sat with us, quiet as a stone, carefully picking through a meager helping of mashed potatoes and beef hash. Considering he was Lunch Meat, the self-proclaimed human garbage disposal, it was odd to see so little on his tray.

When a bright spot of a table of friends grows dim, everyone notices. Mickey, the usual one to cheer up everyone, gave it his best.

"All right, so this priest is holding confession, right? And he's listening to this gorgeous skirt, who just reeks of wine, spill her guts out."

Most of us at the table smiled, picking through our own trays. Not really from the joke he was telling, more from just knowing he was trying to lighten the mood.

"'I'm an alcoholic and a diagnosed nymphomaniac. I forked fifty men last month, most of 'em were married. Worst part is, Fatha, I got this memory condition, too, and I can't remember no names and no faces.'

"Priest says, 'You're tellin' me you can't remember a single one?'

"'No, Fatha, not a one,' the lady says.

"And the priest says, 'So, uh, you like Italian food?'"

I laughed, and a little milk came out my nose.

"Get it? Get it? 'You like Italian food?'"

The one laughing hardest at the table was the one who told the joke. That, too, made me almost lose it.

Coop grunted, looked to the ceiling, then back at Mickey. "I don't get it."

"Jesus, Coop!" Mickey said, clearly offended. "I gotta explain fucking everything to you? Even Nosebleed got it! He's asking her out 'cause he wants to poke her! She already said she doesn't ever remember . . . I mean, Jesus!" he trailed off after that, and reverted to his meal. "Cock knocker."

"Screw," Coop said.

But Benny didn't laugh. He just stared back and forth between his tray and the Sucrets tin, which he held in one hand. It was like he never even heard the joke.

CHAPTER
twelve

Some of my fondest memories of my father (not that there are many to choose from) are of the times we played cards. At four years old, while other children learned how to spell, I was taught how to play five-card draw. As you might imagine, this didn't thrill my mother, who was of a more conservative nature. She always told me I learned my suits and numbers long before I ever learned to spell. Dad saw to that. After all, what good was it spelling *full house* if you couldn't count the cards that made up one in the first place?

As I grew older, the games came with more frequency, so that by the time I was in third grade, I could best many of my father's friends at poker. And on more than one occasion, I ended up in the principal's office for winning lunch money from my friends during recess sessions of five-card.

We were in the bunkhouse, crowded around Benny's and Mickey's beds. They were just a little farther down from mine, which meant they were just a little farther down from the bathroom. Elmore Holling currently stood at the entrance, making an unpleasant face as an even more unpleasant smell wafted from one of the inside stalls.

"For God's sake, Professor, the stench is brutal," Mickey said to Coop, falling back on his bunk and pretending to strangle himself. I tucked away a letter from home; it was just as plain and dry as the last. Coop provided entertainment by struggling through another magic trick. It was a card prediction trick, but what Coop didn't know was that Mickey was screwing with him, repeatedly denying the last card turned was his. Everyone was stifling laughter, and when Coop finally figured out what was going on, he said, "You assholes."

We couldn't hold it any longer, releasing a burst of laughter at the guy's expense. "Sorry, man, but you should have seen your face," I said.

Coop gave me the finger.

They began to talk about who was better: Elvis or Buddy Holly. The Coasters or the Zodiacs. There was a brand-new song we kept hearing on Cal's AM that Benny loved, from a little group called the Beatles. And then, it was the Babe or Mantle. Being a White Sox guy myself, I voted for Shoeless Joe. Benny had gotten a letter from home, and was rolling the Sucrets tin around in his palm. Something inside it rattled.

"All right, Benny," I said. "What do you keep in that thing?"

He just smiled at me. "Nothing much." He went back to the letter.

I picked up Coop's deck of cards.

"Holy shit, where'd you learn to do that?" Mickey asked. I didn't know what he was talking about, but then I saw each of the guys staring at my hands. Without consciously realizing it, I was doing a one-handed cut and shuffle. As many times as I'd done it before, it was as natural as breathing.

"I saw a guy on TV shuffle like that," Benny said.

"Pretty slick, Nosebleed," Coop said. He smiled and pushed up his glasses.

"Here," I said, and with that, a tradition was born. I dealt cards to each of them and myself. "Everybody know how to play seven stud?"

Benny asked, "Seven what?"

I kept dealing. "Stud. Time to learn."

Mickey finally picked up his cards. "All right," he said, "I'll play. But don't go thinking you're my fucking best friend." His look said he wasn't joking.

"Yeah," I said. "Heard that already."

Mickey already knew cards. Coop had only played a handful of times, and Benny hadn't a clue. But he was quick to learn. I coached them through the first hand, and when it was time to lay down, Benny said, "Hey, lookit that!"

"What, did I win?" Coop asked.

Mickey shook his head. "No, Professor, you didn't win. We all have trash hands, but Nosebleed takes it." He made to scoop up the cards and go again, but Benny stopped him.

"No, that's not what I meant," Benny said. "See? We each had a king. Weird, right?"

I shrugged. "What's so weird about that?"

"Dunno," he said. "Just thought it was neat. There're four kings, four of us."

We played until it was time for dinner, then played again afterward, until lights out. When the games first started, most of the talk was of the game itself—which hands beat which, rules for betting. Benny ended up digging out a cloth bag of peanuts he'd snuck from the mess hall, which proved to be just as good as poker chips or coins.

Our nightly card games gave us something to look forward to, and it was through those games that I finally began to feel accepted in their group. Even Mickey started to warm up, calling me by my real name.

One evening, we managed to talk Cal Jenkins into a hand. He sometimes shot the shit with Mickey, maybe since they were both from Missouri. Cal had a face for poker; the guy could bluff with the best of them, and, man, did he. In one hour, he took nearly half the peanuts and a few of Benny's apples, too. He told us how he was going to Las Vegas someday, to sit in a casino and smoke cigarettes and play twenty-one all through the night.

"I hate the bunk fights," Cal said once, during a card game. "I even tried to stop them for good one time. Nearly lost my job, if you can believe that."

"I believe it," Mickey said, flipping down two and drawing from the stack. "You tried to screw with tradition."

"Warden Barrow." Cal lit a cigarette and took a heavy drag. "You'd have thought I tried to rape his daughter."

"Barrow has a daughter?" Benny asked, eating one of his peanuts.

"I'm just saying, Fritch. You know? But I'd shut my mouth before going too far with it. This was right before he made Frank Kroft his right-hand Jesus Christ. Another guy was head guard then—Radle—and he took it farther than I had. Went right to the top and questioned Barrow's authority about the whole damn thing. He said Barrow had no right to let the fights go on, gambling on them like that and all. Threw out words like *illegal* and *immoral.* Barrow took him back into his office, lit up that pipe, and pulled a damn gun on the guy. We heard he just sat that way for minutes on end. Smoking his pipe, that pistol pointed straight at his head guard's chest. Radle told us the son of a bitch even cocked the hammer about five minutes into it, maybe just to break the silence. After that, we had a change in staff, and Kroft took the job." Cal pulled another cigarette and tossed two peanuts into the pot. "Call," he said.

Across the room, someone raised their voice. It was Bobby Pettigrew. He was talking to Eddie Tokus, who looked ready to take a swing. "Sit down!" Bobby said. "What, you wanna make more of it?"

Eddie shook his head. "I don't care what he lost!" He was looking at Silas. "He ain't got no right! I fought him best as I could!" He was standing now.

"Then maybe you should have done it the way I told you," Silas said. "Maybe you should have listened, or don't your ears work?"

"Screw all of you," Eddie said. "I ain't working off no debt 'cause I lost out. I ain't your fucking boy." And with that, Eddie turned, and huffed away into the bathroom, ending the evening's drama.

We turned back to the game. "Yeah. Vegas," Cal said. "Don't know how much longer I can stay around here."

"I know the feeling," Coop said.

Cal tossed his hand on the cot. "I'm out." He took his cigarettes, and pulled out of the game. He stepped outside, pulling another from the pack, and stared up at the night sky as the door swung closed against his ass.

None of us noticed Silas Green get up and follow Eddie into the bathroom, or that neither of them ever came out. None of us noticed anything, really, until Eddie was already screaming.

"No!" It came steadily enough from the bathroom opening. And that one word just repeated. *"No. No. No."*

We went for a closer look. I glanced behind me, waiting for Cal to rush in, and saw Bobby Pettigrew standing there, looking proud of himself. He'd slid Cal's billy club into the handle, preventing the door from opening. I'm not sure why I didn't go and confront Bobby then. I'm not sure why any of us didn't. But I think it was mostly curiosity. By then, we could tell something bad was going down, and we were all drawn to it like moths.

Silas had a choke hold on Eddie Tokus. They were lying on the floor, Eddie in Silas's lap, almost like lovers. With each breath, Eddie was barking out the same plea: "No."

Silas had his fist curled around Eddie's left ear. He was pulling on it, stretching it as far as he could, and at first I thought he was waiting on Eddie to cry uncle.

"No" turned into *"Please."* "Please, Silas," he whispered now. "Please, please. Don't do it, please."

But Silas just shushed him in small breaths, as calm as a librarian.

"Stop it!" Mickey yelled.

Silas pulled harder, and Eddie screamed.

There was a tearing sound, like canvas, and blood ran down Eddie's cheek.

"God!" he screamed. "Oh, *GOD*!"

Eddie broke free of the loosened grip, and rolled on the floor as though he were on fire. Silas just stood, and then held something up in the air: Eddie Tokus's ripped-away ear. A trophy, simply for being cruel and maniacal. It was smeared with blood, and something white protruded from the top of it. Cartilage, maybe.

There was a crash behind us, and four guards bull-rushed into the bunks, Cal Jenkins leading the way. Elmore Holling took Pettigrew to the ground, and the others took Silas. I heard more voices coming from outside, but nothing in that moment could match the screaming that was coming from Eddie, still rolling on the floor, hand clamped to his head.

CHAPTER
thirteen

I MAY HAVE BEEN ONLY THIRTEEN, BUT I WAS BECOMING QUITE A regular Mr. Fix-it. Thank God for Benny Fritch, who was right there beside me all along, teaching me how to bind, set, and section a fence; how to frame the side of a new shed; how to paint a barn. Yes, there is a right and a wrong way to paint, as it turns out.

Still, even under Benny's watch, I was a work in progress, many times finding myself with hammer-pounded thumbs and wearing more paint than I brushed onto the barns. This was how I looked when Silas first approached me.

We'd already eaten dinner and were in the middle of a seven-card stud game. The biggest pile of Benny's peanuts was in front of me, but Coop was having a good night, too.

"Hey, faggots." Silas walked up to my bunk, hands in his back pockets.

Mickey was the first to respond. "Oh, hey, you don't want to stand there. Only hermaphrodites stand there." Even after what had happened to Eddie Tokus, Mickey was as brash as ever. It was awe-inspiring.

Silas's hint of a grin vanished. "Warden and Kroft want to see the walking paintbrush. I'm here to collect."

❖ ❖ ❖

THE LAST STREAKS OF DAY PEEKED OUT FROM OVER THE WESTERN ridge, and the temperature was dropping. Silas led me past the main house and farther back toward the northern pasture, out behind the barns. I'd never spent much time there, just once when I took a couple of riding saddles out to the fence for the guys who were working inside.

Now, as we approached, I saw two men behind the fence. Warden Barrow was on a mammoth of a horse, but he still looked too large to be on it in the first place. He wore a wide-brimmed black hat and a gun on each hip, like he was ready for some sort of damned shoot-out in Tombstone.

"Mr. Sheppard. Glad you could join us."

I only nodded. Behind me, Silas too was quiet.

"Tell me, son, how are you settling in so far?"

Standing beside the warden, Kroft wore no particular expression.

"Things are okay. It's hard work, but it's okay."

"Good. That sounds like a positive attitude." He pulled the pipe from his shirt pocket and lit it, cupping his hand around the opening. "Now . . . you understand, Mr. Sheppard, that the more cooperative you are, the easier your time here will be. Frank tells me you're interested in joining the breakers. Wanting to work a little closer to the action."

"Yes, sir."

"It's unusual for a boy to get his chance when he's only been here a handful of months. You know that, don't you?"

I nodded. "Yes. Guess I do."

"Unless . . . certain provisions are taken. Certain . . . allowances, by me."

"I don't understand."

"You beat the shit out of Eddie Tokus."

"I defended myself. That's all."

"No, you did a hell of a job. The fights are no secret, William. Call it a tradition, if you like. But I do have to tell you, I lost a bit of a gentlemen's wager. Mine was on that chubby little pecker." He took a few draws from his pipe. The sun was now setting directly behind him. It reminded me of the painting in the holding room. "We have a new guest arriving soon. From Texas. I want you to try your damnedest to win, no matter what. Hell, fight dirty if you have to. I have more fun playing the long shots." Fingers of smoke filtered from his mouth and nose as he exhaled.

"What if I don't want to fight?"

"Oh, you'll fight. And if you win, you're on the team working the horses. There might be a hell of a dollar on you. I hope to God it pays off."

My composure crumpled. "Go to hell with your money. I'm not fighting."

Silence.

They were either too surprised or too outraged to reply. Behind me, I heard Silas draw a gasp of breath.

Barrow smiled and dismounted the horse. He handed the reins to Kroft. As Barrow stepped toward me, I braced for the blow. He reached with a firm hand and slapped it against my shoulder.

"That, son"—he leaned close to my ear—"is why I brought the boys along." He walked past me, and off into the twilight.

Kroft climbed onto the tall horse, settled into the saddle, and secured his boots into the holsters. He reached over to the opposite side of the saddle and took a handful of rope.

"Silas," he said.

The punch caught me on the left side, and knocked me to one knee.

"This is to let you see what sort of hell your life will be if you refuse," Kroft said. He twirled a lasso over his head, and the rope cut into the evening air with a thin hiss.

I rose, hoping to run, but never got the chance. I didn't fully comprehend what happened until it was too late; the lasso slung around my chest, cinching tightly around my ankles. Kroft yanked with fantastic strength and I was immediately pulled to the ground.

"Hyah!" he screamed, or maybe it was Silas—I couldn't tell.

A heavy thunder filled my head as the horse bolted to an

immediate gallop, yanking me directly behind. The earth raced everywhere around me, scraping my body against every rock along the tattered field.

I lost my breath. I flailed my arms toward the rope, as if that might end it. Underneath the cutting rocks, underneath the beating hoofs of the scrambling horse, even underneath Frank Kroft yawwing the animal on, beneath all this, I heard Silas. Laughing at me as I was dragged across the north pasture like a doll.

CHAPTER
fourteen

"WILLIAM. WILL. COME ON, NOW."

Somewhere, in the darkness, I heard "Earth Angel" playing at low volume. I wanted to sleep more, to rest. But the voice, again.

"Will."

Miss Little eased over me; her eyes peered down into mine. I lay on my side, and felt something taped to my back. My head swam and my leg burned.

"There, now," she said with that gentle voice. "Thought we'd damn near lost you, child. A miracle. That's what it is, all right. Nearly believed you were going to sleep forever. Those drugs sure had their way with you."

Looking down, I saw a stretched jigsaw of bruises and tattered skin that used to be my left thigh. Judging from the pain, I could already tell that my back looked even worse.

"Trust me," she said, "looks better than it did. That's the truth!"

She helped me sit up, and I thought for sure I was going to pass out. Lightning whipped across my leg and back, and tears welled in my eyes.

"I've done dug all the dirt and rocks out of you, child." She shook her head. "But, it looks worse than it is, miracle of God. You'll stay here for a few days, and you'll probably scab over something awful."

"I feel like I'm on fire."

"You'll live, no doubt about that." She began gathering rolls of tape and gauze. "Don't understand this forsaken place. Send one away with just one ear on his head and they send me another with his back nearly sliced away. Wonder I don't leave in the middle of the night. Just slip off like I was never here."

"Why do you stay?"

She placed the rolls of bandages and instruments in their drawers, and put her hands over mine. "I suppose . . . we all have our reasons for what we do, child, even if we keep it secret from others. Me, the guards, even you boys. Do you understand? You just leave it alone, now."

I shifted, trying to find a position that didn't make me feel like passing out, then came close to it anyway, falling onto my side.

"Boy's torn up from head to toe, and they call it an accident." She helped me turn over, as gentle as my own mother might have. "We'll change these rags again in the morning. Trust me, you'll be right in no time, honey."

"They want me to fight. Someone I don't even know."

"New boy. I heard. What you going to do?"

"I don't know. I told the warden I wasn't going to. That's what earned me this trip here."

"You have to make up your own mind, sugar. Boys don't always fight, you know. I usually see them in here anyway once they've made that decision."

"It doesn't matter what I do, then," I said.

"Sure it does! What you mean it don't matter? Matters a great deal, child. It matters to yourself when all's been said and done. You'll know what I'm talking about. You may not think it, but it matters to the other boys, too. Some will hate you for it, but some might respect you, too. You're right, though, not always up to you in the end. If they don't get to you, they always seem to get to the other one. If he decides he's going to fight, you may not have a choice at all."

She helped me off the table and stretched a loose T-shirt over my head. It was white and had SWOPE across the front in small block letters.

"Just be careful, sugar," she said, and rustled my hair with a soft hand, then helped me to a crooked-looking hospital bed that looked like it came straight out of a World War I medical tent.

IT WAS STRANGE TO HAVE THE LUXURY OF A QUIET AND PEACEFUL night. But even with the pain medication, I had a difficult time sleeping without all the little things I'd come to be used to—the tick of Cal's desk clock, a wide array of coughing and snoring (Benny's was always the loudest), Coop flipping through a book, trying his best to be discreet. God help me, even the sound of the creaking bunk springs from masturbation. As disgusting as that was, it was familiar, and at thirteen years old and a thousand miles from home, there was comfort in familiarity.

Still, there was something calming about Miss Little's infirmary. It was also her living quarters, and hearing her sleep in the room next to mine made me feel like I was staying the night in a real home and not a prison ranch. It was a comfortable deceit.

During the night, I woke to what sounded like muffled crying coming from Miss Little's room. She called out what sounded like a name, and then another, though I couldn't tell exactly what they were. Her voice came in and out through the soft weeping. It ended, rather abruptly, and was replaced with the sound of rustling sheets and slow footsteps on the floor.

As the door opened, I narrowed my eyes and pretended to sleep. The room I was sleeping in was more of a nook, really, and allowed me a view of the open space of the infirmary. Miss Little crossed the room as silently as a ghost and opened a tall cabinet door.

"Mind if I light a lamp, sugar?"

I opened my eyes and whispered, "How did you know I was awake?"

"Just knew." She turned on a short table lamp, and the soft light betrayed her puffy, red eyes. Her voice sounded old, and tired. "Just came to collect a little help." A few items in the medicine cabinet toppled as she plucked a small bottle of tablets from the back.

I shifted and my back burned. The pain pills were wearing off, and I let out a sharp cry.

"Might as well change those bandages since you're up," she said. As she worked, she began to hum. It was a familiar tune, something my mother used to sing when I was younger. I closed my eyes, submitting completely to her care.

"You're comfortable around me, child."

"I guess so."

"Remind me where you're from, now."

"Chicago."

"Never been. I'm a Southern girl, myself. From—" She paused, as if deciding whether to tell me. ". . . just outside Savannah. That's Georgia, understand."

"Yes, ma'am. I know."

"Reckon you do. No, quite a few boys around this rooster house aren't too terribly comfortable as you are. Guess they don't think much of a colored woman seeing to them."

"You really think that's it?" She was so warm and gentle, I couldn't imagine anyone shying away from her. Yet I remembered Eddie Tokus, and how he kept pulling back each time she touched him.

"Course that's it. Only black-skinned soul on the ranch, ain't I? It don't bother me none, though. I've found there's a good deal of gentle souls here as well. Doesn't that just sound funny to say, in such a place?"

Perhaps a little too quick with my mouth, I asked, "Why do you think they hired you, then?"

She stopped, eyebrows raised, then laughed, wiping her eyes. "Lord. In all the years I've been working here, nobody's asked me that. Not a one." The smile faded, her demeanor more serious. "Good for you for asking tough questions, William. Never stop asking them." She tousled my hair with her long, thin fingers. "Tell you what I think. I think the ones who decided to give me this job didn't give a flop *how* I made the kids feel. Fact, I sort of figure they thought it might be sort of a bonus if I made them uncomfortable. That's exactly what it was."

I was in awe. This was one of the first real conversations I'd held with an adult, and I was surprised how small it made me feel. "If you knew, why did you take it? Didn't it make you angry?"

"Back then, William, I wasn't feeling much of anything. I was just looking for something and something came along. Didn't much care why they gave it to me." She finished bandaging my torso, and placed a loose, half-separated nightshirt over my head.

"Anyways. I've been here nearly a decade. But it was only a few years back that I really earned my stripes, you could say. Tall boy brought to me. Got himself hit upside the face with a shovel and needed a home stitch or two. Must have struck a nerve on that boy. Pricked him harder than he liked, and before I knew what happened, found my sorry self on the floor, blood just pouring out my busted-in nose." As if to accentuate, she ran a finger along the crooked slant of her nose.

"Silas Green."

"Mmm-hmm," she hummed. "Regular Boy Scout, that one. Between you and me, I'll be glad to see that devil go; put his file away for good. Although there's always someone to come along and take his place."

I winced, falling not so gracefully back into the mattress.

"Funny how life has a way of working out," she said. "Scraped my way through nursing school—colored-only program. We all had such grand ideas. Had one friend who ended up in Paris. Can you just imagine?"

"Never thought you'd end up on a ranch in Colorado, I bet," I said.

"Never thought *you'd* end up on a ranch in Colorado, I bet." She wedged an extra pillow behind my head, and produced several pills that were nearly as large as nickels. "This should get you through the morning. Wish I had something stronger for you, baby, but it should help you rest."

She was right. I slept until noon the next day.

Four days later, I was back in my own cot in the barracks, waking to the sound of Buddy Holly's "Oh, Boy!" It was Saturday, and Cal sat behind his desk with a smile on his face, the Philco AM before him. "Rise and shine, ladies," he announced at the top of his lungs. "God's granted us another beautiful Rocky Mountain morning!"

My back itched and stung like I'd slept on a bed of ants. I'd tried my best to stay on my side during the night, but I still woke on my back, staring at the naked bulbs hanging from the ceiling.

I hadn't slept much at all. I kept thinking about the conversations I'd had with Miss Little. I wouldn't have admitted it to anyone, but I felt sad when she released me from the infirmary. I felt welcomed by her, and that was a hard thing to give up. Although it was good to see my friends again. I dug through my footlocker, pausing to glance at the black-and-white of my mom before pulling out my clothes for the day.

The new guy, the big shot from Texas, was arriving that day. And that night? How could I fight, the way I'd been cut up in the pasture? I vowed to try my best, but I was still bleeding and wearing bandages, for God's sake. It would be a joke. But it wasn't just that; I didn't want to fight him out of sheer spite toward those who just wanted another reason to throw their money around, or whatever else they had to wager.

It was the expectation that we must fight each other like hungry dogs that I resented. I'm sure I wasn't the only one who felt that way, yet the fighting survived.

All we needed were sharpened spears. I know I gladly would have taken one.

CHAPTER
fifteen

"WHAT BULLSHIT!" MICKEY SAID. WE WERE AT LUNCH, AND I WAS giving more details of the little ride I took around the north pasture.

"How can they keep getting away with all this?" Coop asked. The morning sun blazed through an east window and caught his red hair, making it look brighter than ever.

"They just do," Benny said. "No one gives a shit about us."

"No." Coop stopped him. "This is a boys' reformatory. And they run it like it's a Mexican prison. We all see what goes on here, but we turn a blind eye and pretend it doesn't happen."

"Damn, we don't turn no blind eyes from anything," Mickey said. "Come on, Coop."

"Yeah?" Coop asked. "Tell me about Frank Kroft, Mickey. You know damn well what he did to Duncan Embry several weeks ago. Elmore Holling saw him take Dunk away, he fucking knew what was going to happen, and he didn't give a shit! The warden lets it happen, too. Besides that, the guards are beating up the kids, yanking us around, dragging us behind horses, throwing us in solitary. What gives them the right? This whole place needs to burn straight to the ground." His Coke bottles slipped just to the edge of his nose, and for a moment, I thought he was going to let them just slip right off.

We were silent. Coop's voice wavered on the verge of crying. I never saw him so emotional and wondered, Why now?

He hiked his glasses back to the top of his nose, picked up his fork and twirled at the soppy noodles. "But you're right, Benny. Nobody gives a shit about us. That's why we've got to stick together."

"That's the plan, man," Mickey said. "I guess even old Shep's part of us, now. Lucky bastard. Hey, there you go, that's exactly what we are, all of us. The Lucky Bastards!" He laughed, trying to lighten the mood.

"No. That's not us," Coop said. "In here, we can be whoever we want to be. Screw the world, it doesn't matter what we did before. In here, we can be kings."

"Kings?" I asked.

And then Coop smiled, and hiked up his glasses again. "Fucking A. Just like the hands we threw down in that card game. We four kings."

"I like that," Mickey said. *"Kings."*

"So what are you gonna do about the fight tonight?" Benny asked. "You haven't forgotten, you know?"

"Of course he hasn't forgotten, Lunch!" Mickey said. "You haven't forgotten, right?"

I shrugged. "Don't know. Thinking about not doing it, or maybe taking a dive, something like that."

"Could be a way out," Coop said, now rubbing his eyes with balled fists. "Or it could just be stupid." He smiled at me.

"Great advice, Harvard," Mickey said, and Coop just shrugged, and picked up his worn paperback. But Mickey didn't let up. "You can't do that, Shep. Seriously! You don't wanna go down like that in front of everyone!" His smile gave away his true intentions, and he started to squint, which was a good indication he was hiding something.

"Yah, yah, yah," Benny said, stuffing a forkful of green beans into his wide mouth. "I'm pretty sure I could guess why you really want him to jump in there tonight," he said.

"Drop dead twice, Benny. You big wet," Mickey said, laughing.

"It's nice to know my friends are ready to turn a dollar off of me," I said.

"Hey, Shep," Mickey said, extending his arms in an extremely exaggerated bow, "we're always here for you!"

"Go screw," I replied.

Benny turned his attention back to another letter from home. He always guarded the precious words written on those pages, never sharing them with us. And when he pretended not to cry while reading them we pretended not to notice.

"Change the subject, Coop. Tell us a story. One of those weird ones you always tell." Mickey propped his head against one hand. He was older than me, but sometimes—when he did stuff like that—he looked so young. Too young to be in a place like Swope, at least.

Coop shrugged, turned a page in his book.

Benny said, "Aw, come on, Coop. A scary one, too."

Coop closed the book, took off his glasses, and sighed. "Did I ever tell you about a guy named Alferd Packer?" He rubbed a hand across his pimple-laced cheek.

We all shook our heads. Mickey shoved a piece of bread into his mouth and smiled.

"Alferd Packer," he repeated. He held up the paperback and flipped it open to the last few pages, then set it down on the table, turning it around so we could see. Across both pages was a crudely drawn map of the Rocky Mountains running through Colorado.

"Almost a hundred years ago, in early 1874, this guy led a group of five men up into the Rockies to mine for gold. While they were up there, an early blizzard ripped across the entire area, and they got stuck. Snowbound. This all happened not even ten miles from here." He pointed to the map, running a finger down from Gunnison to the town of Lake City.

We all ate in silence. It was fun to watch Coop get so involved in a tale; his excitement was contagious.

"Two months pass. Then, Alferd Packer creeps out of the mountains and into town. He heads straight to a bar, and tells his story of survival to anyone who'll listen. He claims he killed one of the men in self-defense, and that the others went on, searching for food, while he stayed to set up a camp. He says they never returned, and he hadn't seen them since.

"So people start talking. Noticing things that didn't really fit with the story. He's carrying a hunting knife that belonged to one of the miners who disappeared, as well as several of their wallets, still filled with cash. And the strangest thing, the most bizarre—"

Now a couple guys from the next table over were listening in, eating in silence and staring at Coop. He could have been sitting next to a campfire, telling ghost stories.

"—was how Packer looked. He was up in the Rockies, in the thick of winter for two months, struggling to survive. Two months. But he didn't look thin, he didn't even look hungry.

"Pretty soon, Packer's brought in for questioning. That's when he changes his story. This time, he says two of the guys died from the cold. And Packer says he ate them—you know, to survive."

"You're shitting me!" Mickey said.

"Then," Coop continued, "he says the other three men died after that, also from exposure . . . and he ate them, too."

"That's sick," Benny said.

"A few months later, the snow melted, and they found the frozen bodies, all mutilated, with ax marks chipped across all their bones. And all the skulls were mashed in from behind. The men didn't just die from exposure. At least, it didn't look that way. Packer murdered them. And ate from the bodies." Coop shut the little book and sat just a little taller, looking quite proud of himself.

"That true, Coop? All of it?" Benny asked, with a mouthful of bacon.

"Of course it's true! I don't waste time with fiction. The truth is more interesting, and bizarre. Like Poe. Everyone reads his stories, but his biography can be much creepier."

"Here goes Coop on another rip about writers," Mickey said, and rolled his eyes.

"Yeah," Benny added, "he's one of those 'cyclopedias, you know? Once he gets going, you better get comfortable."

I never minded. I thought Coop was about the smartest guy I ever knew. Sometimes, when he got off like that—after he finished saying something clever but wasted on the likes of us regarding the style of Ernest Hemingway, or the poetry of Byron—we'd all just stare at each other and crack up. He laughed right along with us, never really getting what was so funny.

"Is that it?" I asked. "Come on, that's the scariest story you can come up with?"

Coop said nothing, but his eyes broke away from his book, and maybe he saw I was kidding around, maybe he didn't.

"I don't know," Benny said. "The mutilated corpses and bashed-in skulls part was pretty creepy, right?"

"Yeah, it was okay," Mickey said. "Not one of your best, but it was a respectable so-so."

I'm sure Mickey wouldn't have said that if I'd kept my own mouth shut. It only added to the critique, though. Coop looked at us like we were traitors.

"Screw all of you! You're the ones who asked for the stupid story, now you pick it apart?"

"Cool it, man," Benny said. "We're just kidding around with you."

"Yeah," I said. "It was interesting. Just not a horror, that's all. No big deal."

Coop's face turned red. "What do any of you know! You guys don't even read!"

There was a lull at the table. Mickey looked to me, I looked to Benny, and we all started giggling.

"Come on, man. Don't be so serious," Mickey said. "You're our bro, always will be. We're just goofing on you."

It seems to me now, though, that Coop was trying to tell us something. Something so important that he almost cried. That we ignored him and laughed at him hurts me still to this day.

Coop picked up his tray and rose to leave. "Kings, my ass." But as he tried to pull his tall, clumsy legs out from under the table, he lost his balance, and fell back onto the floor. The tray toppled, sending his half-eaten lunch all over him. Instantly, shrills of laughter flooded the room.

"Coop! What's into you?" Mickey asked. He was the first one to Coop, hand outstretched. "Come on."

"Are you okay, man?" I asked, standing.

"Just let me alone!" Coop shouted. He wiped at the spaghetti noodles on his forehead and hair, but only succeeded in smearing them. Marinara sauce splashed across one of his lenses, and I couldn't help thinking right then how much it looked like blood. "I'm fine. I'm cool. Just let me alone for a while." He made to get up, but his sneaker caught a pile of the food, and he slipped once more.

Benny was there, helping him up. "Coop," he said. "It's us."

Coop wiped his glasses with the back of his hand. "I'm fine, really!" He grabbed his books. The one with the map of Colorado was ruined, covered with stains. Coop hurried out of the mess hall, leaving his tray overturned on the floor. And as much as I didn't want to believe it, I think he was crying.

"The hell are you all laughing at!" Mickey screamed out to everybody. We sat back down at our table, feeling miserable.

"Did something happen?" I asked. "This morning? Did something happen to him?"

Benny looked at Mickey. "Kroft wasn't with him, right? He didn't go off with Kroft, did he?"

"How the hell should I know, Lunch? I'm no bodyguard. I ain't with him all day and all night! I didn't see anything, but how should I know?"

"What do you mean, Kroft?" I asked. "What does he do?"

No one answered.

"Did Kroft hit him? Is that what you mean?"

"Forget it," Benny said. "Just forget it, Will. Coop's fine. He'll cool off, you know?"

"I don't know," Mickey said. "Coop's just that kind of guy. I don't think he'd tell us if something happened."

My thoughts ran wild and I felt worse by the minute.

CHAPTER
sixteen

JOHN CHURCH WAS PRESENTED TO THE GENERAL POPULATION IN much the same way I had been: through the side door of the mess hall during dinner. But that's where the similarities ended. Before Church, Benny was the biggest guy my age that I'd ever seen. Church had him beat by almost a foot. He stood in the doorway, hands in pockets, blocking out much of the dying sunlight behind. No one said a word.

I guessed him to be over six feet. I heard he was just ahead of us in age, maybe fifteen, but looking at the guy, I thought he was old enough to buy beer and then drive around with it between his legs.

John Church was so large that no one saw Frank Kroft standing behind him until John's body lurched forward, shoved from behind. Church turned to Kroft and gave him a hateful look, but Frank stood his ground. John turned and slunk over to the chow line.

Church carried his tray to a crowded table and dropped it down, waiting for one of the guys to move over. He didn't have to wait long. It was Eddie Tokus who slid down. Eddie, who was back at the same table as the animal who'd mutilated him. Eddie, with a gauze pad the size of my hand taped to the side of his head.

Church sat down like a paperweight on a desk.

Silas just stared at him as though Church were nothing more than an insolent child who didn't know better than to sit at his table without permission. Ruben DeMarco, seated across from Church, folded his hands and said, "Wait, I got it." He laughed to himself. "You're somebody special! Right?"

There was a nervous laugh from most everyone else who heard. "Your shit smells like cinnamon sticks. That it?" Ruben smiled at Silas and the other guys, then reached across the table and took a dinner roll from John Church's tray. "Why don't you just get up and go sit someplace else, Moose?"

I'm not sure what Ruben expected, but I'm guessing it wasn't what he got. Ruben had just stuffed the roll into his big mouth when John reached across the table and slapped an iron hand onto his shirt, reeling the poor guy across the table and into one of the most powerful punches I've seen, even to this day. It didn't stop there. Ruben took a literal beating, not that I felt much sympathy. I'm sure he never even knew what happened until his teeth started falling out. And John Church did this, blow after powerful blow, without rising from his seat. He got in six solid punches to Ruben's head before the first guard even reached him.

It took all of them to get him on the ground and cuffed. The entire cafeteria was blanketed in silence. Everyone's eyes were on the behemoth on the floor; everyone's mouths were open. It was almost cliché. He must have been like dead weight because it took three grown men to lift him up, and it wasn't until they'd led him outside, and the door swung shut, that the room erupted.

"Holeee shit," Benny said.

Mickey looked as serious as I'd ever seen him. "That was the single greatest thing I've ever seen. I can't believe Coop wasn't here to see it."

"Holeee shit," Benny repeated.

"That's the guy I have to fight," I said, looking at Ruben DeMarco's face. It was already swelling up most every place. He just sat there, holding his head in his hands while Cal Jenkins hunched over him. "How am I supposed to do that?"

"Well," Mickey said, "at least now you have a little time to mull that one over."

❖ ❖ ❖

WE DIDN'T SAY MUCH BACK AT THE BUNKS. IT HAD BEEN A LONG DAY, and I wanted nothing more than to just read an old letter from home before falling asleep. I pulled off my shirt, and reached into my footlocker to grab a clean tee.

I noticed instantly that it was gone—the black-and-white of my mom. I'd left it underneath a stack of envelopes along the right-hand side of the locker, but that didn't stop me from pulling everything out. I registered that some of the letters were gone, too.

Jeans, shirts, underwear—all of it lay bare on the floor at my feet. A pain deeper than being dragged across the north pasture sliced into my heart.

"What's up?" Benny asked. "What happened?"

I didn't answer him. I looked around the crowded room, bustling with guys going about their own business. Tears were already welling, and I tried to blink them away.

"What's missing? Tell me," Benny said. "Come on, you're not alone here."

But he was wrong. I felt more alone than ever. I just shook my head, and collapsed onto the cot, wondering who, wondering why. Wondering how anyone could be so cruel as to take the most important possession I had.

CHAPTER

seventeen

WHEN I USED TO HAVE BAD DREAMS, MY MOTHER TOLD ME TO LOCK a happy thought in my mind until I fell asleep. She said to picture it, whatever it was. Think of the sounds you hear, if the wind is in your hair or if the sun is shining warm on your skin. For me, that thought was usually the same: my mother, sitting with me in the cool grass underneath the shade of an apple tree in McGuane Park. She is reading to me, and I close my eyes, tuning out the sound of cars, the laughter, the shouting. I only hear her voice.

This trick didn't always work, but on the nights it did, the sleep was the best. This is what I was doing when I realized Coop was sitting Indian-style on the floor beside my bunk. The lights were long turned out, and most everyone was already asleep. Seeing him made me jump; as pale as he was, he could have been a ghost.

"Coop?"

"Let's say there's this kid," he said. His whispering scratched through the quiet room, and for a second, I wanted nothing more than for him to just go back to bed.

"Let's say he's dumped off into an orphanage in San Francisco. But he grows up a good kid, decent. The nuns there are straight. Hard and strict so that while other kids grow up reading books on Dick and Jane, this kid is taught the New Testament, about how John the Baptist's head ended up on a silver platter."

I looked over at Mickey's bunk, hoping to God he'd be awake by now. "Come on, Coop. You don't need to get into this. You were right, I was an asshole earlier."

He didn't even flinch. "Maybe the more he reads, the more he starts wondering about his own parents; maybe they were smart, too. Maybe they liked to read. Maybe even his mother worked at a university. And then, one night, he's found by the head mother who never liked him. She finds him with a book, and instead of the lashes on each hand, she tells him the truth. That his mother wasn't really an English professor at all. Only a fourteen-year-old runaway who was raped this way and that in a back alley."

Now Mickey was awake. "Coop?" He propped himself on one elbow.

But Coop wasn't going to stop for anyone, and his eyes never left my face.

"And all along, there's a secret. Something that shuts the world out and makes him feel high. It didn't hurt anything, never did. The fires were always small.

"And then, God sends a miracle to the orphanage. By a twist of fate, they see this boy, a man and his wife see something in him. And I bet you wouldn't believe it, but they go ahead and adopt this kid."

A few of the other guys around me stirred. Benny sat up, but he looked as though he'd heard the story before. It dawned on me that he most likely had.

"So maybe this couple, they take the kid home. They give him everything he ever wished for. And each night, the kid prays he won't wake up the next morning to find it's all just a goddamn dream.

"Then, something crazy happens. The man and woman find out they're going to have a baby. The orphan's going to be a big brother. And now, a baby girl is born. She grows up, chasing her big brother around everywhere. The kid loves the girl, would do fucking anything for her. Would die for her, even."

"Coop," I said.

Mickey interrupted. "Let him finish, Will."

"More time passes, and then, how about another miracle? The happy family finds out another baby's on the way. Nobody's happier than the redheaded freak. Maybe Mom and Dad are so jazzed, they go out one night to celebrate. And maybe they leave the kid in charge of the little girl."

Coop was crying now. "Let's say that while they were gone, something happens. After all, he hadn't burned anything in a while, and temptation's just a bitch. And it's nothing. Just some rags in a wastebasket. But then the little girl runs in and sees him. Sees the flame catch. Sees it spread, and starts screamin'. Maybe she runs off and hides somewhere in the house. Maybe the kid tries and tries, but he just can't find her anywhere."

Coop's eyes were glued to mine. He didn't even wipe the tears away.

"He calls her. 'Elizabeth!' No answer. 'Oh, Christ, Elizabeth, please!' And all the while, the flames grow, and grow, and now the whole fucking house is on fire, and no matter where he goes, there's no answer. There's never an answer, not until the end. When someone pulls him out of the house. That's when he hears her. His little sister, screaming. Screaming out his name, over and over, until it eats a hole in his head. And he has to sleep each night after that with the same voice, crying out. Crying out how much she hurts. And he thinks that's just about the scariest story he's ever heard. But it's not about what I think, because it's just about if it's scary enough for you. Is it, Will? You think that's a scary enough story?"

CHAPTER
eighteen

"TODAY THE DAY?" MICKEY DROPPED HIS TRAY DOWN NEXT TO US and slung a leg over the seat next to Coop. "And keep in mind, we've been hearing the same shit ever since her herd trucked in." He brushed something off his bacon before taking a bite.

Coop poked at the hash on his own tray, then grunted. "Course today's going to be the day. Just wait and see." He'd been quiet since that night in the bunkhouse, but he seemed stronger, too. Confident. We were just glad to see him come around.

"The day for what?" I asked.

"Nah," Benny said. "Today ain't the day."

"Screw both of you—just wait. It's close. You know what they say about Rome, right?"

"Yeah, it took fuckin' forever to build, just like you and your horse." Mickey smiled at his own cleverness.

Coop looked momentarily like he intended to slap Mickey, then rolled his eyes and said, "Today. Today."

"Reaper," I said. "How long has it been?"

"Long enough that she may not break at all," Benny said. "I bet they're already talking about selling her untamed."

"That's not happening," Coop said. "I made a connection with her, she's making progress. It's just a matter of time."

"Move on, man. Give it up. I would have already."

"Would you want someone giving up on you, Mickey? Would you have liked it if we'd never let you hang with us?"

"Come on," Mickey said. "That's not the same. Besides, you and Benny both were just waiting on a great guy like me to come along and tell fuck jokes all day."

"And I'm not giving up on her," Coop said. "She's like . . . one of us, you know?"

No one said anything.

"You all know what I mean."

And the funny thing was, we all did.

THAT PARTICULAR DAY CONTINUED WITHOUT MUCH OF ANYTHING TO note. In fact, when I think back on it, I can't seem to remember hardly anything that happened between that morning's conversation, and what came later in the evening.

After dinner, I walked out of the mess hall alongside Mickey. At least, it mostly looked like walking; my cuts were healing, and my legs and back didn't scream as loud when I moved. John Church was scheduled to get out of solitary, and most everyone still expected a three-round special.

We were halfway across the commons, just near the towering flagpole, when we saw a gangly blur of red hair and glasses sprinting toward the barn.

"Wow," I said.

"Yeah," Mickey said. "I had no idea old Coop could run like that." He stopped, and cupped his hands around his mouth. "Hey, Archie Andrews!" he yelled. "What's the fuckin' rush?"

Coop nearly tripped over his own feet when he looked back to us, but he never completely stopped. "Silas! Stole Benny's box! Went to get it back!" Coop stumbled into the barn, and was gone.

"Oh, crap." Mickey yanked my arm, and broke into a run, dragging me along just behind. "This is bad."

"What's inside the box that's so important?" I asked, trying to keep up. Mickey was small, some might even say tiny, but his speed was amazing. He shook his head at my question while in full sprint.

"Don't worry about it," he said.

It's funny about time. Mere seconds can make just about all the difference in the world. If we'd have only been able to cool off Benny, things might have turned out differently.

We pushed through the same door Coop ducked into, and saw a bizarre image at the far end of the barn. The setting sun was picture-framed in the open doorway, and the sharp light revealed the image only as a trio of dark silhouettes. But it was obvious, from the size and shape of their forms, who was who.

Silas stood over Benny, foot on his throat. He knelt, and began knocking Benny's face with punch after violent punch. And behind them (we were just in time to witness this), Coop ran up. Something was in his hands. He held it high, then swung it hard into the back of Silas's head.

It was a pipe wrench. Silas immediately fell to the ground, dazed.

At their feet, in the dirt, was the blue Sucrets box. Even from where I stood, I saw it was open. Benny swiped a hand at it, missed, then reached out again. He rolled over, and began plucking things out of the dirt, placing them back into the tin. He seemed suddenly oblivious to everything around him, and just kept scanning the dirt, running his hands over the ground until everything spilled had been put back into place.

Coop, on the other hand, focused exactly on one thing: Silas. He swung a foot directly into Silas's stomach, and then again. He was gritting his teeth, clenching his fists, and it was clear he was putting everything he had into each strike.

Frank Kroft burst into the barn behind me and Mickey. His rifle was slung over his shoulder, and he practically threw us aside as he passed. "What the hell is this?" he screamed. In that moment, he looked just as crazy as Silas.

Coop's eyes doubled in size when he saw the seven-foot-tall Frank Kroft charging toward them.

Silas was on his knees now, blood seeping through his dirty hair. I could have sworn on the Holy Bible that he was grinning. "Cooper took a gun, Frank!" Silas said. "Get him, he's breaking for it!"

Both Mickey and I screamed Coop's name. Screamed for him to stop as we ran toward Frank Kroft, who was already raising his rifle.

Coop was well into the open pasture, heading for God knows where. The pipe wrench was still in his grip and as he ran, his arms pumped wildly up and down. Silas yelled again, "He's got a gun!"

"Frank!" Mickey said.

The gun recoiled against his shoulder. The sound ripped open the world, and my ears immediately began to ring. I dropped to a knee, noticed a thread of smoke coming from the end of the barrel, and heard the echo of the shot again, and again. Halfway across the field, the outline of a boy dropped to the ground without so much as a sound.

CHAPTER

nineteen

MICKEY LATER TOLD ME THAT I THREW A PAIL OF TOOLS AT FRANK Kroft after he shot Coop. I honestly can't remember. I do recall seeing Benny lunge at our chief guard, punching and kicking in a blind rage. And Mickey was too shocked to do anything but bear witness to it all.

Frank elbowed Benny in the throat, then brought the butt of his rifle down on my head. I was only vaguely aware of them later dragging us to solitary.

The box. It was a stand-alone unit containing three blackout cells that were each roughly the size of a king mattress. The box was painted white on the outside, I guess to contrast what most saw on the inside. Each cell inside was lined top to bottom with concrete. There were no windows, and the only light to seep into each room came through a hair-sized break beneath a solid steel door.

Rumor was, the temperatures were only tolerable just a few months out of the year. The heat was sometimes bad enough (I just thanked God we weren't in Arizona or Nevada), but the winters were just unbearable in the box. A close similarity was being stuck in a meat locker down at the local butcher's. Once, Mickey was there for two days during a mid-January snowstorm, and said the warden had a truckload of hamburger delivered to the cell next to him when the kitchen freezers broke down. "Felt like my nuts were gonna freeze right off, Shep. No kiddin'."

Frank Kroft killed our friend, and for throwing pails and rocks and God knows whatever else I could get my hands on, I got four days in the box. Benny got six in the concrete cell next to me. Call it ranch justice. Call it bullshit. It's all the same.

An inquiry was held the very next day at the ranch. It was privileged attendance, I heard, and only the warden and Kroft were there to meet with the suit from the Colorado State Board of Corrections. Mickey later said they even called in Silas to provide an accurate testimony. Probably just as accurate as Frank Kroft's version of what happened.

I spent the first night in the box grieving. My hands tightened into fists each time I thought of Silas.

I was mad at everyone, at everything. None of them—the warden, the suit, the guards—showed remorse about the boy shot dead with a tool in his hand instead of a pistol. Only an annoyance at having to clean up the mess, settle things over with the state. The *mess*. I really heard the warden use that word.

I couldn't get that image of Coop out of my head. I cried into my open hands, biting my palm so I wouldn't be so loud. I must have finally fallen asleep, because I heard Frank's rifle and saw Coop fall like an animal, and my head jerked into the concrete wall.

Sometime during the next day, I was startled awake by a sound in the darkness. It was Benny's voice, low and muffled, coming over the top of the wall.

"I never told you what happened to me. How I ended up here." His speech was shaky, and interrupted by sniffing. I imagined his eyes, like my own, bloodshot from too many tears. I was glad that I couldn't see his face and that he couldn't see mine.

"You don't have to . . . I don't care." And I didn't. As angry as I was at the world, was I fully aware that included Benny? I think so. I kept thinking had he not chased after Silas, Coop would still be with us. And for what? A keepsake. A tin box.

"I know you don't need to know. But I'm going to tell you anyway." I heard him blow his nose—into what, I have no idea.

I sat with my eyes closed. In the darkness, it didn't matter. I focused on Benny's voice. It sounded so innocent sometimes. Different from the other guys'.

"I have a little brother. His name's Todd. He's four years younger than me. When he was born, there was something wrong with him, you know? The doctors told my dad it was called Down syndrome, and he didn't understand. So they told him it meant Todd was retarded.

"And you should have seen them—Mom and Dad. They didn't know what to think at first. Mom took it the hardest. She started getting a depression about her. Dad, I don't know, he sort of just pretended nothing was wrong. That was kind of the best thing to do, I think. You know?"

I can't say why, but I remember thinking about Coop as Benny spoke. Wondering where he was, right then. Some sort of crude, makeshift coffin? Maybe in some truck, being crated back to San Francisco? Wherever didn't matter. Because he was dead; the life shot out of him like a doomed soldier on a battlefield. I bit my lip and squeezed my eyes shut, and I heard nothing in the world but Benny's words.

"Todd was different, but he was still just a goofy kid, like anyone else. Really, he was happier than anyone I ever knew. My friends never minded him hanging around. And he *always* hung around me, you know? He hated not being by my side.

"One day, Dad gave us some Superman comics. I read them to Todd, and he just about popped his top. He ran around the room like he was Supe, making whooshing sounds, and jumping. It was crazy. I must have read him those things a hundred times. One day, I really thought Mom was going to strangle him when she found him in her bedroom closet. I don't know, he must have been six or seven. He'd taken her best winter coat, this heavy red wool thing, and cut it to pieces. When she found him, he was wearing a big flap of it around his neck, and he started yelling, 'I Superman! See, Mommy? Superman!' She started cryin', but she was laughing, too, right?

"And he wore that thing everywhere. Man, he practically threw conniption fits whenever anyone had the sack to try and take it from him. So most people just let him be. Even by summer, he was still wearing that thing. You should have seen it, tattered and stained and everything.

"Later that year, I gave him a box of jacks for his birthday, right?" Benny blew his nose again. "He loved those things more than that old smelly cape. Really, he took them everywhere. And, I don't know why, but he couldn't say jacks. Always called them 'jakes.' But, it was funny, the way he said it like that. 'Shake jakes, Benny. Shake jakes.'"

I started to have a nauseated feeling in my gut, like I'd eaten a brick. I suddenly didn't want to hear any more.

"Once, he lost the box, so Mom gave him a new one to keep 'em in. The little blue Sucrets tin. Everywhere he'd go, *everywhere,* he took the tin box, and he'd crack up each time he shook it, hearing those jacks shake around inside.

"So, that was his thing. Anytime someone was blue, Todd would shake that box, and say, 'Shake jakes!' And if something was really wrong, if you were really down? He'd open up that Sucrets box, and give you a jack, to keep. Like it was the world's greatest treasure, and he was handing it over to you." Benny let out a long breath. "I always bought more down at the five-and-dime, to restock the tin, but he never knew.

"Mom used to rock Todd every night, reading him stories and stroking his hair," he said. "I listened from my room, on my bed. Sometimes, I closed my eyes and pretended she was reading to me, instead. Sounds stupid, right? I was jealous because my retarded brother got all her attention. Sick, huh?"

I started crying. It was everything—Coop, being in the box, the way I yelled at Benny about the tin of jacks. In only half a year, I'd made the best friends of my life, and now it was all slipping away. They had let me into their inner circle, and I constantly felt like I didn't deserve their friendship.

Benny went on. "One day, everything changed. I was walking home from school and along the way I passed by an open alley. There was a group of older guys, high school guys, hunched over something on the ground. One of those guys was Lucas Hill. Man, he was a certified, grade-A asshole. We all knew about him.

"Guess I should have just kept walking. But I didn't. I went over, to see what they were up to. They had a cat. Big, fat, orange one. They were holding it down while Lucas tied a cherry bomb around its tail.

"They told me to screw off. But that cat, the way it was squirming, and crying out. Man, I was pissed. Lucas turned, he told me to jet before he shoved that cherry bomb up my ass instead. But, you know, I didn't leave."

That was exactly what made Benny Benny. I smiled, glad he was my friend.

"So, Lucas Hill yanked a book of diner matches from his pocket, tore out one. Really, that cherry bomb was going to blow that cat in half. And I yelled, 'Leave it alone! You shits, you got no right!'

"He struck the match anyway, so I picked up a rock and hurled it. Picked up another, threw it, too. And I just kept on, you know? 'How you like it?' I yelled. All of them stood up, forgetting about the cat. Lucas took a few steps to me. 'The fuck is it to you?' he said. And, man, Will. All of them started at me like bulls.

"I ran my ass off. Never looked back once. Two blocks, three. I made it to our dirt drive, was halfway up when Lucas's arms wrapped around my legs. I went down hard. He was alone, the other guys couldn't keep up, I guess. But it didn't matter. Lucas Hill was older, and stronger. He ripped a knee up into my balls, smashed a fist into my mouth, then again into my nose. I tried to fight back, really. But he was just too much. That's all I remember, him yelling, screaming, punching. And then?

"There was this weird noise. Like a cracking noise. And everything just . . . stopped. Lucas just sat there, on my chest, with this mean look on his face. He whispered something. I couldn't understand him. And then he just fell over to the ground.

"Behind him, wearing that homemade Superman cape, was Todd. In his hand was my dad's ball peen hammer. There was something stuck on the end of it." Benny's voice trailed off at that, and he sniffed.

"You should have seen his eyes, Will. 'Superman save day!' Then he said it again. So I rolled over to Lucas, and—" Benny paused, then said, "There was a hole in the back of his head. I saw . . . saw pieces of his skull, and some parts of his brain, I think. His foot twitched, and I threw up right there.

"I started calling out to Todd. 'Oh, God, oh, God, what did you do?'

And he said it again. 'Save day!' Then, right there in my driveway, Lucas Hill died.

"You know what, Will? As soon as that happened, I knew what I was going to do. I never thought twice about it. Like it was instinct. There's no way I was going to let anybody come take Todd. He would have been shipped to some state hospital. He'd have died, not seeing us anymore. And he wouldn't have understood. Never would have.

"So that's what I did. I took the hammer, wiped his prints off it. I've seen *The Untouchables*, you know? I know how all that stuff works. As soon as I finished, the other high school guys rounded the corner. They got one look at that hole in Lucas's head, and they turned white as ghosts.

"That was when Todd got scared. Maybe he finally sensed the wrongness of it all, or maybe everyone else's fear was contagious. But he started to cry. 'Bennee. Bennee!' And then he did something that made it all too real for me. Todd reached up and untied his cape, letting it just fall to his feet. He said, 'I won go side, Bennee!' Big, fat tears rolling down his face.

"Then, my mom came out of the house. The police came pretty quick, too. I told everyone Lucas attacked Todd, and that I grabbed the hammer from the front porch, and only meant to stop him. Only meant to stun him, you know? I told all of them I never meant to kill anyone. That part was true, right?

"Anyway, saying good-bye was the hardest. But, man, when I hugged Todd, he took out that tin box from his pocket. I thought he was going to give me a jack or two, but he gave me that whole damn box. He said, 'Shake jakes, Bennee.'

"I told him I loved him. That I'd see him soon. I don't know. I . . . I just wanted you to know that, Will. I wanted you to know why it was so important I got those things back from that bastard. He had no right to take them. But I didn't mean to get anyone killed."

I couldn't say anything from my side of the room. I was crying and trying to be silent at the same time. I was trying to catch my breath.

CHAPTER

twenty

Benny Fritch and I shared a common bond: an attachment to something we'd do anything to protect—or retrieve. I was reminded of this when I dressed each morning, and undressed each night. The loss of my mother's picture hurt me more with each passing day. I believed Benny when he said he truly never meant for anyone to get hurt. He'd let the fury of being victimized drive him, and I knew I'd do the same.

Bobby Pettigrew called from several bunks down. "Ready to have your ass handed to you, Sheppard?"

It had nearly been a week since Coop's death. Now, for the first time, I was back in the bunkhouse. John Church was there, too. I hadn't forgotten about the fight, that couldn't have been possible. But after Coop, and then the box—I don't know. Everything just ran together, and I began to think perhaps it just might not happen. Until Pettigrew opened his mouth.

I knew there was no getting out of the fight, but more so, I found that I didn't even care. At that moment I decided to give in to emotion. I told myself that it was John Church who had stolen the picture from me. I told myself that it was him who had shot and killed my friend.

"You up to this?" Mickey asked.

I just glanced at him, not saying anything.

Church stretched his left arm across his opposite shoulder, and the room sprung to life; murmuring and whispering turned to electric buzz, and a few whoops and whistles. The middle of the bunkhouse cleared; guys even dragged their bunks out of the way. Cal was off duty that night, and Elmore Holling and another night guard had coincidentally stepped outside of the bunkhouse.

Somebody pulled the AM from underneath Cal's desk and flipped it on—to mask the noise, or maybe just to add to the entertainment. Jerry Lee Lewis sang "Whole Lotta Shakin' Goin' On."

Church came at me like a snot-slinging bull.

"Shiiit," Benny drew out, slinking away.

There's one thing I learned watching guys fight on the streets: always land the first punch. Always. And if you wanted the fight to be over quick, you went for places like the nose, the teeth, the throat. You never took a guy in the balls, though. That was one of the few understood and universal rules, a respect held for even your worst enemies. Only once have I kicked a guy in the nuts during a fight. I did it as a last resort, but that didn't hold any water with my father. He found out, somehow. He took me in the back, made me stand against the wall, and told me to close my eyes. He swung his shoe one time into my crotch and I immediately knew I was going to vomit. Deep waves of pain crept in and up the length of my entire body, and I went down, curling my legs up to my chest.

"Now," he said, "you know how it feels. Go wash up."

The rumbling keys of "Shakin'," each note, hung in the air. It set the tempo for the fight. Everyone was charged, ready to explode. Jerry Lee's voice rolled and climbed up and down the walls, in the air, in my head. I rushed toward Church and saw surprise in his eyes. The soreness and pain still in my back and legs melted away, like a blessing had floated down to me. Or maybe it was just the adrenaline.

Good, I thought. He expects me to roll over; now he's got his fight.

He drew back an enormous arm—I dove at his waist—we tumbled to the floor. The place erupted with cheers, and Jerry Lee Lewis sang.

The piano keys exploded. The beat only got faster. "*. . . We got chicken in the barn, whose barn what barn my barn.*"

I punched his face and heard his nose break. He didn't even react. I followed with two shots to the ribs and another into his teeth. All this, and nothing from him. Blood spilled out of his nose and down the sides of his face. The guy didn't move. He just lay there on the floor, grasping me with those pythons in a locked grip. I stopped when I heard him. It was a sound I first mistook for pain. It would have been better if that's what it was. He was chuckling in broken and chopped gasps. Church looked up with blood running down his face, over his mouth and into his teeth. He smiled, and that's when I pretty much knew I was screwed.

It wasn't a crazy smile, like I would have gotten from Silas. That wouldn't have bothered me as much. You can write that off as being loony tunes and not knowing when to stop.

This was different. He was jazzed; he was having fun.

Oh, shit. He's just getting started. A thought screamed through my mind as John Church picked me up and threw me across the room. *The nuts! Kick him in the nuts!*

I don't know if that would've even made a difference. The guy probably had balls of cast iron, for all I knew, considering how things were going. I came down hard on Mickey's bunk, and before I could register anything but my flaring pain, I was yanked up onto my feet. One punch into my eye, another into my nose. I had that one coming.

I blocked his third punch, and drove a hook into his throat. He dropped me, holding his neck. I wasted no time and launched punch after punch at his head and ribs. It sounds crazy to say, but I swear every swing was to that beat. Jerry Lee, it was perfect. I shook my head; Church was smiling. God help me, it must have been contagious, because I think I was smiling, too. I don't know why, but through the pain and the blood, I was letting it out. The anger and the grief. For the first time since coming to the ranch, for the first time since Coop died, I was really letting it all out. I was fighting John Church. I was fighting Frank Kroft and Warden Barrow. I was fighting the ranch. And oh, holy shit, *it felt good.*

He busted my lip.

"Shake it, baby, shake it."

I busted his ear.

Tumbling. Again the piano and Jerry's voice in my head and everywhere, we went round and round, punching, kicking, bleeding.

Then, suddenly, the song died. A piercing whistle replaced its tune. "Enough!" Cal thundered. He looked like he had just run all the way from the residentials. "I said enough of this bullshit!"

Everything stopped. I later learned that prior to that night, a guard had never stopped a bunk fight before.

I lay on the ground, pinned by Church and out of breath. Blood ran into my eyes.

Church nodded his head. "Good fight." He drew his fist and landed a final punch to my head.

As I was helped out of the room, I heard someone ask, "So who won?"

"Who do you think, numbnuts? The big fucker. He's still standing, ain't he?"

CHAPTER
twenty-one

THAT WOULD BE THE LAST TIME I'D EVER SEE CAL JENKINS. AFTER leading me and John Church to the infirmary, he laid his pistol on Barrow's desk. The continued tradition of boys beating the shit out of each other like clockwork was a large part of it, but really, I think it was Coop's death that set it all in motion. That last fight was just the proverbial straw.

Cal's departure from the ranch wasn't easy on any of us. As I said before, we all liked him. And when the one person in authority who's not a complete asshole flies into the wind, his absence doesn't go unnoticed.

When I returned to the bunks that night, Mickey was sitting on his cot with his knees drawn up to his chest. He didn't look sad, only tired. Benny lay stretched out, hands behind his head. They looked at me in a funny way as I hobbled up, and it made me feel as though I'd just navigated a dangerous rite of passage that left others staring at me in awe, if just for the simple fact that I hadn't died.

Mickey told me what happened. How he'd seen Cal walk into the bunks one last time, rummaging through his desk. I initially wondered if maybe he had driven west to Las Vegas. Window down, a cigarette in his mouth. Radio blaring.

"Pisser," I said.

"Nah," Mickey said, and looked to the desk, where Joe Addison sat now instead. "It's not like you can be broken up about it or anything."

"Well, I'm gonna miss him, right?" Benny said. He looked like a droopy dog that just lost its master.

Mickey sighed. "No way, man. Cal was a prisoner here just as much as you or me. I'm glad he made it out."

And Mickey was right. If I had to pick one extra person who was a part of our group, crazy as it sounds, it was Callahan Jenkins. I wish we all could have gone with him, wherever he went.

An odd thought suddenly struck me: in a way, Coop had made it out, too. It made me feel dirty to think that way, but at thirteen, that's all I had.

And Coop's death was harder on me than I thought it would be. It wasn't just his empty bunk or the vacant seat at our table in the mess hall. I don't know, maybe it was those things for Mickey and Benny. For me, it was the stud games, and how I always wanted to deal that extra card.

IT WAS MARCH OF 1964. I'D BEEN AT THE RANCH FOR JUST OVER half a year, and the winter months had been hard. I'd known cold in Chicago, but winter in the Rocky Mountains was something else entirely. There was a dark isolation to it that made those months worse. And when everything is covered under four feet of snow at ten thousand feet, it's hard to remember the outside world even exists. The bunkhouse, thank God, had plenty of oil heaters, as did the mess hall. Work duty was when you just about froze to death. You had to be smart about keeping your feet dry and insulated if you didn't want to lose any toes to frostbite. And the atmosphere inside the bunkhouse was not too different from the outside. Bleak, quiet.

The only indication of Christmas—or that previous Thanksgiving, for that matter—was the turkey and cranberry sauce at dinner. That was fine with me; I never wanted to associate the ranch with holiday memories. As bad as my home life had been, I still held images—treasures, really—of me and my mother. Moments that I branded into my mind, if even just to save them for when my days were filled with abuse and ugliness. Times such as when we trimmed the Christmas tree and I lost my balance, toppling into it, sending ornaments and branches everywhere. I pulled myself out of the mess, expecting a hurt, disappointed look on her face, but she was only laughing. So hard there were tears streaming down her face. Or the time I shared an ice cream with Carrie Francello on the steps of our building. How the sunlight shone through her hair, the way she squinted when she smiled at me. In that moment, she truly looked out of place in our tired, dumpy neighborhood.

Many of these images and memories preoccupied my thoughts during those weeks. I'd lose myself in the daily chores, focusing not on the missing, but on those I would see again after my time was up.

But there were deeper emotions twisting inside my body, and I often didn't know quite how to feel. It was my father, and how I'd tried to kill him. The thing that began to bother me the most was that I did not regret any of it. I won't lie, I felt worse that I'd let my mother down. Because I'd acted out, she was now there alone with him.

The guys and I were in the bunkhouse following another gourmet dinner, listening to Ruben DeMarco brag about his girl back home. He was laying it on pretty thick, maybe hoping the guys would forget how he ate John's knuckles in the mess hall.

We were deep into another card game, while Ruben ran his mouth to whoever would listen.

"Did you really?" Bobby Pettigrew asked.

"Shit, yeah! I laid her twice that night in the backseat of my old man's Chevy. We were catching the double feature at the pit when outta nowhere the movie cuts off—broken tape reel or some shit. Ten minutes later and we're doing the backseat bingo."

"What? In front of everybody?" Eddie Tokus asked.

"Man, you don't know nothing! Everybody's doing it."

Pettigrew asked, "So what's it like? Did she have big tits?" There were nods of agreeing wonder.

Back in the corner of the room, Benny studied his cards like he was about to take a pop quiz on them. "Raise."

"Fold." I tossed my cards. "You think Backseat Bingo over there's really been laid?"

"Nah, I bet it's all bullshit," Mickey answered.

Ruben went on. "Gina's tits were the best. Swear to God! She's only fifteen, but those puppies were so big and bouncy I thought they was gonna burst like water grenades. And when she let me slip it in, oh, *maaan*, there ain't nothing like it. I'm telling you."

"How long's it last?" Eddie asked, wide-eyed in amazement. He no longer wore a bandage over what was left of his ear (which, incidentally, wasn't much. Only a nub of healing flesh).

"Dunno. Ten, fifteen minutes. Didn't have my old man's watch, you know?"

"God, that doesn't sound so long," Bobby Pettigrew said.

I looked at Mickey and Benny, and we all cracked up.

John Church, lying on his cot with his eyes closed, said, "That's because it's not long, Bobbo. He just popped his top too quick."

Ruben was smart enough to avoid another beating from Church, but at the same time, he didn't want to lose face. "Hey, as long as I have a good time."

"Don't sweat it, Ruben," Silas said. He was walking through the bunks on his way to the head. "To him, a hot date means using both hands."

John opened one eye. "All you do is *talk . . . talk . . . talk.*"

Everything went quiet. I looked over to Cal's old desk; the guards were engaged in their own conversation. Church caught Silas by the arm.

Silas started to say something, but never got the chance to finish. John was already twisting Silas's arm behind his back at an odd, cartoonish angle. He bulldozed forward, leading Silas with a locomotive's momentum into the bathroom. Each one of us had the same choice to make: follow them, and attract the guards' attention, or miss entirely what was to happen next. Nearly thirty boys rushed after them.

The guards, of course, did notice, but by the time they barked and elbowed their way into the long and narrow bathroom, it had already happened.

John Church had Silas on his knees in the nearest open stall. Silas's feet thrashed out like two striking snakes. His head was in the toilet bowl. The long, ornately tiled room was filled with echoes of yelling, cursing, laughter, and sloshing water.

Elmore Holling threw Ruben DeMarco aside, then Aaron Gumm, hastily making his way toward the main event. John Church flushed the commode just before Holling's metal flashlight cracked into the back of his neck. John let go of Silas. And with that, it was over.

The blood rushed into Holling's face, and he looked ready to start swinging that flashlight into a few more skulls. "Goddammit, if I'm not wrangling up the motherhumping horses, it's you fucking kids!"

Silas was on his knees at the edge of the commode, looking like he was going to puke at any second. I waited for him to pounce at Church, who was still on the floor, rubbing at his neck and looking confused. But he didn't. Instead, a bizarre calmness washed over him. Silas stood up, not making eye contact with anyone, and retreated to his wool-covered bunk.

John Church had just moved into legendary status. To the boys in the bunkhouse, he had just become a god.

CHAPTER

twenty-two

On a wet spring morning in early April, Benny and I were, surprisingly, in the stables, cleaning out the stalls. I was actually getting pretty damned good at it. After seven months at Swope, I could turn a stall in less than twenty minutes. I was already looking forward to the coming afternoon, when Benny, Aaron Gumm, and I would be constructing a set of feeding troughs. Honestly, anything at all sounded better than pitching piles of shit and piss-soaked hay.

The talk at the ranch—all the talk, really—was of John Church. You'd have thought a celebrity had come to live with us. Guys even came up to me asking what it was like to fight him. The gossip flowed through the reformatory like a strong current. And yes, I'll admit it, I was right there, along with everyone else, wondering aloud who John Church really was. So was Mickey, who, by the way, earned yet another cigar gambling on the fighting. Only this time he bet against me. When I gave him shit about that, he just looked at his feet and said, "Nothing personal, Shep."

There was one guy on the ranch who never got caught up in the John Church obsession. When I asked him about it, Benny only shrugged.

"I don't know," he said. "He's just a guy, like you or me."

I laughed. "He's not like me, man. Come on, you saw how he took control, when he showed Silas how it really was. That was nothing but cherry."

Benny's smile faded a little. "I guess. Doesn't make him no Jesus Christ, though, does it?"

"You know what I mean," I said. "I just think it's cool how he doesn't care about anything."

"Why is that cool?" Benny asked. "That's how you want to be?"

I didn't say anything at first. It had rained hard that morning, and the horses were all still inside the stable. We were giving each stall a half-turn, which just meant we filled water troughs and scooped any extreme piles of manure. "Maybe," I finally said. "What if I do? What difference does it make?" I dropped a new salt block onto the floor of the stall.

Benny worked two stalls down. "What's wrong with the way you are now?"

"Forget it, Benny," I said. I shook my head and opened Reaper's stall. "You wouldn't understand." I stepped in, and Reaper immediately went into a good one—pitching a hell of a fit, even though I moved slow. I thought of Coop, who always proclaimed he would be the one to break her. She still wouldn't take a rope, and more than ever, guys were thinking she wasn't going to make it.

I shoveled what I could, staying as far away from her as possible.

"I understand," he said. "I bet I understand more than you think. You think if you didn't give a shit about anything, it'd be easier for you to sleep at night. It'd be easier to remember what happened to you back home and not feel like a knife was in your own chest, right?"

I was stunned. It was like he had slapped me. "What do you mean?"

Reaper snorted. I slung the bag of grain from my pail into her trough, then backed out to grab the water hose.

Benny didn't answer.

"Benny?" I asked again.

Finally, he let out a sigh, and from inside a far horse stall, said, "Mickey told me."

"Mickey? How did he find out?"

Benny emerged from the stall, dragging his own hose behind him. "Come on, Will."

"How did he find out!"

He paused, and stared up at the ceiling. "Miss Little keeps most of the records and paperwork in her office. He took a peek at yours before we even met you."

I couldn't decide if I felt betrayed or relieved. "Why didn't you guys ever just tell me?"

Finally, he looked me in the eyes. "I don't know. We figured you'd tell us yourself, when the time was right. But we don't ever judge, you know? I know you have your side of the story."

"Of course I have my side of the story! He liked to get drunk and beat the piss out of us! How's that for my side? I never knew when I was going to wake up in my bed to find him slinging a goddamn belt at me. I'd have to wear three pairs of jockeys just so he wouldn't find out I'd pissed all over my sheets. I watched him break my mother down for over ten years, and I had to stuff toilet paper in my ears to block out the noise of him raping her up like she was some kind of nickel-and-dime hooker. How's that for a fucking side?" I jerked the hose from Reaper's stall and lugged my wheelbarrow to the next one down. I realized I was breathing heavy, and that my hands were shaking. "I just . . . I can't believe you guys pretended not to know. All this time and all."

Benny looked dumbstruck. "I'm sorry about all that, Will. But we didn't pretend nothing. It just never came up. I wasn't going to ever ask you about it, right? Neither was Mickey. We didn't care. But we know it eats at you. I've seen how you stay awake at night. You know, it's the same way I am when I start thinking about all the shit." He disappeared into another stall.

"Well, you don't have to worry about me, Benny. I don't give a shit about what I did, and I'm aces now. You and Mickey can worry about yourselves, or anyone else you want to." I was angry, but didn't really know why.

"That's not you talking," he said, two stalls down. "I haven't known you a long time, right? But long enough to know that's not *you* talking."

"Maybe I'm not the only one who needs to learn a thing or two from John Church," I said. It came out soft, and I only half meant to say it.

After a moment, he said, "Is that it? That what you really think? Maybe if I acted more like him, I could have fought off Lucas Hill myself instead of having my kid brother do it for me?"

"That's not what I meant. That's not fair."

"Maybe," he went on, "if I acted like him, I could have shown Silas how it *really* was; maybe I could have shoved a horse bit up into his mouth instead, right?"

"Benny—" I wanted to say something to make peace, but in that moment, I just couldn't find the words.

But it was Benny, after all. He showed the promise of a smile, and just waved me off. "Hey, Nosebleed. Don't forget your bucket."

I looked over my shoulder at my rusty wheelbarrow's empty handle on which I usually hung the wooden grain pail, next to Reaper's trough. By now she'd probably nosed it around to the back.

"Forget it," I said. "I'll grab it later."

But he opened her pen himself. She snorted as he sidestepped to the back of the stall. I listened as he whispered something, and followed it with a shushing sound. "I guess we should have told you, you know? I mean, you're one of—"

I heard Reaper whinny, then buck her hind legs into the wooden bucket. The sound was like a clap of thunder. I flinched, inside my own stall, and cried out in surprise. I can't describe it any better than if someone had taken a sledgehammer and teed off on the bucket.

I winced and stepped out of my stall, closing the door behind me. "Hey, Benny . . . I didn't mean anything by all that. I know you mean—" The rest of the words just hung in my mouth. A sick feeling welled inside of me, and I realized what I'd heard wasn't a bucket being cracked apart. It was Benny's skull.

"No," I whispered, half paralyzed.

He lay at the back of her pen, and a deep crimson line ran across one side of his forehead, exposing a glimpse of cracked skull. Blood seeped down his face. His eyes were locked in an upward stare, as if he, too, were trying to peek up at his mashed forehead.

He was dead. That's all I knew. I'd heard the impact, the strength in its sound. He'd have had a better chance taking a bullet.

My first urge was to run to him, but I stopped. What could I do? Bone was sticking out of his head, for God's sake. There was something gray behind the bone, too. Something soft. I turned and stumbled out of the barn, to the first group of people I could find. Under the porch covering of the main two-story house were a few guards.

Time slowed, in opposition to my racing heart. A group gathered outside the stable, with all the guards inside. From somewhere within, I heard four faint words that made me absolutely sick: "Jesus, he's still alive."

And then Miss Little was there. She took complete control of the insanity with her steady voice and focused demeanor. She asked Elmore Holling for a blanket, and Joe Addison for ice. All the while, she whispered to Benny. I'll never be able to explain how, in that moment, I saw and heard only Miss Little.

I heard her say, "Not now, baby. You gots to lay still for me, child. Just lay still now for Miss Little." My stomach wrenched as I realized he must have tried to move. And then she did something so motherly that tears welled in my eyes. The words of "You Are My Sunshine" came soft and slow. I knew it meant he was dying.

Holling came back with the blanket, followed shortly by Addison with the ice. She gently covered Benny, tucking the edges under him with the utmost of care. All the while, singing. She took the ice, and built it up around Benny's neck and broken head. I expected someone to race back to the main house and radio for an ambulance, but they never did. We all waited, silently. In the distance, beside a pasture fence, I saw one-eared Eddie Tokus run to Silas, telling him the news. I saw them smile, and laugh, and a blaze erupted inside my gut.

Miss Little yelled for Kroft to pull a vehicle around. It was the first time I heard her voice so cold and sharp. It was absolutely commanding. They were going to drive Benny out. The closest hospital was in Gunnison. I tried to remember how long it had taken me to travel from Gunnison to the ranch, a lifetime ago, when I first arrived. I guessed that through the twists and turns of the mountains, it was over an hour.

An extreme amount of time to ride in the backseat of a car with your head cracked open.

Mickey ran up, out of breath, and just stared openmouthed. When I whispered Benny's name, Mickey held his head and squatted, as though feeling every ounce of the pain himself.

It was my fault, I wanted to say. I may have even mouthed it, but Mickey didn't see. Guilt flooded my heart as the scene replayed itself inside my head. It had been my fault. I turned to vomit, and when nothing came, I fell to my knees and cried instead.

CHAPTER
twenty-three

At dinner, Mickey wanted to know every detail, every part of why things happened the way they did. I told him about the argument, about me forgetting the grain bucket, how Benny called me Nosebleed again. Everything except Benny telling me he knew what I'd done to my father. Finally, Mickey stopped me.

"It wasn't your fault," he said.

I pushed away my tray. The thought of eating was absurd.

"Will, it wasn't your fault." He put a hand over my arm, and when I looked up, I only saw a scared little boy, and realized I must have looked the same way. "He should have been more careful around her," he said.

"Okay," I whispered. Did I believe him? Not in that moment. Not at fourteen.

After dinner, I approached Kroft. I found him smoking a cigarette outside the mess hall. The setting sun was eclipsed by the peaks above, and the slanting shades of scarlet and amber cast a glaze over the ranch grounds, and on Kroft himself. It made him look even more menacing. I didn't want to talk to him any more than I wanted to shoot the weather with Silas Green, but the one thought dragged me forward.

"Mr. Kroft?"

An uncomfortable silence followed. His slow, held gaze made my stomach tighten. In that moment, I forgot who I was talking to, forgot he was the head guard. I wanted to leave, I wanted to fall down. I wanted to have not approached him at all.

Yet my mouth opened, and I pulled the thought from my mind. "What's going to happen to Reaper?"

Nothing. Just a look of contempt.

"I know she's been here awhile, and now—with all this."

He held his fingers tight to the glowing cigarette, as if at any moment it might take flight like a bird. But when he let go, it fell to the ground, limp, and dead, and he squashed it with the heel of his boot.

"William Sheppard," he said, as if registering who I was for the first time. He reached out and placed his leathery hands tight on my shoulders. "It's none of your concern what we do with the animal, not even if we put a shell between her eyes." His hands found their way from my shoulders to the sides of my face, and he stroked the bottom of my ear with his thumb.

I felt my heartbeat inside my neck, and I fully expected to piss myself at any second. Rumors, circulated stories, floated to the forefront of my thoughts like ghosts. Stories I'd heard from other guys because Mickey and Benny never wanted to talk about it. Stories about Frank Kroft, and the things he did.

In slow monotony, he said, "Get your ass to the bunkhouse, and out of my face."

I whispered, "I could work with her. I could do it."

After seeing Benny trucked off the ranch, I knew what fate awaited the wild horse. Something inside became clear, and everything all just fit together: taming her was what I was meant to do at the ranch. My responsibility. For Coop, and now Benny, too.

He ran his long fingers through my hair in slow motion before clinching a handful of it in a sudden yank. "You couldn't tame a shit," he said. He released me, and fell into the shadows, pulling a new cigarette from his pack.

"HE'S GOING TO PUT HER DOWN. I KNOW HE IS." I TOLD MICKEY most everything, but I couldn't bring myself to say how Kroft had spoken. How he'd touched me. I don't know why, but I was embarrassed, and ashamed.

"Yeah, but . . . maybe it's not the worst thing."

"Are you kidding?" I asked.

"Dunno. I mean, why do you care so much? After what happened?" He was on the bunk next to me, shuffling the deck of cards. It sounds strange for me to say we tried to play cards again, but we did. After Benny left, we were about to go crazy with grief and anxiety. We didn't even know if he was alive. No one knew. But we had each other. And it was his idea to try and force a card game, just to keep our minds off everything else going on.

"Come on, you act like it was personal. She was going to be Coop's horse, man."

"Yeah."

"Just tell me this," I said. "You think Benny would want her head shot in?"

"Benny's not here to answer that."

I looked him in the eye. "Neither is Coop, but you already know the answer."

Mickey looked down at his hands, at the cards, and was quiet. We were still using Coop's old deck. It felt sad to use them rather than trying to find a new pack, but we considered it more of a tribute. I'm sure Mickey could have found one. It was immediately apparent that we were at a crossroads: either recruit a couple of wet ends, enough to play seven stud, or choose a new game.

"Okay. Blackjack it is," he said.

"I'm not going to let them kill her, too."

"Or Go Fish," he said.

"Come on, Mickey. Help me think of something?"

When he looked up, I thought for a moment he was going to cry. He dealt the cards out on the cot, and when he was finished, there was nothing left in his eyes but a weary confidence.

"Can you bet in Go Fish?" I asked.

"You can bet on anything in this world, man," he said.

And with that, I knew Mickey would help no matter what idiotic idea I thought up. So we let the conversation go, and just held the cards. It no longer mattered what we played; we shared the same thoughts. Where was our friend? Was he even alive?

When the lights-out call came, the bunkhouse was quieter than ever. I listened to the wind roll through the valley outside the windows. I stared at the ceiling and tried not to think about Kroft, and the fear that had gripped me when we spoke. I tried not to think of Reaper, or Benny, or the way he lay on the ground with his head opened up. The way his eyes kept looking up into nowhere.

But it was impossible not to think of those things.

CHAPTER
twenty-four

IN ALL THE YEARS OF MY LIFE, I NEVER FELT CLOSER TO ANYONE—other than my wife—than I did to my friends at the ranch. It was the pinnacle of the 1960s, and even now, if I turn on the radio, thumb it to the oldies, most of what I hear takes me back to my childhood. Herman's Hermits, the Beatles singing "I Want to Hold Your Hand." Elvis, of course, was king, and Eddie Cochran. When I hear these tunes I can close my eyes, and I'm suddenly back at the bunkhouse, playing seven-card with Mickey, Benny, and Coop, listening to the gods of the airwaves through Cal's AM. Or I'm shoveling horse shit in a rusted-over, half-red wheelbarrow, or trying to beat the hell out of John Church while savages surround us, screaming and laughing and having the time of their lives. We were sheltered in a veil of stark confinement, blind to everything else going on in the world: a civil rights movement, Vietnam, a fucking space race. No, for me, the apotheosis of my adolescence was sneaking into the stables at night to try and tame a wild horse that everyone called Reaper. It only took several days of convincing before Mickey began to listen, which really meant that I just bugged the apeshit out of him until he realized I wasn't going to shut up about it.

❖ ❖ ❖

Mickey wrinkled his nose, and asked, "Do you realize the shit we'd both be in if we're busted?" It was sort of funny to see him so serious and concerned.

Sitting just outside the stable, smoking a pack of Winstons, was the sole reason we were able to sneak away from the bunks—old Gus Grimsley. He hadn't taken much convincing. I think, mainly, he felt sorry for us. After Cal left Swope, Gus was the next best thing to being a sympathetic ear.

On the way to the pens, Gus told us more or less why he'd agreed to help. "I'm seventy-eight years old, boys. Sort of like an old cow, not much use anymore. Think most everyone else around knows it. But between us, I think they're just waiting on me to kick over."

"So why are you waiting around for it?" Mickey said.

"Easy for a young piss to say," Gus said. "I like this land. Don't want to go anyplace else. I worked this ranch years before the state came in throwing the cash in our faces. Now I wake up every day wishing I hadn't sold it."

I stopped, thinking I hadn't heard right. "Wait, this ranch was yours? You sold it?"

"Yuh," he said. "Partly mine. And I guess maybe that's why I've stayed. This's always been home for me, kid. Maybe . . . I just feel guilty for selling it off the way I did. Maybe I deserve to see all it's become."

"Damn," Mickey said, staring up at old Grimsley with renewed wonder.

"But, none of that means I'm going to take any kind of heat for you. Last thing I need is that big bastard yelling up and down on my face." He pulled a rag from his back pocket and blew into it. "No. Anyone comes asking," he told us, "it's your ass in the sling. People don't give too much of a shit about me, but it'll probably be the box for each of you, or worse. Just so you know."

He was resigned to sitting low, holding up the stable wall outside, and dragging on his cigarettes. He told us up front that he didn't want to know the particulars of what we were up to inside. As time went on, we noticed Gus would sometimes even abandon his lookout, just to return when it was time to get back to the bunks. He never said why he left. Maybe it was just to see if we would get caught. That was the thing about Gus. He was usually a decent fellow, but he could also be frustratingly indifferent. We liked him just the same.

"You get all that, right?" Mickey asked me again. "You know how serious this is?"

"Yeah. I know," I said. "But if you want to know what I really think, you're acting like a pussy."

Mickey made a face, and smiled. I hadn't seen that smile in a long time; it was a welcome sight. He said, "Well, hell, what are we waiting for?" He stepped behind a stack of hay bales, near the cluttered corner of the barn, and reemerged with a glass kerosene lamp.

"Where'd you come up with that?" I asked.

A sheepish grin spread from cheek to freckled cheek. "We've all got our secrets, Shep." He took a box of matches from his pocket, and when the flame caught, I watched the way his shadow stretched across the floor and up the wall. For a moment, he was far taller than four and a half feet.

"I'm starting to think you could get a girl in here if I asked for it, the way you get everything else," I said.

Mickey just beamed. "It's a good thing you haven't asked! Do you realize the seriousness of sneaking in a hooker? I'd never get out of this place!"

"Thanks for doing this for me," I said.

"Forget about it. But don't go thinking you're my fucking best friend," he said, and smiled so widely I could see every one of his teeth.

AS USUAL, SHE THREW A TANTRUM WORSE THAN ANY THREE-YEAR-OLD from the first instant I showed up, proving just who was in charge. She snapped her teeth, and I thought twice about being away from the bunkhouse. Her hoofs beat into the dirt so hard I felt it in my legs. She snorted, stomped at the ground, and tightened her muscles like she was going to flat out charge at any second. It all scared the shit out of me.

For two hours, I sat. Nothing else. My back against the stable wall, Reaper snorting and pacing. I had no idea how talkative Mickey was until that night. It didn't matter that no one else was outside the stall with him; he talked for the both of us. I listened to him argue (with whom, I have no idea, but he argued just the same) how Mickey Mantle was the all-time greatest. After that, it was a theory of how Abbott and Costello performed in a traveling circus before being discovered.

I never said a word. Those were my strict orders. The only thing I could do was to watch her, and try my best not to get trampled.

"Last night was easy," Mickey said at the breakfast table. "I mean, let's face it—you sat there with your thumb up your ass." He smiled, and his freckled cheeks rose up to his eyes. We smiled and joked because it was better than the alternative of grieving for Coop, or worrying about Benny. And we still hadn't heard any update. We truly would have gone out of our minds if not for that white horse, and breaking her became not just a priority, but a need.

"I really didn't have my thumb up my ass, all right? I was getting off to thoughts of your sister."

He didn't even have a sister, but I still got a punch in the arm. "You're still a cock knocker," Mickey said. "Guess you always will be."

"That's fucking A with me," I said.

"Yeah, me too."

Three nights later, I went back, and again sat in the stable. Then again, and again, for close to two weeks. On the last night, something different did happen. It was subtle, but to me it meant all the difference in the world. I hadn't even noticed it until Mickey was halfway into how he'd once gotten a girl to take off her shirt.

I whispered, hoping not to make a scene. "Hey!"

"Hold on, this is the best part. She was wearing this lacy bra, I dunno, something with flowers on it or some shit, you know?"

A little louder, and sharper. "Mickey!"

He paused. "What, you have to take a leak or something?"

"Listen, dumbass," I said, smiling by now that he hadn't already noticed, even if he was on the other side of the wall.

"I don't hear nothing. And what's with—" He must have finally caught on because he suddenly popped his head over the top rail of the gate.

We both just stared at Reaper and beamed. She wasn't stomping. She wasn't pacing from one side to the other. She wasn't doing anything. And it was brilliant. It was the first time she had settled with me in her pen. In fact, she'd even taken a few paces closer. Her nostrils flared and I knew she was trying to figure me out—just who in the hell was this damn kid and why was he in her place?

"Just stay still!" Mickey hissed. "Don't do nothing to spook her."

"This is great." And I truly meant it.

Naturally, I took this as inarguable proof of my extraordinary skill and ability. A sign I had gained her trust.

Jesus, even now I'm laughing, shaking my head at just how stupid I was.

CHAPTER
twenty-five

"What is it with you today?" John Church's voice hovered out of the horse stall like a distant, rumbling thunder. It was the first time he really spoke to me.

It was a lonely thing, conducting my morning chores without Benny to keep me company. That Church hardly spoke only made it seem more unbearable.

"I'm fine," I said, yawning.

I stabbed a pitchfork at a clump of soiled hay, and fresh horse manure rolled onto my shoe. The nights Mickey and I worked with Reaper were getting to me, or really, it was the morning after, I should say. Gus always had us back before lights-out, but I was exhausted all the same.

"You're dragging ass. You're leaving more work for me," he said, hoisting his wheelbarrow past me. "That's what you are."

"Just can't wake up, that's all."

He stopped, and turned. "I can come slap the shit out of you. That might wake you up." He readjusted his grip on the wheelbarrow's handles, and pushed it out of the barn. But there was the hint of a smile on his face when he said that. Either he thought the joke was funny, or it was the thought of hitting me. I couldn't tell which.

❖ ❖ ❖

HE WAS RIGHT, THOUGH. I WAS DRAGGING. AT LUNCH, MICKEY SAID he felt the same way.

"This is busting my nuts, Shep," he said. "We don't even play cards no more. I hope you're getting more out of it than me. That white bitch better turn, soon." He nibbled at his sandwich.

It was so odd to sit at the table without Coop and Benny. We shared it with other guys now, but it wasn't the same. It never would be.

"She'll turn," I said. "We just need a few more nights. I know I'm getting close." I felt guilty that by recruiting Mickey's help I'd taken the card game away from him. I think he had come to depend on them as much as I did before I grabbed hold of my new obsession.

And it *was* an obsession. To do what Coop wanted to do himself, to tame the horse that had sent Benny away—it's something that's still hard to describe. It was almost like stealing small pieces of my friends back. Something just felt right each time I tried to do the seemingly impossible.

"Man, you sound more like Coop every day." Mickey took another bite of his ham-and-cheese.

THAT NEXT NIGHT, I ALMOST FELL ASLEEP IN THERE, THAT'S HOW bad it was. Reaper still didn't appreciate me in her space, but she no longer threw her tantrums. I felt ready to make the next move, even though Mickey said she wasn't anywhere near ready.

And so I sat in that pen, my back against the door. Mickey shushed me like a seasoned librarian each time I tried to talk. I didn't care, and he eventually started talking back. We couldn't see each other because of the wall, but just taking part in the conversation was a welcome change to the previous nights.

I clammed up, though, when he changed the subject.

"I already know what you did," he said. "I . . . guess you didn't know that, but I wanted you to. Hell, maybe Benny said something. But I should have told you sooner. I just felt weird bringing it up, Shep."

He waited. I couldn't think of what to say.

He said, "What you did doesn't matter. Okay? We never cared about that."

"Benny did tell me," I whispered. Reaper snorted. "But what's on my file . . . it's just words, just facts. It's probably not what really happened. You know?"

Mickey laughed. "You don't have to fucking tell me! I know you have your side to it. Benny and Coop knew, too. The files are always black and white. They never tell the story. Hell, I bet I could guess what most of 'em really mean. I bet you came from an abusive home. I bet your old man swung anything he could get at you. Maybe even at your mom, too. I bet he was drunk most times. Maybe sometimes he wasn't."

He went on, but I was biting my lip, trying to keep my eyes from welling up. It wasn't just because he read me so clearly, or because of the memories he stirred. It was those things, but it was more. It was feeling the guilt of not trusting them in the first place, and sharing the things in my life that kept me up at night.

"Take me," Mickey said. "My file's open and shut, just like every other JD here. 'Assault with Intent to Kill.' What bullshit! Honest to God, it really says that.

"Sometimes I think I was just destined to end up here," he said. "Sounds bananas, right? But I'm telling you, man. I was on a bad path. If not here, I would have ended up somewhere else, maybe worse. I used to lie awake, wondering where it all went off track, you know? Then, I started thinking maybe I never was on track.

"Maybe it would have been different if Mom hadn't died," Mickey said. "I was only two when she got sick. It's weird, I don't even remember her now."

I stared at Reaper, hearing Mickey's words float into the stall. I tried to imagine him, his home. But in all of those thoughts I saw myself, my own home.

"So how's a kid supposed to have a chance with a fucking deadbeat for a father and an older brother who wants to be just like him? My mom was the one who held the family together. Must've been a saint to do it as long as she did."

"Yeah," I whispered, thinking of my own mother. "Know what you mean."

"I remember the day my father came to me and said, 'Got laid off, Mickey. It's time for you to pull your weight.' He'd already arranged for me to shovel the horse stables down at the track. He was a regular down there, knew a few people.

"So that's what I did. I raked horse shit and pitched the hay. Ironic, right? That I'd end up here, doing the same damn thing?"

"Yeah," I whispered. Reaper swished her tail.

"So here it is. I'm shoveling up one day, and I hear these two voices outside. I knew one of them. Joey T, loan shark to anyone in need. Also ran a seedy nightclub in the middle of East Saint Louis. He was with this other guy, Joey T's leg breaker. They pass by the stall I was in. Joey T calls out, 'Ain't you Freddie Baines's kid?'

"I said I was. I was still holding a full scoop of manure in my shovel. Joey T starts to rag on my old man. Told me to give Dad a message about how he owed Joey T sixty-seven dollars. He calls my dad more names."

Reaper swung her mammoth head left, then right. I enjoyed imagining that she was listening, too. Mickey's voice was becoming softer, and he paused, letting the memories marinate.

"But, you know me. You know I got a temper. I mean, here was this prick. I'd never seen him before in my life. And he's calling out my dad, to my face! Yeah, my dad's a zero, but family's family, man."

I cringed, but didn't say a word.

"Then he pressed me. Said, 'Come on, kid. You got that, or you too stupid to remember? Maybe you got too much of your old man in you.'

"So I said, 'Fuck you, you fuckin' dago.' Oh, man. The leg breaker stopped laughing right there, Shep. Joey T said, 'Got a mouth on you, don't ya, kid?' And he pulled a snub-nose from his back pocket."

"Shit," I whispered.

"Yeah," Mickey said. "I was scared, man. I thought I was punching my ticket, no kiddin'. Bad things happened in that part of town, no matter how old you were.

"But then, Joey T gets this smile on his face. He sees I've just about pissed myself, with his gun in my face and all, and he says, 'Not so tough now, are ya? But I'm a nice guy, really. Ain't I a nice guy, Jack?'

"Leg breaker says, 'Yeah, real nice.'

"Joey T says, 'Tell you what I'm gonna do. I'm gonna forgive you for insulting me. Even better, I'll forgive your father's debt. All you have to do is one thing for me, kid.' He picked up a lump of manure. He said, 'Just put this in your mouth.'

"I don't know, Will," Mickey said. "We barely had enough to eat back then. Dad was broke, in debt, out of a job. It was hard enough, man."

He paused, then said, "So I say, 'I do this, everything's square?'

"Joey T smiles, and says, 'As a cube.'

"I took the piece of horse shit, and I just looked at it for the longest time. I kept thinking, no one would ever have to know. So just like that, I put it in my mouth."

I closed my eyes, hearing Mickey's voice, and all the sounds of the stable. Reaper, the other horses, the wind outside.

Mickey let the words dwindle, letting their seriousness settle over me. "Then Joey T said, 'Chew it up.'"

"No way," I whispered. "No way."

"I shook my head no," Mickey said. "He cocked the gun, and said it again. And . . . you know, all I saw was that gun. So . . . I *chewed* it, man. Gagged. Chewed again. All the while, that pistol was shoved in my face.

"Joey T said, 'Now swallow it, kid.'

"And I fucking swallowed it. I did." Mickey started to cry on the other side of Reaper's stable door. I heard the hitch in his voice and what sounded like him dragging his sleeve across his face.

After a moment, Mickey said, "So, you know, after that he put the gun away. He said I did good. He said Dad was off the hook. And when he went to leave, he slapped the leg breaker on the back and said, 'I made Baines's kid *eat shit*!'

"So after all that," Mickey said, "I go crazy, and I get this idea in my head. I go out that night, to Joey T's club."

I laughed. "You didn't go in any nightclub."

"Not *in* the club, behind it. I lifted his red Caddy from the parking lot."

I laid my head on the stall door, smiling. "Sincerely, don't lie to me, now."

"If I'm lyin' I'm dyin'," Mickey said. "Swear to God. And that car was cherry, Will. Damn, it was fine. Cream leather seats, rag top, rich chrome everywhere. I drove away as quiet as a snake in water."

I smiled, imagining a Cadillac pulling out on the road with nothing but a head of messy brown hair behind the wheel. "Didn't anyone see? Some stupid kid driving a Caddy?"

"Nah. It was late. I took all the back roads. Lucky, too, I guess. I'd done it a few times before, with my brother riding shotgun. And I knew exactly where I was going—a warehouse, down near the river. I'd been there before with my dad.

"I take the car and go see Uncle Marty. No relation—just another lowlife my dad sometimes did business with. But he's big-time. Hell of a reputation, you know? Long story short, I walk away with seven hundred bucks."

"Now you're shitting me!" I couldn't even imagine such money. I never carried more than a wrinkled five-dollar bill in my own pocket, and that was on my birthday.

"Yeah, I know. Car was worth at least a couple thou on the streets."

I shook my head. Mickey Baines had a way of getting hold of things no fourteen-year-old kid had any business doing. I'd never met anyone with such balls.

"I go to the track the next day, couple hours before the first race," he began again. "I find a guy to place a bet for me. Didn't look too respectable, but I didn't want to find someone too trustworthy, you know? They'd just report my ass."

I agreed, just amazed by the story.

"I tell the guy I'll give him a hundred bucks to place the bet, plus another hundred when he gives me the ticket."

"What if he took the money and bolted?" I asked.

"He could have. But I also told him Martin O'Connor was my uncle, and if he ran, I'd turn Uncle Marty on him. Like I said, Uncle Marty had a reputation around town. The guy actually believed me and placed my bet. Five hundred bucks on a horse named Union Bill."

Back home, Mickey would have been called big league. I laughed in disbelief when he told me Union Bill won the race by two lengths. Mickey had won just over three thousand dollars.

Three thousand dollars. In 1963, three thousand dollars could buy a lot of things. It could buy a brand-new car, almost pay half of a house note, and here was a fourteen-year-old with it stuffed in his blue jeans.

"That wasn't even what did me in. There at the track, through the crowds, I see Joey T and his fucking sidekick cashing out a ticket. I followed them back to the stables, behind the track.

"I picked up a piece of rusted pipe, walked up behind them, and got the fucking drop on them like you ain't ever seen. He didn't have no gun in my face this time, and I sure as hell never gave him the chance to go for it, either. I beat the ever-living piss out of each of those two bastards. All I saw was red, Shep, the whole time. You ever hear a person say that?"

"Only on TV," I said.

"Yeah. But on TV, it's just actors. I ain't ever hit anybody the way I was hitting those guys. I guess Jack Dikeman, the leg breaker, got off easy enough. In the end, I heard I broke his arm, his leg, couple ribs. But Joey T . . . man, they rushed him off in an ambulance with the gumballs flashing. Heard during my trial about his injuries; some lawyer listed them off like a fucking grocery list. Broken jaw. Broken nose. Missing teeth. Broken arm. Cracked kneecap. The last swing I took at him with that pipe—it cut across his head and tore away part of his scalp.

"After I went at them like that, I just sort of stepped back, looking at what I'd done. Joey T was unconscious, and Dikeman started scuttling back toward the corner, like a beach crab. He was looking at me with crazy eyes, just scared to death. Seeing him look at me like that made me feel sick.

"I ran, Shep. Have you ever wondered how far you could run if you had to?"

I told him I had, which was true. I thought about running plenty when the ambulance came for my father.

"I made it for two days. Knew they'd look for me at my house, so

I never went home. I never saw my dad again. The day I was picked up by the cops, he was shot in an alley. They never found out who did it."

Where would you be right now if you were still running? I thought. Where would I be if I *had* run? But sometimes, life is just too damn short to care about such things.

IT WAS GETTING LATE. GUS WOULD KNOCK ON THE STABLE'S FRONT door soon, ready to take us back to the bunkhouse.

I stood, and was taking small steps toward Reaper.

She immediately perked her ears and snorted. It was a deep, grumbly noise that spoke of her uneasiness. Something was different, though. I could feel it.

"Will?" Mickey asked. I heard him jump from the floor and grab the top of the stall door.

I took another step.

"Keep your hands down—hands down!" Mickey whispered. His words were sharp and full of energy. "Don't look away, either. Keep eye contact."

A chill swept over me as I thought of Benny, walking behind her. I took another step. More than anything, I didn't want to show fear.

Another step.

Her ears dropped, and she looked away. Believing she was ready, I reached out an arm.

Behind me, I heard Mickey. "What're you doing? Aww, man!"

She raised her long head, and I could hear the breath whoosh out of her flared nostrils. She neither backed away nor made toward me. A good sign.

The feel of her mane was electric on my fingertips. Reaper's breathing quickened. I brought my hand down along her muscle-lined neck, feeling the strength ripple just below the short, flat hair.

"Easy," I whispered, trying to sound cool as a breeze. "Easy, girl. It's all right. It's just me. Just Will."

If Mickey was breathing, I couldn't hear him. Everything had stopped. The collective sounds in the barn, the wind outside.

"Hi, there," I whispered again. "Hi, girl. You didn't mean to hurt him, did you? I know you didn't. We both know."

No one had ever stroked her neck like I was at that moment. That thought opened a door to newfound confidence.

"You see? It's all right. Don't want to hurt you, girl."

I was going to add how beautiful she was, but the thought never survived the journey from brain to mouth. With the quickness of a bolt of lightning, she snapped her head, and I felt a stab in my right shoulder. Then a stomach-twisting *CLACK*—the sound of her teeth against my collarbone.

I went to the ground, my shoulder numb. I clinched my eyes from the pain, and when I opened them I saw hoofs, just inches from my head. Benny's broken face flashed into my mind and I was overcome with terror.

"Stay still!" Mickey yelled.

Above me, Reaper didn't budge an inch, just daring me to move.

After a moment, and after finding my breath, I did move. Slowly, I rolled away, onto my side, and quietly stood. I fully expected my knees to give out. Keeping my front to her, I retreated toward the stall door.

"My shoulder," I said, once Mickey shut the door.

"No shit, your shoulder," he said. "I thought she'd bitten it clean off."

I was flying. Adrenaline coursed through my blood and my heart was lodged in my throat. "That was *incredible,* Mickey. Did you see it all?"

"See it? I might have to check my shorts for chocolate skids."

In spite of the burning pain in my shoulder, I laughed. I wouldn't feel the real pain until later, when the rush wore off. In the meantime, I felt *important.* Like I had accomplished something monumental.

"I didn't think that bitch would ever let anyone lay a finger on her," he said. And the way he was looking at me then—it was almost like admiration. "Come on, you're bleeding on your shoes, toilet wipe."

I pulled my torn shirt aside and looked at my shoulder; the pain was just beginning to sink in. What I saw made my stomach drop to my feet. Purplish tears outlined where each of her teeth had cut into my skin. The flesh hung loose, blood swelling around it.

"Don't worry, it's just a love bite," Mickey said. "We better go see Little, though."

CHAPTER *twenty-six*

After the third knock, we turned to leave for the bunks. Maybe I could just keep something pressed to my shoulder and hope for the best. Lord knows I wasn't about to go to a guard for help.

We'd just stepped off the porch when I heard her voice. "Who's out there?"

"It's Will," I said. "And Mickey Baines."

The infirmary door unbolted from the inside, then creaked open, just enough for Miss Little to see the mess on her front porch. Her dark face emerged from behind the door, careful to look from left to right.

"It's what you might call a covert incident, ma'am," Mickey said.

She scanned the darkness once again, then held the door open. "Covert. Mmm. Devil knocks at my door and I am cursed to always answer. Ain't that just the truth."

We filed into the infirmary feeling like refugees. The warmth of the front rooms washed over us. Miss Little saw the blood seeping through my shirt and winced.

"Child! What you gotten up to tonight!"

"Only you and guard Grimsley know, ma'am," Mickey said. "We're trying to save a horse."

She paused, sensing there was more to it than what Mickey had given. "And just why is it so important you save this horse?" she asked, motioning to the examining table. I was getting to know the infirmary fairly well, and knew just where to go.

"Breaking that horse was important to Coop," I said. "So now, it's important to us. And what happened to Benny . . ." My voice sort of trailed off at the thought of him. "I don't want to waste this chance to do something for them. Not after we couldn't help them before."

Mickey smiled, and said, "Besides, what else are we gonna do in this place?"

After studying us, Miss Little picked up the telephone and dialed. A feeling of betrayal flooded my heart as she cradled the receiver in her long, slender hands. She was calling the guards; going to tell them what we'd been up to.

"This is Little, at the infirmary. I have two of your boys. I'll send them back with Grimsley when I'm finished. That's right. They're here with me now." She hung up and regarded us.

"All right, boys. You're not raising any eyebrows tonight." She pushed a pair of wire-framed glasses higher on her nose, and focused her soft eyes onto my shoulder.

"If I may pose a question . . ." she began, threading a long stitch into my cut shoulder. "Does it eat at you? Trying to save a thing that was so important to one friend but left another for dead?"

I flinched. She gave me a shot to numb some of the pain, but I could still feel the needle and thread lancing through my skin all too well. "It did at first," I said. "But we know Benny. He wouldn't want her killed, either. What she did to him, it was an accident."

"Shame what happened to that boy," she said. "Got too comfortable, let his defenses down. That's rarely a good thing."

"Have you heard anything about him?" Mickey asked. "Nobody's told us nothing. I know he's probably . . . maybe . . . But no one's talking."

"Sugar, the South could rise again and I wouldn't know up from down about it. News don't exactly travel too quick up this mountain. Only news I get is from my AM/FM, and I keep the old girl pointed straight to my sweet Louis Armstrong and his etceteras."

She dabbed a swab of peroxide over the stitching and then blew on my shoulder. A chill rolled across my back, and in that instant I longed more than ever to be home with my mother. Visions I had no business drudging up—skinned knees, Mom bandaging me—rustled from deep down like dead bodies pushing aside dirt.

"Yeah, but you didn't answer the question," Mickey said, taking a sip of his tea.

She stopped her delicate work, leaving the curved needle lanced halfway through my skin. I could have slapped Mickey if I'd had the reach.

"You're right, I didn't answer the question, did I?" I felt a pinch as she fished the needle through. "The only thing I know is that Benny Fritch was alive when they reached the hospital. Such a shame. Lord, I ain't felt such pain for a child since . . ." Her soft eyes blinked, and with her even softer hands, she snipped at the thread and finished the stitch. "Well—enough of that." She pulled another white SWOPE T-shirt over my head.

"What would you boys say to a slice of apple pie?"

We looked at each other, not sure we'd heard correctly. "Yes, ma'am!"

"But not a word to the others back at that bunk, now. Not running no treat stand here."

It was sort of funny—us all sitting there like that at her table. Apple pie on our plates, hot tea in our cups. We were quiet for the most part, listening to her talk about boys who came before us, her years nursing at the ranch; she even talked about the things she hoped to accomplish one day, dreams of a life after the ranch, if there ever was one. "Sometimes," she said, "I feel as trapped here as you boys must."

Next to the small round table was a phonograph sitting on a rickety stand. My mother had one very similar; it could have even been the same model. Across from us was Miss Little's kitchen. I call it a kitchen, but really, it was no bigger than some modern-day walk-in closets. Room enough only for a sink, range, a General Electric icebox, and a cabinet.

Mickey kept stealing glances all around the infirmary, until Miss Little finally said, "Now you look like you got something on your mind, Michael Baines."

He looked down at his plate, face reddening, but he said nothing.

"Out with it, boy! Say what you have to say."

Mickey clinked his fork on the plate, and met her eyes. "Well . . . You read up on each boy that comes to the ranch, right?"

She stared at him for a moment, and was quiet.

Mickey continued. "So, after time, we all get to know each other. Usually, we hear what everyone did. But there's one guy here . . . one guy who's never told."

"And you want me to oblige," she said before taking a sip of tea. "Want me to just open up and have a pleasant conversation about a boy's private records, do you?"

Mickey stammered, "Yes, ma'am. I do."

Miss Little laughed at his directness. I almost did, too. But instead, I just kicked him underneath the table. "Shut up!" I hissed.

"I suspect you're referring to Silas Green," she said.

Mickey nodded, didn't even blink. I took the last bite of apple pie from my plate.

"Let me tell you something, boys. And I want you to listen *real* good. The less you know about that dog, the better off you are. I already told Will to stay clear, and I'll tell *you* the same."

"We wouldn't tell a soul how we found out," Mickey said. "We wouldn't tell a soul we *did* find out." He was practically pleading with her at this point. I just wanted to stay out of it.

I was curious, no doubt about that, but Mickey was already doing the talking, and if he couldn't get it out of her, I didn't stand a chance.

Miss Little took the last bite from her plate, letting her fork scrape across the ceramic. She pulled the fork from her mouth, slowly, then pointed it at Mickey. "You know something? I believe you. I really do. I don't think you *would* tell a soul."

We eased toward her, forgetting all about pie and tea, and waited for what we were about to hear. After several seconds of us staring at her, she shook her head.

"No. I'm not going to tell you, boys. So you might as well sit back and close your mouths."

"But you don't like him any more than we do," I said.

Her chair creaked as she pushed away from the table. "Now, I think you boys best be getting back to the bunks, don't you? Tell Holling guard Grimsley was with you but wandered away. Lord knows, he'll believe it."

Mickey and I were at the door when he turned back. "I guess I understand why you can't tell us. Thank you for the snack, ma'am."

I thanked her, too, and we left. I looked over my shoulder as we made our way down the path, and saw her looking at us through the parted doorway. She smiled and shook her head before turning to close the door.

"SHE GONE?" MICKEY ASKED.

"Huh?"

"You just looked around. Is she still in the door, or at the window?"

"No," I said. "She's gone. Hey, I can't believe you—"

Mickey grabbed my good arm and yanked me off the path. "Let's go, hurry!" He did a sort of tiptoe run back toward the infirmary.

"Hey, wait!" I hissed. "What are you doing?" When he didn't answer, I followed.

Even though we were cloaked by an overcast night sky, I felt vulnerable, and knew any second a guard would spot us. I caught up to him, just behind the infirmary building. I crouched, and whispered, "What the hell are you doing?"

He put his finger up to his lips, then spoke so soft I barely understood. "She keeps his somewhere else, not with the others. I wanna know where she keeps it."

The inside curtain was pulled just far enough for us to see where we had stood just moments ago. I placed my head next to his, feeling guilty that we were spying on someone who had just given us tea and pie.

She was out of view, but I could hear the clink of the plates and silverware. She was in the cramped kitchen, whistling. It was an almost familiar tune. "Come on," I whispered, "Not a good idea."

Mickey didn't budge.

It was suddenly quiet for a long moment. I was about to stand up and yank his shirt back. Just then, we saw her feet come into view as she entered the room. We both crouched, and heard her footsteps draw nearer, right up to the window. Quiet, again.

I barely breathed. Mickey was biting his lip, staring at me. All I could do was shake my head and silently curse. She wasn't moving, we'd have heard her. No, she'd seen us. My mind wheeled. Do I stand, give myself up? Run? Crawl away?

I was about to run when I heard her move away from the window. Mickey eased back up to the glass. I saw his eyes narrow, then widen. He motioned his head at me, and I joined him at the window once again.

There, inside, was Miss Little. Her back was to us, not more than five feet away. I could have poked her with a stick if the window were open. In her hands was a manila folder, opened around a cluster of papers. She flipped her way from page to page.

"That's got to be it," Mickey said, barely audible.

"What?"

"The files," he said. "She moved them from the last time I broke in." He bobbed his head and smirked. "She's always moving them."

Inside, Little gave a small *harrumph* sound, and turned. We dropped like a couple of bricks to the ground. Footsteps neared, and I waited for the window to rise open above us. Instead, I heard a rummaging sound, and then the footsteps faded into an adjacent room.

"Come on," Mickey said. "Let's go."

And we were just on the verge of slinking away into the night, when we heard something from inside. It was music. Etta James.

It was coming from the phonograph by the kitchen table. Granted, not many guys at the ranch would have known just who the hell Etta James was—but she was one of Mom's favorites. And the song was one that I almost knew by heart. My mother had played it over and over, until I thought she was going to wear the record out.

Something amazing happened that night on the ranch. Amid all the violence, all the hardness and grit . . . amidst the death, Mickey and I were witness to a stolen moment of sheer warmth and tenderness. And it made us fall instantly in love with Doreen Little. I say "stolen" because we had no right to see a side of her she never would have intentionally shown.

The song was "Something's Got a Hold on Me," and Miss Little began singing right along with it. She started slow, soft at first. But as Etta picked up the tempo, Miss Little picked up the volume.

Her voice grew even louder, and then she came into view. She wasn't just singing the lines—she *was* Etta James. Belting every word, meaning every one. Moving her feet, her arms, her hips. We couldn't look away.

I'll tell you what it was like. It was like walking across the hot slab of an immense, empty parking lot and, right in the center, finding a perfectly formed, unnaturally beautiful sunflower shooting straight up through the pavement, reaching for the open sky despite having no right to have been growing there in the first place. That's exactly what it was like.

She spun once during the performance, and the smile on her face was something I still think about at odd times. It was like she forgot how to smile until just that very minute. I wanted to steal it from her, to keep for myself while at the ranch. And I suddenly felt guilty for watching.

"We should go," I whispered.

Mickey nodded in agreement but remained glued to the window.

"Come on." I pulled away, pulling him with me. "My shoulder's killing me." We slunk away, returning to the path that led to the bunkhouse.

CHAPTER

twenty-seven

ON THE NEXT OCCASION THAT I CLIMBED INTO THE STABLE WITH Reaper, I probably twitched more than she did. Every swing of her head, every step, I flinched. I waited as though it were inevitable that she'd go for me again. Maybe finish me off and just be done with it. But she didn't. This time, she just stood there, waiting for me to do whatever it was I'd do. That's how things started out with Reaper: small, hard-fought victories. With each progression, we celebrated, and told ourselves Coop would have been proud.

One particular night, she let me stand near her for almost twenty minutes, stroking her neck and back. Maybe she finally understood I wasn't giving up. Coop had worked with her for weeks on end. It had taken me just over three months.

Not that any of it was easy. She just about pitched a temper tantrum the first time I tried to slide the damn saddle over her back, and I was lucky to get out of the way. Trying to break that horse was like dancing a cha-cha. We took little steps forward, big steps back. Sometimes she'd let me go just a little further than before, and sometimes she wouldn't.

And then, all the late nights and long days finally paid off. I was in her stall, in the very spot where she broke open Benny's head, to be exact. It was hard not to think about that.

"What are you, crying or somethin'?" Mickey hissed.

"Screw off," I laughed under my breath. Sweat ran into my eyes and, along with the sharp cut of manure in the air, stung like hell. She was saddled, if you can believe that. I was standing right next to her and I hardly believed it myself. It was just the third time she had let us sling the thing onto her, and only the second she actually let me strap it underneath.

Standing there, eyes red from the stench and the sweat, I brought my left foot up and wedged it into the dangling stirrup. Reaper grunted.

I stole a glance toward Mickey, who was clinging to the outside of the stable door like an insect. His face, just barely visible over the top rail, was a bleached sheet. "Jesus, this is it!" he whispered. "It's been nice knowing you, Nosebleed. You weren't such a douche after all."

I reached up to grab around the base of her neck, and that's about when she decided she was done with the formalities. I saw it coming, too. Saw how the smooth hair on her neck twitched like I'd touched a live wire to her.

She reared, and kicked, and through it all, I somehow managed to hang on. At one point during all this, my left foot slipped out of the stirrup, and my right one found its way in instead. Reaper screamed, over and over. I'll swear to that, too—it was no whinny. It was a pissed-off, honest-to-God scream.

I tried my best to throw my free leg over the saddle. It was the best bet. If I let go, I'd easily snap my ankle, which was tangled in the stirrup. On top of that, I'd be risking a few hoofs planted into various parts of my body.

She started circling, like a dog chasing its tail, in an effort to be rid of me. And it should have worked. I should have found myself on the ground half buried in manure, but at that last moment, I reached out with an open hand and came up with a fistful of her white mane.

She screamed again, and snapped her teeth at me.

That was when I threw my leg up over the saddle, and ended the scenario facing the wrong direction.

This, of course, was all met with a release of laughter from the other side of Reaper's pen. "And you want to be a breaker?" Mickey yelled. "Oh, damn, this is just the best!"

Reaper slowed, apparently just as confused as me. "Shh, shh, shh," I whispered. "'S okay, girl. It's okay. Nothing to worry about." I stroked a hand along her flank, and watched her skin twitch. "Nothing at all. We're gonna make a great team. You'll see, girl. You just wait and see. Shh."

She stopped circling and snorted. It sounded appropriate, at least. Mickey's head rose above the gate as he climbed back up to watch. His mouth was open almost as wide as his eyes.

"You're doing it!" he said. "Holy balls, Nosebleed, you're riding that bitch after all!"

I was riding the unrideable horse. I was facing the wrong way, but I was riding her. For Benny, and for Coop. I stroked her flank. "You'll see, girl. You'll see." She swung her head back to look at me, as if she finally understood.

IN SPITE OF OUR PRESUMED CLEVERNESS, CERTAIN PEOPLE DID BEGIN to notice things—how tired we always were, Grimsley calling us out at odd times so that we could steal away to the horse pens. Ruben DeMarco even asked me why we didn't play cards as much anymore.

Once, Mickey fell asleep at lunch, and I kicked him in the shin just before guard Addison walked by. But only one person came out and asked.

"Really, what is it?" John Church stabbed his pitchfork in the dirt, and then propped a foot on the stock. "You're half awake. You and your little friend are yanked out of the bunks here and there. What gives?"

"Nothing," I said, and shrugged. "Just working, that's all."

He pondered this for a moment, then scratched his chin. "That's not it. But you keep your secret."

It was hard to believe John Church was only just a few years older than me. If I didn't know any better, I'd swear he was a high school grad. I wondered what it felt like—to be so strong, so intimidating to everyone around you.

Ever since his arrival, we all formed our own theories about what he had done. Mickey swore Church must have held up a First National and gunned down every man in sight. Benny once said Church probably ran a motorcycle gang, like James Dean. Me? I wasn't sure I wanted to know what he did. Whatever it was, I didn't think it would live up to the legendary stories already circulating the ranch.

"Man, how do you do it?" I asked. I posed the question before I had time to reconsider.

He turned around after hanging a bridle on the wall. "What?"

I paused, trying to find the right words. "How do you not let anything ever bother you? The things . . . here, at the ranch. Whatever it was you did to get here . . . how do you act like it doesn't ever bug you?"

He looked at me, then laughed, shaking his head. "You're such a faggot."

I laughed, too. "No, really. Nothing ever gets to you. How's that possible?" I tossed my manure-covered shovel aside and slunk to the ground, back against a stall, to take a fiver.

"Really," he said. "You're such a faggot. How do you know nothing gets to me?"

"Because you're too cool for any school. That's what everyone thinks, anyway."

"Yeah. And what do you think?"

I was so tired, I wanted to lean over and sleep in the dirt. "I don't know."

He went into a stall behind me, carrying a salt lick. "It's not that hard. Who gives a shit what other people think? You should try it sometime."

"Right," I said.

"What?" he asked. "You sorry for what you did, or you sorry you got caught? Which is it?"

I didn't say anything.

"You're sorry for what you did, right? Yeah, I knew it. See, I'm not sorry for what I did, *and,* I'm not even sorry I got caught. You know why?"

"Why?"

"Because fuck the world, that's why." He laughed at that, and I sort of did, too. "What, you cry yourself to sleep each night, wishing you could be back home with Mommy and Daddy?"

"Go screw," I whispered. "Just go screw."

"Yeah, that's it," he said from the other side of the wall.

"That's not it," I said, "Just so you know."

"Then what is it, ya baby?"

"Maybe I just haven't figured it out yet. I will, though. I . . . I did something, to my father, and . . . I'm not sorry I did it. I'd do it again, a thousand times again, but . . . I think I'm starting to feel guilty about it. Even if I'm still not sorry." There. It was out. I never told anyone how I felt inside, not even my closest friends. But there I was, confessing to John Church. He would understand. He would show me how to deal with it, how to be cool with it.

I waited for his response. For his sharp words, or maybe something insightful. After all, this was the slickest cat of us all. He was John Wayne.

He started laughing as though I'd just told him one of Mickey's jokes, and my face reddened.

"Starting to feel guilty?" He stepped out of the stall and stood over me. "What's there to feel guilty about?" He squatted down to me, so that his eyes were level with my own. "Fuck your old man. Who cares what you did? Grow some balls of your own." He spat on the ground next to my shoe, then rose.

"Feelin' guilty," he said, walking out of the stable.

I wanted to hate him for laughing at me that way. Maybe I even did, for a few seconds. Was it possible he was right? I couldn't see that at the time, so I told myself to just put my dad as far out of my head as I could.

HERE'S A FUNNY THING. I WAS ACTUALLY IN THE STABLE WHEN Frank Kroft confirmed what I'd feared was coming. This must have been August, and even though Swope Ranch sat at an elevation of thirteen thousand feet, it was damn hot.

I was pitching horse apples out of a stall when Warden Barrow stepped inside the barn, Frank behind him. I turned into a rock, just out of sight. A pile of manure was still loaded on the spade of my shovel, but I held it steady, listening.

Frank Kroft wanted to put Reaper down. I heard words like *ordinance, responsibility,* and *lost cause.*

I wanted to run out and tell them everything. How I'd been sneaking over, working my ass off with her, how she was coming around. I rested my shovel in the straw and made to do just that. With my hand on the gate, I stopped at the last second when Frank started talking again.

"I've never turned one free in ten years," Frank said. He sounded defiant.

Warden Barrow took a draw on his pipe. Finally, he said, "I could still get a small price for her, even if she's still a tornado. There's *always* someone else who wants to try."

They were standing outside Reaper's stall now, one looking on her with troubled eyes, the other with contempt. Reaper snorted, and stomped her front hoofs into the dirt.

Kroft added, "But it wouldn't be much."

"No," Barrow said. "Wouldn't be much." The smell of his pipe rolled into every part of the stable like thick, sweet fog. "You going to clean it up? I can't have a carcass lying around."

"I have just the boys in mind to clean it up," Frank said.

Barrow nodded. "Do what you want, then. We're not looking at a marginal loss here."

"You're still talking about the horse, right?" Frank asked.

The two men broke into a low laughter, and agreed to meet back in the morning. But I was thinking about Coop, running, falling to the ground. Frank Kroft, running his fingers through my hair, rubbing my ear. I'd avoided him the best I could after that night, trying to pretend he hadn't touched me at all. But it was the thought of him touching my horse . . . putting a gun to Reaper's head. That made me want to vomit. Not just because I had become so close to her during those weeks. It was how he thought he had the right.

CHAPTER *twenty-eight*

"No way he'll listen, *especially* to you," Mickey said, plucking a card from the pile. For the first time in two months, he looked rested. We decided at lunch that too many nights had passed since shuffling Coop's deck of cards. "Besides," he said. "He wants to do it, anyone can see it. You can hardly blame the guy, it's just in his nature to be a slimy prick."

I half smiled, and threw down a queen, taking an extra turn. "There has to be a way. Some way to show them what I've done. How far she's come."

"You douche, you still can't ride her out in the pasture. You're just not to that point, man." He looked at his cards, then down at the discard pile on the bunk, and shook his head. "Fucking crazy eights."

"Listen," I said, "I'm not going to let this happen. I'll just have to figure something out."

Mickey took a card and laid down his hand.

"Hey," he said. "Keep it up and maybe Frank will get some extra target practice, just like he did with Coop. That make you happy? It's hard for me, too, you know? The thought of that fuck putting her down makes me sick. But that horse isn't Coop. And she isn't Benny."

"Just help me get her in the morning."

Mickey threw his cards in my face. "You're crazy! You even hear what I just said?"

"It's hard to explain, man. When Coop went down . . . man, we saw it happen right in front of us like some horror picture."

He stared down at the cards for a long time.

"Okay," he said, and nodded his head. "Okay. You don't have to make me choke up. Just don't get me killed, too." He turned around and elbowed a kid on the next bunk. "You believe this guy?" he motioned my way. "Thinks he's Harry fucking Houdini."

WHEN FRANK KROFT AND WARDEN BARROW WENT TO THE STABLE to collect Reaper, I can only imagine the stunned look on their faces when they found the empty stall.

Well, not entirely empty. Gus Grimsley was there, having been summoned by a certain four-and-a-half-foot-tall juvenile delinquent. "You should head to the south pasture," Gus said. "Something going on out there you might want to see."

"And what might that be, Gus?" Barrow asked.

"Well-sir, seems your horse is already out and about," Gus said. He later told us that when Kroft elbowed past, he heard the rifle's bolt unlatch—the same rifle used to murder Coop.

As they drew up to the fence, I heard the warden mutter, "Sweet Jesus." Kroft never said a word, but even in dim light, I saw his face flush.

There was something about that moment that, to me, verges on the miraculous. I'd sat on Reaper before, in her stable. But when Kroft and the warden approached that evening, it was the first time I'd ever really ridden a horse, and the first time Reaper ever obliged. Yet there I was, in the south field, trying my damnedest to look like I knew what I was doing. I was scared to death, no question about it, and even though I'm sure she sensed it, Reaper never once tried to throw me. I can neither explain nor make sense of it.

I rode her along a line, turned, and drew to a somewhat shaky trot.

I thought my heart was going to pop at any moment, saving Kroft the trouble of having to shoot us both. I don't know if they saw who was controlling who, but as long as my ass stayed in the saddle, I guess it didn't much matter. I'd only slipped a halter over her, not a riding bridle. I didn't have the balls to shove that metal bit into a mouth that still snapped at me.

I nudged her toward the fence, and by the grace of God, she complied.

"What is this bullshit?" Barrow yelled out.

The rifle was tight in Frank's hand. He looked eager to raise it.

"I know I'm supposed to be working, and I have no business being with the horses. But I just had to show you, both of you, what I've been doing. This horse isn't a lost cause. I've been working with her, by myself." I wasn't about to throw Mickey's name out.

"It doesn't matter what you've accomplished, you little shit," Kroft said. "You weren't allowed to work her or any other horse. We have rules. Looks to me like you've been breaking your fair share."

"I couldn't stand the thought of you putting her down. She's a good horse."

"It's not your concern what we do," Kroft yelled. "She's still going to end the day with a hole in her head." He went to crawl through the post fence, rifle clenched even tighter in his knuckled fist.

Barrow had caught Kroft's arm in a single grip. "No, Frank."

Frank looked like the warden had slapped his face; his face turned a deeper crimson, and a large vein swelled above his eyebrow.

"Remarkable," Barrow said. "How long have you been at it, boy?"

"Almost fourteen weeks."

"Fourteen weeks. Lord's mercy." Barrow propped his foot on the fence railing. "All right, Mr. Sheppard, take the animal back to her pen for now."

Frank interjected, "You know how I feel about this, sir."

"I know exactly how you feel, Frank. But let's remember who's in charge. Last I heard, I was the warden and you were the chief guard. I know money when I see it, and if we can sell a tamed horse, I'd say that makes more sense than putting a fifty-cent round in her head."

Frank lowered his rifle to the ground, but he never took his eyes off me. "Yes, sir. Suppose so."

"When you're done putting the animal up, Mr. Sheppard, wait there until Frank comes to collect you. He'll be more than happy to escort you personally to solitary. Rules are rules and you just put yourself in more trouble than even the Almighty would ever care to see."

"Yes, sir," I said. I nudged Reaper in the sides. For a second, I was sure she would buck. But she settled, and with a reluctant grunt, slowed to a bizarre sideways trot toward the gate.

"And Mr. Sheppard?"

I stopped, and turned to Barrow.

"When you do get out, I want you to stop wasting your time shoveling horse shit and report to the central pen. We might have use for you over there."

I couldn't stop the smile that spread across my face. "Yes, sir." And when I saw Kroft's reaction, I smiled even wider. I'd probably pay for it later, but I didn't care. That moment belonged to me. For the first time in a long time, I was proud of myself.

CHAPTER

twenty-nine

"HOPE IT WAS WORTH IT," FRANK KROFT SAID, THROWING THE butt of his rifle into my back like a battering ram. The blow sent me to the ground. As I rolled over, the door slammed shut, extinguishing all light.

The air in the cell was thick with the smell of shit. That, along with the punch to the back, took my breath away.

I crawled around the room, keeping one hand against the concrete wall. It smelled like a rotting carcass was in the room with me. My eyes began to adjust, and I could just make out my hands in front of me. After a few steps, I bumped into the steel commode, nearly sticking my hand inside. The toilet was almost half the size of a conventional one; I never understood that. As if finding the thing in the dark wasn't hard enough. Also, there's no plumbing in any of the cells in the box. Each commode is pretty much a dressed-up bedpan. Upon release, it's your responsibility to yank up the removable basin and clean it out for the next visitor.

The smell from within sliced through me, even though I breathed solely through my mouth. There was no doubt its contents were left especially for me. After putting Reaper back into her stall, I'd waited nearly half an hour for Kroft to come. Enough time for someone to have come and left the gift.

I crawled to an opposite corner and threw up.

My breath was returning, and I tried to focus. On what, it didn't matter. As my eyes continued to adjust, I realized the commode was in a different corner in this cell. Then it dawned on me that I was in the same room as Benny when he told me about his brother. How long ago was that—three months? Four? It suddenly didn't seem long ago at all. I drew my knees close and tried to gather positive thoughts.

Reaper.

I saved her from a murderous bastard. She took a saddle in the open field. She let me ride her. I didn't know if Mickey had seen, but I told myself he had. I thought of us playing crazy eights the night before. Then, my thoughts transcended the ranch. I thought of Jimmy Curio from back home. Playing ball. Carrie Francello wearing a new dress. I thought of my mother.

Suddenly, in the dark, I thought I heard Benny's voice, whispering to me. The voice was so real, so alive. It made me feel for the first time that he was truly dead. I had never wanted to believe that, but months had passed. I had seen the inside of his skull. Maybe his ghost was back to keep me company. I know how that sounds. But there, in that pitch-black cell, things were different. You heard better, I swear you did. As if your ears made up for what your eyes couldn't show you.

"Anyone over there?" I whispered. I was afraid to ask, afraid of what might answer back.

Silence. The wind, outside. Rustling leaves.

I was relieved, but saddened all over again. His image formed in my mind. Our last talk in the stable. The way he once ate raisins with filthy hands.

One of the worst things about going to the box is how time loses its meaning. There's no concept of it, really, as daytime is just as bleak as the night. Waiting for a day to pass was enough to make your mind break. Really, there are only two options you have: sleeping or thinking. And sometimes, I couldn't tell exactly which I was doing.

I leaned my head against the wall, closed my eyes, and drew in more thoughts. Miss Little, singing Etta James. Playing cards with Coop's Bicycle deck. Reaper's mane in my fingers. I thought about what things would be like once I got out. Is it odd to admit I began to think of getting out as in out of the box, and not the ranch itself? Probably. But still, I imagined myself in the central pen with Mickey and the rest of the breakers. Riding the horses in the pasture.

Somehow, despite it all, I must have drifted off. Thank God for that. Anytime you can sleep in the box, it's like fast-forwarding time.

During the middle of the night, I awoke. And I say middle of the night because even though everything around me was still black, the cell door was wide open, revealing a canvas of stars in the glimpse of sky. Something shifted next to me, and then a boot punched into my ribs.

Multiple hands dug into my shirt and under my arms, pulling me from the floor. A face drew up to mine, inches away. Someone struck a match, casting a glow across the entire cell. And there, before me, was Silas Green.

"What are you doing?" I asked. It was a stupid question, but all I could manage.

"We're having a blanket party," he whispered. "And guess what? You're the guest of honor." He looked past me, over my shoulder, and with that, the dim world disappeared completely. It was a bunk blanket, I could tell from the feel of the scratchy wool. Something else—a belt?—drew tight around my stomach and arms. My confusion and frustration was immediately replaced with pain.

The punches came from every direction. I kicked my legs at nothing, trying to roll away, trying to push off as best I could with the bunk blanket tied over my head and chest. "No!"

They kicked and punched at random; lightning exploded in my head, my shoulders, my back, my mouth.

"Pleeeze!" I was weeping, and curled up on the floor. The assault finally slowed, and then, silence. There was a rustling, the sound of zippers. Everything was suddenly wet. To me, wrapped in the wool blanket, it was the sound of rain streaming onto a tent. They were pissing on me, all of them. I felt it splatter against me, against the blanket, and

then soak through. I felt it in my hair, against my neck, on my nose. I lay there, unable to move, to even roll away, and waited for it all to end.

One of them kneeled close to me, put his head right next to mine. Silas said, "That's from Frank. He wanted you to know that. I hope you liked it."

They unstrapped the belt, then shut me back in alone. After some time, I pulled the blanket away and slung it into the far corner next to the shit-filled toilet. There was nothing to do but stare into the darkness until I fell asleep.

On the morning I was released, I staggered into the sunlight carrying the used toilet basin. I didn't even get sick as I cleaned it out with the hose. After, I made my way to the bunkhouse with my hands shoved deep into my pockets.

My lower lip had ballooned, as had my left eye. On top of that, I reeked of piss. Despite all this I managed to smile at Mickey, who was waiting for me on my cot.

"You okay?" he asked.

I was too embarrassed to tell him what happened, the specifics, then realized he probably had already figured it out. "She let me ride her," I said.

He smiled. "I know, I was watching."

"Yeah?"

He looked away. "Look, I'm—I'm sorry I didn't come out and tell them I helped you. I shoulda taken the blame, too. Shoulda been in there with you."

He waited on me to say something, anything. "Whoever said we were fuckin' friends?"

He laughed.

"I didn't want you to take any blame," I said. "I never told—"

"Hey," Mickey cut in. "Listen, something's happened.

"Don't tell me I missed something."

Mickey shrugged. "You could say that. It's Benny. He's . . . he's back."

I felt like someone suddenly swung a baseball bat into my gut. He was shitting me, he had to be. "No way, man. The guy punched his ticket. Come on, Mickey, don't play around."

He looked down. "I didn't know how to tell you. Because, the thing is, he's . . . different. He's not the same guy, Will."

I stared at him, not knowing if I wanted to hear. "What do you mean?"

"Someone said they had to cut out part of his brain, but . . . that's just the talk going around. You know how it is."

I sat on a bunk and stared at nothing, trying to digest the news.

Benny. Back from the dead.

"I don't know," Mickey said. "He's just not there. Almost like—aw, I dunno, just someone else."

I had a strong feeling Mickey wanted to say "almost like his brother, Todd," but I didn't ask. I suddenly wondered if Benny remembered that I was there the day of the accident.

"Where is he now?"

Mickey shook his head. "Don't know. Haven't hardly seen him much at all. He's been spending a lot of time at Miss Little's. Guess they're still kinda figuring out what to do with him. I was waiting on you to go over there with me."

I needed to see him. And at the same time, I couldn't stand the thought of seeing him. I was afraid he'd remember why he went into Reaper's stall in the first place. Worse, I was afraid he would blame me for what happened.

CHAPTER
thirty

Miss Little was keeping Benny to herself, it seemed. Considering ourselves to be somewhat in a higher caste than the rest of the prison ranch population, we decided to just walk over and ask to see our friend. After all, we'd sat in Miss Little's kitchen, eaten dessert with her.

Mickey knocked on the door, and my heart crawled up the back of my throat. I suddenly felt guilty, as though I'd crippled him myself.

Footsteps drew near, and the door cracked open only wide enough to frame her thin body. "How can I help you boys?" She didn't smile; there was no warmth. It was a completely different face than the one I'd seen singing, all those nights ago.

"We came to see him," I said.

"Just for a second," Mickey added. "Just to say hi."

But she only shook her head. "Absolutely not. You best be running along, now." She made to close the door, and Mickey shot a foot into the doorway. When he saw the look in her eyes, he withdrew it.

"Just . . . for a second?" he asked.

Her face softened. It would be difficult for others to have seen this, but we caught it. "Not now, boys. He's not ready just now. Be patient." She closed the door and locked it.

And so, we were resigned to wait. And it was all we could think about for the remainder of the day.

ASIDE FROM THE ANXIETY OF HOPING TO SEE MY FRIEND, THE NEXT day was everything I'd hoped it would be. I worked alongside Mickey, I worked with Reaper, and I gained the respect of the guys for how far I'd come with her. Only Silas Green looked at me with dead eyes as I led the great white horse around the pen. She resisted a few times, but nothing like she could have. Just a jerk here and yank there, but I held the rope tight, and kept whispering. The other guys thought it was a miracle. I knew it was just luck. There was still a raging fire in her, and I knew better than to ever forget that.

I learned about technique and how to further develop my skills. I learned more about the horses in that first day than I had since coming to the ranch. I learned for the first time that Mickey—as small as he was—needed help getting up into a saddle. He glared at me and said he'd jump down and punch me in the nuts if I so much as smiled. It was wonderful.

Aaron Gumm tried to show me the finer points of roping, and I entertained everyone by embarrassing myself. I took it in the stomach when trying to file hoofs, and ended up vomiting my breakfast all over the dirt.

I realized after all this that the rest of the breakers had looked forward to my first day almost as much as I had.

When lunch hour finally arrived, Mickey took it upon himself to point out every single thing I'd done wrong that morning; I hadn't seen him so happy in weeks.

"Not so easy, is it!" He wasn't really asking my opinion. That was obvious. "Yeah. Not so damn easy at all! I think now you'll appreciate me just a little more." I wasn't even smiling, and it took everything I had not to throw my glass of lukewarm milk in his face.

"You're hilarious," was all I could say. "A real piece of work."

He laughed at this, and took it as a compliment. He looked around the room as he wolfed his sandwich. I knew what he was looking for because I'd been doing it ever since we sat down at the table.

"Why do you think they sent him back here?" I asked, digging a pickle out from between my bread.

Mickey put down his cup. "Really? Come on, you have to ask?"

"Getting nearly killed should have been his ticket out of here."

"No way. You know Barrow, and Frank . . . shit, they'd see letting him walk as a sign of, what, weakness or something. You know? Kroft would rather set loose a horse than one of us."

But none of it made sense. "Yeah, but it couldn't just be up to Barrow or Frank. Sending a guy back to this place . . . after having his head kicked in—that's got to be a decision someone else makes."

Mickey shrugged. "Who the hell knows? Maybe they're waiting on paperwork or something like that before they transfer him."

I think he meant that as a joke, but looking back on it, all these years later, I think Mickey could have been more correct than he knew.

I pushed the thought from my head, and shifted on the hard plastic bench. The bruises I'd already accumulated were making me feel like an old man.

That afternoon, I was told to take Reaper back to the stables, and grab an extra halter while I was there. Inside the musty barn, surrounded by the heady aromas of fresh-cut hay, dust, and manure, I met Benny Fritch for the second time in my life. I say that because, just as Mickey said, he was not at all the same person I knew before.

He stood near the stalls, his back to me, separating a tangle of bridles. His hair was different. That was the first thing I noticed. A spot the size of a grapefruit had been shaved across the broad side of his head. The bristled, blond hair was growing back, but it wasn't long enough to cover the roadmap of scarring that stretched across his scalp. And it wasn't just the scar I noticed. His head was misshapen. Mashed in from the kick.

He turned around and looked directly through me; I turned to make sure nobody was behind.

Then, his eyes changed, just a little, and a smile curled up along one side of his mouth.

"Will!"

His voice was broken, rough. At that moment, I wanted to run away. His life was ruined because of me.

"Will?" he asked, as if now unsure who I was.

I wiped my eyes, and tried again to look at him. "Benny. I'm . . ."

There was a patience in his eyes unlike any I'd ever seen.

". . . I'm sorry. It was my fault you . . ." I didn't know how to finish.

His eyes turned toward Reaper and his smile faded. He recognized her. I thought he might be angry, or scared, but his expression turned to wonder.

"She's a pretty horse. I wasn't careful."

His words were simple, and he said them differently now, like he had had to relearn how to speak. For all I knew, maybe he had.

"I can't believe you're back."

"Yuh," he said. "Yuh, I'm back. From the . . . hospital." He placed the bridles on the ground and went to Reaper. Amazingly, she stood still.

"Careful, man," I said. "Careful. She might snap."

He raised his large hands with a finesse I never saw in him before. Reaper turned her nose into him while he rubbed the side of her face. I winced, and waited for her flip out—she still hadn't let a soul touch her besides me. But she only snorted.

His smile returned. "It's . . . okay, girl. Okay. Benny A-okay now. You're . . . a good girl." He looked back at me. "Not your fault . . . either."

He slipped Reaper's lead from my hand and took her into her stall.

Even the way he took off her halter put me at ease. I shook my head in wonder. Without a worry in the world, he stroked her neck, and talked to her like an old friend.

"You hurt me . . . real good. But I'm not mad," he said, just within earshot. "Was my fault. My fault. You didn't want to hurt me." There was a red handkerchief shoved into his back pocket. He pulled it out after closing the gate, and wiped it across his sweat-beaded forehead.

Reaper turned twice inside her pen, then stuck her head over the gate to watch us, and grunted.

"I used to be . . . good with animals," he said. "When I's a boy. You know that? Real good."

"I think you told me once," I said. He had, in fact. Just before Silas Green threw him to the ground and yanked a horse bit into his mouth.

"I forgot. For long time. Daddy used to say I was . . . blest."

Blessed. "Maybe you are," I said.

His stare went distant again, and he picked up the pile of bridles from the floor. "Still got work to do. I get on it."

"Okay, Benny. I'm glad you're back. I—" My voice faded into a hushed tone. "I was so scared. I didn't know what to think."

He smiled, nodding his head. "Sometimes, when I'm dreaming. Remember it happening. Sometimes I cry when wake up. Didn't like waking up . . . alone. I get scared, Will."

I let out an exhaled laugh. "You won't be alone anymore, I guess." I left the barn thinking how amazing it was that things can change as much as they do.

We were all together that night at the table. I never knew until that moment just how much I missed that. It was like having the gang together again, almost. Except, of course, for Coop. But Benny Fritch was alive. *Alive.*

It was like catching your second wind to hear Benny's hee-haw again. That laugh was so deep, so resonant. Once, he laughed so hard that he stopped and put his hand to the caved-in side of his head. I thought he was having a stroke or something, right there and then, but he just smiled, dropped his hand, and the laugh returned.

"Hurts sometimes," he told me later. "Hurts me, and think I'm going to fall asleep. And then . . . it goes back."

"Goes away?" I asked.

"No. Goes back. Pain hides back in me. Somewhere. Can always feel it hiding. But sometimes it comes out and hurts me. But I'm still here. Benny's still here."

I once heard Frank Kroft tell the warden how he never turned a horse free, how he'd rather kill it. To turn it loose before its will was broken, or to even sell it untamed, was seen as a failure. Maybe Mickey was right. Maybe that's how it was with Benny.

CHAPTER
thirty-one

"I HEAR BENNY'S A RETARD. SHIT FOR BRAINS. SURE AS HELL LOOKS true to me." Silas Green threw a saddle over an Appaloosa mare, never once looking me in the eye as he worked.

Mickey stood at my side, sharp on his toes as always. "What the hell do you ever know, cockbreath?"

Ranch guards worked alongside us in the training pens, but none within earshot paid attention to us. Not that any of them cared.

Silas's eyes narrowed on Mickey. "Oh, you're just asking for it, aren't you, faggot? Don't worry. You're gonna get yours." He went back to the mare, leading her around the pen.

"Forget him," Mickey said. "I heard he's only got another five months, anyway. Then he's outsville."

"Five months?" That would leave me almost a half year after he was gone. I marveled at the thought of nearly six months without Silas Green around.

"Yeah, thought you'd like that. He doesn't even know it yet, so this is way classified. I just weaseled it out of Gus. They're sending him to a juvy hall back east for another few months, then from there, I guess, he's home free. Released back into the wild, or some shit like that, right?"

"Yeah, something like that. Scary thought—Silas Green running around loose."

ON HIS SECOND NIGHT BACK, BENNY CONVINCED ELMORE HOLLING to let him switch bunks with Brian Barhorst, whose bed was just before mine. Benny told Holling he sometimes got scared in his new bed at the end of the row because it was darker there. My end of the bunkhouse received a constant wash of stale bathroom light, which was sometimes comforting and sometimes annoying.

Holling looked at him like he was waiting for the punch line. When none came, Elmore Holling smiled anyway, still amused. "Hell, Benny," he said. "Don't let me stop you if you need a night-light." That drew a few stifled laughs around the room.

Benny turned red. "I know it sounds . . . funny, but I can't help it. Just feel bad, sometimes. In the dark."

Brian Barhorst didn't give much of a shit. In fact, those were his exact words. He was glad to switch out; he had a few pals at the other end of the building.

So Benny grabbed his things and dragged his footlocker across the concrete floor to his new cot, a small grin on his face. He sat down and said, "Now show Benny, again. Show me the poker . . . game." And so, for the second time, I taught my friend how to play cards. Surprisingly, it didn't take as long as I thought.

"Hey," Mickey told Benny. "All you need now is a cigar in your mouth and you're big-time." He laid down his winning hand, allowing time for me to roll my eyes and curse his mother. "I was thinking," he said. "What if we stuck together after we get out of here? Wouldn't that be boss?"

I shuffled through the deck and dealt them across the cot. "Yeah, and how would that work? We're not all exactly from Saint Louis."

"Why . . . not live here? In Col . . . Colorado? Live here, and . . . still work, with horses. But for money." Benny's eyes were as large as silver dollars. "All of us. Right, Will?"

I threw him a card.

"Shit, yeah!" Mickey said, accidentally flashing his cards. I knew he was bluffing me. "We could make a killing doing this stuff. Real jobs. Plus, can you imagine all the girls I'd get if I ran my own place?"

"Yeah," I said, laying down my hand. "I've often heard shoveling horse shit is a huge turn-on for babes."

Ideas like that were fun to get caught up in, but we knew the more likely truth, even if one of us wouldn't admit it: we'd all go our separate ways. Benny smiled through all this, as if he didn't entirely get what we were saying, but he laughed right along with us.

"Well, maybe . . . someday," he said. "Maybe then I can . . . help you guys. Help you with those horses."

BENNY TOLD ME HE USED TO BE GOOD WITH ANIMALS, BUT NOW I know he was being modest. Fact was, he was really more of a genius with them. Whether he was just as good with horses before he came to the ranch, I'll never know—prior to his accident, I only saw him turn out dirty stalls.

On an early July morning, I was in the main pen with the other guys. We were with a chestnut-coated mare that sometimes showed good behavior, and sometimes threw a hell of a tantrum. On that morning she was fighting each one of us.

Primarily, she was Silas's project, but he was making slow progress. We watched him slip a lead rope around her neck, and then we watched the horse absolutely lose it when he started to yank her forward. She snapped her teeth and reared up on her hind legs, as if to further scare the shit out of us.

"Whoa, whoa, whoa," Silas whispered, not letting go of the rope.

Frank Kroft motioned everyone back to the fence, giving the mare all the room she needed. "Let's go, let's go," he shouted.

At that moment, Eddie Tokus opened the gate to join us. Slipping in like that wasn't uncommon, even with a manic horse inside. Only, Eddie tripped. He was carrying a couple of bridles and some coils of rope, and he somehow wound his foot inside the dangling harness straps. He fell into the gate and sent it swinging open like it was spring-loaded. The steel frame banged against the fence, and that was all it took to send the horse completely over the edge.

The lead ripped out of Silas's hands as she went off into a full tantrum around the pen, bucking and kicking and suddenly breaking into full gallop. She pointed straight at Eddie Tokus, still on his knees, and the wide-open gate.

"Oh, shit on me!" he yelled. He wobbled to his feet and pawed at the gate with his fat arms.

"Close it! Close the gate!" Frank screamed at the top of his lungs, grabbing everyone's attention but the horse's.

Eddie tripped again trying to swing it closed. His face came down hard on the bars, causing it to slam shut and bounce back open. He rolled out of the way just as the horse came thundering down. I still can't figure out how he didn't get trampled.

The horse collided at full gallop. The impact was so great, the gate separated completely from its hinges. She cried out and barreled directly toward the barn, and toward Benny Fritch, who was heaving a wheelbarrow of horse manure and straw.

I saw it coming. We all did. She was going to knock him into next week.

Benny let go of the wheelbarrow, sending horse shit all over the ground. He raised his arms up to the horse and stepped into her path. He made a series of low moaning sounds, the way a dog might do after getting grazed by a car.

When the horse was over him, something bizarre happened. She eased up, enough for Benny to reach out and catch the lead rope. He kept at it with the odd sounds, and she further slowed to a trot, yanking the guy right alongside.

With a free hand, Benny reached high along the mare's neck, and ran his hand down, then up again. Grooming her, with his fingernails instead of a brush. He was still saying something to her, but none of us could hear any more. It was just a whisper now, and I knew he was speaking some kind of magic. He must have been because that mare stopped, whinnied once more, then hung her head. Once she was calm, Benny led her back to us, still chanting in her ear. It was unbelievable.

Inside the pen, he paused, then reached up to give the horse a scratch behind the ears. "You're okay, now," he said with a soft voice. A few of the guys laughed at this, but not me. Not Mickey. "Just . . . stay by Will," Benny went on. "He'll keep you s-safe." With that, he handed the rope to Kroft. "Here . . . you are. She okey-dokey now." Then, he turned and walked out, back to the overturned wheelbarrow.

"Okay, what was that?" Mickey asked.

Frank shook his head and stared at Benny like he was nothing but a freak.

Benny Fritch had the touch. He had a way with the horses that I'd never seen before or since. It was like they just understood what he wanted them to do, just by hearing him whisper some kind of voodoo into their ears. Really, it was a thing of complete and absolute beauty to observe, like watching a painter create his masterpiece. That was just Benny.

CHAPTER

thirty-two

ONE FRIDAY NIGHT IN AUGUST, WE ALL GATHERED INTO THE MESS hall for what was to be an organized announcement and special event. Usually, that meant some sort of new work detail. Punishment for God knows what.

Only we received the surprise of the year. In the middle of the mess hall, sitting out of place on one of the long tables, was a film projector. We all poured into the room in long antlike lines, and the mess hall became filled with a collective air of excitement.

Along the walls and bookending the doors, bringing everyone in, were Frank Kroft, Elmore Holling, Joe Addison, and several others. They all waved their arms in guidance, like shepherds who'd traded in their robes and staffs for tight button-downs, pistols, and billy clubs.

"Come on, ladies," Holling bellowed. "Let's go, before the show's over already. Move your asses!"

It took all of ten minutes for the entire juvenile population to enter the mess hall and take a seat. I ended up with Benny at a table near the projector. As close as I was, I still couldn't make out the title of the movie hanging on the reel. The anticipation was killing me.

From behind, someone called out, "This a Marilyn Monroe?" Simultaneous laughter erupted.

Once everyone was seated, the lights flicked off and the projector sprung to life, whirring and clicking. The bare wall across from it was immediately transformed into an almost authentic movie screen.

It was a Bogart. *African Queen.* Not what you'd expect a roomful of teenaged boys to enjoy, but we did all the same. I'd never seen it, but I did catch him in *The Maltese Falcon* and thought that one was slick. Bogart was good. No Bela Lugosi, but he was good.

We were nearly halfway into it, just as Bogart was piloting the *Queen* past a group of Germans, when the picture blinked off, leaving only the sound blaring. The responses were immediate.

Kroft gave the projector a once-over the way he might check under the hood of a ranch truck. "Keep your panties on, ladies. We've got another bulb in the supply room."

Benny, maybe just because he was closest to the projector, said, "I could go get it. Could bring it back."

I expected Kroft to look past Benny and over to me, or maybe even to Joe Addison, who was standing at the mess hall entrance. But he didn't.

"All right, Fritch. Get your ass over there. Little green box on the third shelf from the left. Think you can remember that?"

"Yes, sir. Third shelf, green box. I can be fast."

Kroft nodded to Addison. "Tell them outside. One going to the supply room and back."

Benny pulled himself off the seat and hurried out like an agreeable pet.

A collection of whispers and laughs filled the dim room as everyone passed the time. I leaned over and saw Mickey two tables down. He shot me the finger.

After five minutes went by, Kroft motioned again to Addison. The two whispered, then Kroft walked out the door. Maybe Benny got confused and couldn't find the bulb. I pictured him fumbling through the closet, rummaging through every box he could find. I wished I would have tried harder to go with him, or that Kroft had sent a screw to get it instead.

The lull in the room turned to a good murmur, and Addison barked at us a few times. Minutes came and minutes passed. Kroft should have been back by now. The supply room was only fifty yards away, connected to the east side of the main house. A minute's walk at best. I let my thoughts get away from me, and imagined Kroft yelling at Benny for being stupid and wasting everyone's time.

After almost twenty minutes passed, the door finally opened. In walked Benny, but something was wrong. Something was very wrong. He walked slowly to the back of the room instead of returning to the empty seat next to me. He walked differently. Not with a limp, just unusual. Gently, maybe.

He was crying. Not in a loud way, but I could see his cheeks were wet with spent tears. Benny found an open spot at one of the back tables and eased down.

The room was absolutely silent. Frank walked through the door and directly to the projector. A small box was in one hand. It took him all of thirty seconds to change out the bulb and turn the movie back on. Behind us all, over the sounds of Humphrey Bogart shooting his rifle, I heard Benny weeping. The proud look on Kroft's face made me sick, and I knew he'd done something horrible.

WHEN THE MOVIE ENDED AND THE CREDITS APPEARED, THE MESS hall erupted in applause. The warden could have thrown a hokey love story on the wall and I don't think the cheering would have been any less enthusiastic.

Mickey made a beeline for Benny, still sitting at the back. The last few times I glanced back, Benny's head was down on the table, buried in the tangle of his arms. I was going to go, too, but a firm hand clamped down hard on my shoulder.

Kroft said, "Keep your ass in your seat, Sheppard." He turned back to the projector, removing the reel, and I stole another look.

Mickey had his arm around Benny. His freckled face was the shade of an apple, and his fists were clinched. I can't remember ever seeing Mickey so furious.

What happened next will always stay with me.

Mickey walked to the mess hall's window and took a metal food tray from the return rail. Tray in hand, and before anyone else realized just what was happening, he was standing on a table at Frank's side. There was an earsplitting *THWACK* as the tray shotgunned into Kroft's face. Frank staggered in slow motion to the ground, confused. The tray swung down again, and again. Mickey lost all the composure that had held him together during the second half of the film. He was on fire.

"I'll kill you!!" The tray came down again. Kroft's nose was bleeding. *"How could you do that to him?" THWACK. "You piece of shit—you* raping *piece of shit!" THWACK.*

Only on the last swing, the tray didn't come back up. Frank caught it—caught Mickey's arm, to be more exact. And that was the end of the show. Thank you, good night. Now it was time for the Frank Kroft feature to begin.

Not even Addison said a word. Nobody in the room believed what had just happened.

Frank's arm was faster than a striking snake, clasping around Mickey's throat. Even with blood running from his nose, the son of a bitch smiled, showing those brown and yellow teeth.

The look in his eyes reminded me of a movie I saw as a kid called *The Turn of the Key.* It was about a guy who was thrown in the loony house, only he wasn't crazy. He met a man who was nuttier than a squirrel—and that guy had crazy eyes and a psychotic grin. That's what Frank Kroft reminded me of. I thought right then and there that he was going to kill Mickey Baines.

He threw Mickey to the ground and leaned in—right up to his face. I heard him distinctly say, "You . . . crazy . . . faggot." And then he started to laugh. He bled onto Mickey's face the way water seeps out of an old spigot. He drew back a large, knuckled fist and piled it with firecracker strength into Mickey's face.

"Get this piece of shit out of here," Frank said.

Addison and Holling finally found themselves, and crept toward Mickey—now unconscious—as though stepping through a minefield.

I knew all too well where Mickey was headed. I just didn't know for how long. He had earned at least a week in the box. Maybe more.

"All you pussies stand up!" Frank yelled. He didn't even bother to wipe the blood from his face.

We filed out just as we were told, and Benny stumbled in beside me as I hunched through the door. Outside, I put my arm around him. I didn't know what to say, besides the first stupid thing that instinctually came to mind. "You okay?"

He didn't say anything. He just walked.

"Benny? Hey, Benny, man, you okay?"

His eyes were empty. Finally, he whispered, "I t-told Mickee—" His lip started quivering. "He p-pulled my p-p-pants . . ." Benny collapsed to the ground, weeping, fists balled up into his eyes. My heart broke all over again. "D-Don't wanna t-talk about it! Will! Okay? Not ever! You promise?" He whispered the last part like a terrified child.

A hand reached down, and we looked up to find Joe Addison. His eyes were wide and glassy, and it took both of us to help Benny to his feet. After Joe walked ahead, I whispered, "I promise, Benny."

He couldn't stop crying, and although I knew what had happened in that supply room, I didn't want to believe it. I didn't want to hear the details and was secretly thankful Benny didn't want to share them. It didn't matter—details never matter. I already knew what was important. Frank Kroft was a monster.

Later that night, I slipped into the bathroom to find it empty, except for Silas Green. He was at the far end, leaning against the counter with his back to me. He held something in his hands—a piece of paper, maybe—looking at it the way a guy might gaze at his first love note. He turned, and for just the briefest of moments, I saw only emptiness in his eyes. It was the hollow stare of someone who is lost.

But then, like a light switch, it was off. Gone. Replaced by coldness.

He returned to the thing in his hands, and without hesitation, stepped into a toilet stall. The sound of swirling water broke the room's stillness, and in that instant, my suspicions screamed that he had just flushed away my mother's picture.

He said nothing as he passed.

What's worse, neither did I.

CHAPTER
thirty-three

I WAS WRONG. MICKEY SPENT TWO WEEKS IN THE HOLE, NOT ONE. Two weeks. That's more than most cons get in Joliet. When he got out, there was no doubt he'd had visitors. His left eye was swollen shut, the color of a ripe blueberry. His nose, too, was swollen, and noticeably crooked.

When we got a chance to talk, it was at the south pasture fence, near the barn. He didn't say anything at first, and that was okay. He looked smaller to me in that moment, certainly not the brash, cocky guy I was used to. This Mickey was quiet, reserved. There was a way about him that suggested he'd either built stronger, higher walls around him, or given up completely. The fact that I couldn't discern between the two worried me.

The thought of Silas's blanket party sped through my mind like a passing truck. "Silas?"

He just lowered his eyes, as if in shame. "Kroft."

I waited for him to say more.

"He came in twice," he finally said. "He . . ." But Mickey couldn't finish. He only shook his head and stared at the horses running in the field. I watched with him. Lately, it seemed time was moving even slower than usual. Not that it ever passed quickly, but still.

"I think sometimes we forget where we are, Will."

"No way, man. I don't think that's possible." I was half thinking he was bullshitting me.

"No. It's true. We've gotten used to this place. Become comfortable. We accept the fate we're given, we carry out the work, we break the horses. And along the way we've made friends . . . and—" He pursed his lips, licking the dryness off of them. "And then, when we aren't expecting it, this place rakes us right back into reality. Kicks us both in the ass and the head. Rips our hearts out, just for fun. We're in a prison, Will. There may not be cinder block walls and cell blocks, but it's a prison just the same."

He couldn't have spoken the truth any more than if he had read from the New Testament in my footlocker. I knew exactly what he meant. I saw it daily with my own eyes.

"But there's nothing we can do about it, is there?" I stated, more than asked.

He just turned and looked me in the eyes for the first time since being released from his two-week stint.

"We try and make it to the next day," I said. "It's all we *can* do. They can't keep us here forever."

"But what if we're not ourselves when we get out? This place takes the life out of you." He turned his face back into the soft wind, back to the horses. "None of us will ever be who we were before."

That comment, more than any other, has stayed with me throughout all my years. I have forgotten neither its commanding truth nor the scared little boy who said it so matter-of-factly.

With our backs against the barn's wall, we stared out at the horses, trotting and grazing in the pasture as though they were still on the wide-open plain.

CHAPTER

thirty-four

Toward the end of August, or maybe even early September, talk started to float around that there had been a roundup and a new herd was on the way. Two dozen horses, maybe a few more, were trucking in from northwestern Colorado. I hoped it was true; it felt like a lifetime ago since the last full herd was brought in, and anything different would be a welcome change.

Frank Kroft finally confirmed the rumor. "That's twenty-six, ladies," he said, standing in the pen with us. "Two for each of you."

It dawned on me that I made up the thirteenth member of the group. I never really considered myself superstitious, but once I realized I was number thirteen, I couldn't get it out of my head.

Benny was scrubbing out stable troughs when Joe Addison walked by. Work would be slow with the breakers until the herd arrived, so Mickey and I volunteered to help him and John Church. Benny was thrilled to have the company.

"Special assignment for a special person," Addison said.

Benny looked up, sweat beading on his misshapen brow. "Yeah?"

"North pasture needs some fencing work, on the far side. Some of the posts are rotten'r than a corpse's cooch. Think you can handle that?" He wore a smile that might have been contemptuous, but with Addison it was always hard to tell.

"Fence . . . work?" Benny asked. At first, he scratched his head, as if what Addison said didn't make sense. Then his eyes lit. "I done some of that before. I could do a good . . . job."

"Bet you can," Addison said. "And it'll be a backbreaker, Fritch. Lots of postholes and lumber carrying. You may not be good for much else, but you'll do a damned fine job with the laboring."

Both insult and compliment were largely lost on Benny. He grinned the way a kid might. "Yes, sir. I'll . . . fix that fence up good!"

Addison nodded, pleased with himself. "And just so you don't fall over dead again, why don't you go ahead and pick someone to help you out."

"Any . . . one?"

Addison nodded again.

Benny's face concentrated, deep in thought. I can't say I was too surprised when he pointed his knobby finger in my direction, though Mickey seemed to be. Like I said, any change in routine is a welcome one.

WATCHING BENNY BULLDOZE THE POSTHOLE SHOVEL DEEP INTO the ground was like watching an ox at work. I'd have bet money he could pick me up and snap me in two with hardly any effort at all.

"So how'd you do it?" I asked.

"How . . . what?" he asked. A bead of sweat clung to the tip of his nose.

"Calm that runaway mare the way you did. I never saw anything like that before. No one here has."

He smiled, and went back to plunging the hole digger into the ground. "I can't tell you . . . Will."

"You can't put it in words? Is that what you mean?"

"No," he said. "I can't tell you . . . won't believe me."

"I'll believe anything you tell me, Benny. That's the truth." And it was. I'd expect Benny to lie to me no more than I would to my own mother.

He only shook his head, and after nearly a minute passed

by, I figured he was pleading the Fifth. But then he said, "I can feel . . . what they're thinking. I can . . . help them not be scared, right? After that . . . don't know, really."

The image of him leading the runaway mare back into her pen came to mind. She didn't even flinch that day. There was something different with him now, beyond the physical. It was something in his soul. A gentleness and warmth that made me think of home. I didn't understand it then, I don't understand it now. It just was what it was.

"I always been good . . . with animals. Just never got much of a . . . chance, to show anyone."

There would be no defining Benny Fritch. I've heard terms over the years to describe what he had, the things he could do. "Horse whisperer?" That could be a stretch, but maybe. I want to believe there *was* a little magic involved within it all. To think otherwise would make my memory of him smaller, and I don't want to go down that road. To me, Benny was pure, in every sense of that word. And finding something clean and unmarked in the noxious world of a reformatory ranch *is* magical. I guess I shouldn't have even brought it up. I smiled, and accepted Benny simply for what he was: my friend.

He squatted down to hoist a fence post from the pile, and then paused. "You believe in d-dreams? Will?"

"Brigitte Bardot, all the time," I said. "I'll never get her naked on my bunk, though." I started to laugh, thinking Mickey would have appreciated my stupid humor. I stopped when I saw Benny didn't get it.

"Had a dream last night."

"Were you shoveling horse shit?" I grinned, wanting to once again lighten the mood. I think somewhere I was afraid to hear what Benny dreamed about. I dropped another post at the base of the fence.

"We were walking . . . on a trail. I was in back. Then—rain, and rain . . . and something from the woods . . . an animal . . . was following us. We were going to a hole. To hide, right?"

"A hole?" I asked.

"Yes!" Benny said, his eyes lit. "And I . . . saved your life. In my dream—I saved your life somehow. But I don't remember. Then you said we was friends. Isn't that . . . a strange one?"

"Yeah, that is weird," I said. But I didn't want to hear any more. I didn't want to hear him say anything crazy like seeing me trampled, or finding Mickey dead on the ground. As if simply saying those things might make them true.

"Maybe . . . someday I will."

"You never know," was all I said.

Benny and I drove the posts into the ground and set them. There were only two more spots we needed to address. From the looks of things, it had been a considerable time since the pasture fences were given any worthwhile attention. It amazed me that none of the horses ever busted out. Barbed wire would have been easier to maintain, but most ranches avoided it. A cut-up, bleeding horse isn't an easy horse to sell.

"Re-member that song, Will? That . . . Platters song, 'Great Pretender'?"

I did know it. And do you know how hearing a song, or even thinking about it, can stir up memories? It made me think of riding in the backseat of Jimmy Curio's older brother's Dodge, windows rolled down, flying down backcountry roads outside the city. We were on a fishing trip weekend. Jimmy and I were in the back, his big brother and Steven Polson in the front. The radio was cranked, throwing out tunes like "Come On, Let's Go," "Peggy Sue," and of course, "The Great Pretender." Anthony Curio bragged the whole way how he'd taken Suzy Micheli to the drive-in (only he always called the drive-in the submarine races) the night before, popping her cherry on the vinyl seat Jimmy and I were sitting on. He laughed with yellow teeth and we all cracked up. I wanted to be in that car again, greasing down the hot blacktop. Wanted to feel the sun burn on my arm while I propped it out the window, making crazy swimming motions in the rushing wind.

"Everybody knows that one," I said.

"Sometimes . . . I hear it. In my dreams. Don't really 'member ever knowing it. Before. But when it comes, in my dreams. It's like I've . . . known it, all this time."

"Weird," I said, and waited for him to say more, but he never did. While we worked, I wondered if Benny's dreams meant anything at all. I wanted to believe they didn't. I wanted to believe all they represented was nonsensical dream shit. Stuff that floated into a guy's head at night just because it could.

Believing this made it easier to feel my own bad dreams didn't mean anything. And despite what I'd told Benny, most of them weren't wet dreams of Brigitte Bardot. Many times, it was Coop, falling face-down in the pasture. It was Silas Green, pissing on me, and Frank Kroft, loosening his belt. It was my father with that Davy Crockett pocketknife hanging out of his side.

"You're sad . . . now," Benny said. "I don't re-member some things too good. But you weren't so sad, before."

I could not respond. Mostly, it was because those words came from *his* mouth—Benny, who had more reasons than anyone to be sad.

I paused, resting against the fence. "I guess a lot of things have happened."

Benny plunged the shovel back into the hole. "Yuh. Lots of things. Right?" A sweat streak raced down the back of his shirt, and in the glaring sunlight, working as he was, Benny suddenly looked older to me. As if time had sped up while he was at the hospital. "But . . . I thought it was something else. Maybe . . . bad news, from home."

"More like no news," I said. "It's been a while since I've gotten any letters. Scares me to think of my mom there, alone with my dad."

Benny just looked at me, and I didn't know if he had caught anything I said, or perhaps understood perfectly. "Will?" He pulled something out of his jeans pocket. He knelt, and placed the Sucrets tin on the ground, carefully holding it in place, lifting the lid as if it were eggshell. "Here . . . want you to have . . . one. I t-told you about them, right?" He stretched out his left hand. In it was a single jack. "This is for you."

I took it, and gently rolled it between my finger and thumb. "Thank you, Benny," I whispered.

CHAPTER
thirty-five

THE TRUCKS AND TRAILERS PULLED IN JUST AFTER BREAKFAST, having stayed the previous night up the road in Gunnison. Everyone, not just the breakers, was excited about getting a glimpse of the new four-legged inmates. It was a beautiful group of mustangs with various coats. There were Appaloosas, a mix of copper-colored chestnuts, reddish bays, and a couple of golden palominos. One of them was solid black except for a dotted streak of white along her nose.

All the breakers and guards lined up outside the barn to watch the trailers unload. The wranglers in charge had their work cut out; getting the horses from trailer to stable was always an entertaining show, no kidding. We hung on the side of the fence and watched like it was some kind of rodeo. The horses neighed, snapped, reared, and fought as best they could, but in the end, they had about as much chance at escape as we did.

After lunch, while I was baling blocks of hay with a couple other guys, Elmore Holling walked into the barn and called my name. "Sheppard! Little wants you in the sick house."

I knew, then, that something was wrong; something inside my gut just didn't feel right. And when I reached the infirmary door, hand outstretched and fingers against the handle, I paused. Intuition told me not to go in. I wanted to turn around and run, to anyplace but where I stood.

I turned the handle and walked inside.

Miss Little sat in the corner, behind her cramped and cluttered desk. She looked up. "William. Come inside, sugar."

I went to her desk and sat. At first I wasn't able to look her in the eye. The second hand of the clock behind her ticked with a noticeable jerking sound, breaking the heavy silence in the room. She looked distant, staring through me.

"Did you know I used to have children of my own?" she asked.

I shook my head, and whispered, "No, ma'am."

Her head went from up to down, slightly, only once.

I felt small. I sat uncomfortably and waited, not wanting to listen, not wanting to be there. There was a palpable sadness in the room. So heavy, I could feel its draping weight on me like a winter coat.

"Will, honey, I have news from home. Isn't going to be easy to hear."

Somehow, at that moment, I knew. I knew before she even said it.

"It's your mother, child. She's passed away."

There. It was out there. I don't know how long I sat in the silence, pressed down by the ticking of the clock; it was only moments, but it felt like years. The word *no* played on a phantom turntable inside my breaking mind.

"There was an automobile accident. We got the news from your grandfather, James McVey. He sent word, but I'm sorry to say he didn't provide many details. He said he's sent a letter for you, too. Should arrive soon. You're going to be staying with him after you get out."

Grandpa Jack. The last of my remaining grandparents. He lived in Cleveland.

I was sure I was going to pass out. My legs went numb and my ears burned. *Car accident. Grandpa Jack.* There was no mention of my father. Sitting in Miss Little's office, I tried my best not to break down, but felt it coming like a hundred-year wave, swelling just over the horizon.

"It's okay to cry, William," Miss Little said. "Don't ever let anybody tell you different. It is through tears and emotion that we bare our souls, did you know that? Sissa Ree told me that when I lost Samuel and Matthew, all those years ago.

"They stole away from me on a July morning. I was hanging sheets on the line and when I turned 'round . . ." She shook her head from side to side; her dark eyes were distant. ". . . they's gone. Thought they's hiding. Turned out, my little ones had gone behind the house, down to the river, two days flooded." She paused, drawing in a slow, deep breath. I couldn't look at her. "We found 'em. Next day we did. The whole lot, everyone, James—*especially* James—looked at me with that hate. All but Sissa Ree. It burned in their eyes. I saw it. Saw they was right to hate me. My little angels drowned. A part of me drowned with them. And my soul was bared to the world, child."

Tears welled down my face—hearing her, but seeing my mother instead. My mother with her empty face and her cast arm. Standing beside the Greyhound, that was the last time I saw her. The last time I would ever see her.

"We carry these things with us, child. People say places be haunted, but pay no mind. It's us that's haunted. We carry around our own spirits. We haunt ourselves with the past. Shame is my ghost, baby. Don't let it be yours. You couldn't help your mother. Oh, yes. I know your story, sugar. I know about your home, I do. Nothing more you could have done to help her. So, you cry. You weep as you should. But don't carry that haunting around with you the rest o' your life, way I do. It eats at you till you can't hardly remember why you do what you do in this world. These are things meant to be left behind."

I wish I could have done that. I wish I could have listened to her.

She turned to the narrow window, staring at nothing at all, and said, "Sometimes I still wake up calling their names, seeing their little heads bobbing up and down in the river like Daddy's fishing corks. I feel hollow inside when that happens. Hollow like a rotten tree, child.

"I've been watching you, kiddo. William Sheppard and his Roundabouts. You boys are the only few who don't look at the color of my skin. Did you know that? I watch you boys, I reckon, as I'd watch over my own. If I still had them."

She crossed to me, sat, and held me in her arms. She cried with me. "I'm so sorry, sugar. So damned sorry. You stay here long as you need to. I'm just so damned sorry."

I don't want to tell you too much about my mother's death, or how it affected me. As important and as personal as those things are, their place is not in this story. That is a window into my soul I cannot open. As many years have passed since then, thinking about it, let alone writing about it, is still far too personal, and painful. Can you see? After forty years, I still feel guilty. I tried to kill my father, but it was my mother who died instead.

I will tell you what you can probably put together on your own—I grieved, just as any fourteen-year-old kid would. I returned to the bunks, walking like a zombie, and lay down. I thought of the picture I'd brought with me. How it was stolen. How Silas Green likely flushed it down a toilet. I felt cheated, and longed for something, anything, that I could hold in my arms that would have connected me to her. So I did something that would sound silly, I suppose, to almost anyone. I did it on instinct. I opened my footlocker and took one sneaker of the pair I'd worn to Swope. My mother saved three weeks to buy them for me. I lay on my bunk with the shoe in my arms, and wept.

CHAPTER

thirty-six

I BEGAN TO FEEL CLOSER TO BENNY AS THE WEEKS DRAGGED ON. I began to take it upon myself to keep watch over him, whether that meant keeping jokers off his back or helping him out with his chores when possible. I guess you could say I still felt somewhat responsible for what happened to him; maybe there's some truth to that.

But I didn't mind. In a way, looking after him that way helped to fill the jarring void in my world after learning of my mother's death.

I didn't realize the depth of my dedication to Benny, though, until he found me in the stable one afternoon. "Will! Will!" he called, excitement in his eyes. "Bobbee wants to . . . help Benny . . . be a breaker. Gonna help me." Bright strawberry welts covered both cheeks, and he looked as if he had just run five miles.

"Hold on, Benny, hold on," I said. "What's wrong with your face?" He could have been stung by a dozen bees and it wouldn't have looked worse.

"I'm fine, Will. Gonna be a . . . breaker now."

"What are you talking about, man?" I asked. "Who told you that?"

"Bobbee Petty Gr-Grew. He did. Told me 'bout the . . . nishee-ashun."

"Nishee-ashun?"

The marks on his face were blooming up the sides of his face.

Beads of sweat crowned along his forehead and dripped as he sucked in a lungful of air.

"Nishee-ashun, to be . . . a breaker," he said. "Hurts, but I'll be . . . a breaker . . . with you guys."

"Initiation? Is that it?"

His eyes lit and he smiled even wider. "Yuh! That's it."

"What's the initiation?"

"Bobby gets to hit Benny. Slap my face . . . for the day, right? Then I'm a breaker. He says they all did it . . . before."

I saw red, but I wasn't looking at Benny's face. I imagined Bobby and the other guys hauling off on Benny with full strength, slapping his head, making him think it was okay, making him think it was fun.

"Let's go," I said.

"Where?" he asked.

"To see them all."

He shook his head, confused, then started ahead of me, huffing toward the barn, pulling a half-eaten apple from his ragged pocket. Inside, Bobby Pettigrew, Aaron Gumm, and a couple other guys stood in a circle, each with a shovel in hand. When they saw Benny, they all began to smile with their dumb mouths and dumb eyes.

"Gonna be a breaker, Lunch? You're doing great!" Bobby said. He was a stout little bastard whose hair was always neatly combed, no matter the time of day. As we neared, Bobby handed his shovel to Aaron, edged back, and ripped the palm of his hand across Benny's face, drawing a pervasive laughter from the group.

I shoved Benny aside, hooked an arm around Bobby's throat and swung him into the wall. He slumped to the ground with deadweight. I took the shovel from Aaron Gumm's hand and swung it hard into the side of Bobby's face. I thought neither of my actions nor their consequences. I only did what came naturally.

"Don't ever fucking touch him again," I said, and turned away. "Come on, Benny."

Benny followed me, turning every other step to look back at the mess I'd left on the barn floor.

CHAPTER
thirty-seven

Aside from plunging Silas Green's head into a commode and living to tell about it, John Church celebrated another, even more monumental feat. He became a breaker in only five months' time. He could do practically anything. I couldn't help but admire him even more.

He'd already once told me where he was from—the rural mountains of West Texas. Alpine. But what I didn't know was that he was raised on a ranch. He grew up learning how to train horses and care for them. With a background like that, it was only a matter of time before he joined us in the pens.

He wasted no time establishing his solitary nature, speaking to no one while I tried to rope a horse for the first time. With every throw, the mustang dodged left, then right, as if he knew the trick to avoiding the damn thing. Then he'd prance around the pen as proud as can be.

"Come on!" I yelled, losing what little composure remained. I was frustrated more at myself than the horse; nearly a dozen pitiful attempts can do that to a guy. Mickey's stifled laughter didn't help.

I had scratched the rope out of the dirt to give it another go when Silas Green jumped down off the railing and approached.

"You're not throwing your wrist right," he said. "Look."

I just sort of stood there at first, half expecting Silas to throw a punch.

"I got it," I said.

"Yeah, you got it, all right," Silas said. "Watch." He took the rope, gathered out the slack, and twirled it above his head. "See my wrist? You're okay with the rope. Your arm just sometimes goes wrong." He flung the rope over the mustang's head, instantly throwing it into a rage. Silas held tight, dug his feet into the dirt, and waited for it to calm. From the looks of it, we were in for a long wait. The copper-colored horse reared on its hind legs, then kicked them out high as he could, trying like hell to jerk the rope from Silas's grip.

"Come on!" Silas yelled. "Come on, motherfucker! That all you got? I said, *Come on!*"

No one said a word. It was unnerving to see just how bright Silas's fury raged; it was more intimidating than the struggling horse. He yanked on the rope, then harder again.

"Gotcha! Gotcha now, fucker, don't I?" he screamed. He jerked the rope again, and the horse neighed and nipped. Then it slowed. The kicking stopped, and the mustang just paced, to the left and right, and after that, there was nothing but the air flashing in and out of its flared nostrils.

Silas Green looked ready to move from the mustang over to one of us; didn't matter who. And then that look washed away, like a mask being pulled from his face. He just smiled at me, and handed back the rope.

"Here. He's all yours," Silas said.

As he walked back to the fence, I turned. "What was that?"

Mickey shrugged, just as dumbfounded.

Silas's odd behavior didn't stop there. Before the afternoon was over, he'd even gone as far as to ask Mickey for advice on a mustang he was working.

"OF COURSE I DON'T BUY IT!" MICKEY SAID, LATER THAT NIGHT. WE were back at the bunkhouse, pulling a hand of five-card before the lights-out call. "He's up to something."

"It's weird how sincere he was, you know, before he went nuts." I sat Indian style on my bunk, guarding my cards. I'd just wrapped up a Green Lantern comic that was currently being passed around the bunkhouse. I'd read it before, but was trying to keep my thoughts preoccupied with anything besides my mother. I didn't really get into comics the way some other guys did, but they were our equivalent of skin mags that get snuck into state prisons. That actually happened, too, but only once, when Mickey produced a *Playboy* the way a magician yanks a rabbit from his hat. That was the first time I had ever seen a naked woman. The featured girl lay in front of a fireplace; the stark exposure of her breasts, her nipples was something I had only dreamed about until then. The sight of her bunched pubic hair was almost shocking, and I don't think I was the only one to stare openmouthed, marveling at the most important secrets of life so blatantly displayed. The Secret of the Titty Book lasted an entire twelve hours before the cat was out of the bag and Cal Jenkins claimed it as his own. Where did it come from? Mickey wouldn't have said if you tortured him with boiling wax.

"You should both be . . . careful, Will. Around Silas," Benny said, taking a fresh card from the scattered pile.

"We're always careful," I said. "And keep your cards up. Mickey's been eyeing them since we started."

John Church was several bunks away, lying on his back and staring at the lightbulbs. We'd asked him if he wanted to be the fourth in our game, but he just sighed loudly, and said, "Don't think so." I wondered how he was able to be such an island among us all.

"I ever tell you guys how I got the scar on my leg?" Mickey asked, killing us with a full house. To accentuate, he rolled up one pant leg clear to the knee. Just along the outside edge of his little leg ran a zigzag line of whitish tissue, maybe four inches in length.

Benny looked up into the ceiling, as if trying to remember if Mickey *had* told him about it.

"Camping trip, Cub Scouts," Mickey said.

"You ain't no Scout!" I laughed.

"God's honest," Mickey said, running his finger along the scar with half-squinting eyes. "It was only for a summer, though. One of the best of my life."

"Even better than . . . last summer? Mickee?" Benny asked. He wore an absolutely serious expression on his face, but nonetheless, Mickey and I both cracked up. Benny only sat there with a bemused expression, not sure what he'd said to set us off.

"Yeah, Lunch," Mickey said. "Even better than last summer."

"So what happened?" I asked. I scooped the deck together and began shuffling.

"Boom Harris. Meanest son of a bitch you ever knew. We was down by the lake by ourselves one night, skipping rocks. Somewhere down the shore, we hear a scream. Really scared the shit out of us, you know? It was late, and dark. Mr. Kendricks, the scoutmaster, was back at the camp with the other guys, telling spook stories. So we go check it out. Well, we come across a couple older guys, Boom and his dickhead pal, Hoover Weiss. Boom was big, and I mean John Church big. The guy had greasy hair, and stunk to Ohio. He was the head bull of his gang, but there were only two of them that night. Pinned underneath Boom's legs was a kid, I don't know who."

Benny's face looked almost sad. I wondered if somewhere in his mixed-up mind he remembered how Silas had done the same thing to him.

"Boom had a cigarette in his mouth. I could see the orange tip glowing from where we stood. Saw him take it out and bring it down onto the kid's arms. The poor guy screamed bloody murder. He couldn't do anything—Hoover Weiss had his arms pinned and Boom was on top. The shit was laughing, I remember that. Just laughing, and torturing this kid who probably didn't even do a damned thing to him. So I couldn't just stand by, right?"

We nodded.

"Me and the two guys I was with start running over along the shore. It was maybe fifty yards. Halfway there, four older guys come barreling out of the trees like jungle soldiers and pile drive us to the ground. They'd been there all along, just waiting. Now we was the ones who were pinned. Boom and Hoover got up, laughin', and walked over. And the kid they were holdin' down? Just another dick in their gang, pretending. The whole thing'd been theater. Fuckin ambush. They was waitin' on me just to come out, knowing I'd probably do what I did. I'd had a couple run-arounds with Boom's gang before. I guess he just had it out for me, wanted to screw with me. He pulled his switchblade that night. Said he was gonna give me a special tattoo. And I guess he did."

"Shit," I whispered.

"That was the last camping trip I ever been on," he said.

I saw Mickey's scar wasn't just an accidental cut. It did have some design to it. Could have been a snake, maybe a dragon. I didn't ask because it didn't matter.

"Thing is, I learned a lesson. That's why I'm telling you this shit. Always keep your eye on the woods when you're going to throw swings. You know, someone might just be playing a good one on you. Don't forget it, Will. You either, Benny. Don't you think for a minute that piece of shit Silas Green is trying to turn a new leaf. Tomorrow, I'll show you what I mean."

"How?" I asked.

Mickey just shook his head. "Tomorrow. Now, deal again. Who knows how many more games we got in this place."

LIGHTS-OUT CAME AND WENT, BUT I COULDN'T STOP THINKING OF Mickey's story. Nearby, Benny tossed. In the dim light, I saw something was in his hands, occasionally catching a muted reflection—he was rolling a jack between his fingers. After a moment, he slipped it back into the little blue box, then slowly shook it from side to side. He whispered something to himself, and then closed his eyes.

I curled my legs up and buried my head in my pillow, thinking of my mom. What her funeral had been like. Her casket. If they'd given her a nice dress.

Mostly, I was able to keep from crying during the days, but nights were always different. I think the pillow muffled most of it, but once I caught Mickey looking over at me, then playing it off like he hadn't seen anything at all.

I tried to play Peter Pan and think happy thoughts. The one I always liked best was of me and my friends, dealing those damn cards. I like to keep that memory close, even now.

CHAPTER
thirty-eight

"EVERY DAY, MISS LITTLE SPENDS AN HOUR IN THE OFFICE NEXT TO Warden Barrow's. Sometimes more. Paperwork or something, I don't know." Mickey scanned the stretch of hillside between us and the infirmary. Most of the boys were in the mess hall shoveling dinner into their faces. A few were still scattered about, finishing chores. Joe Addison was the closest guard to us, and even he was preoccupied, helping sort out a mess of bridles and harnesses Benny had just happened to drop.

I rubbed my head. "You really think this—"

"Come on!" Mickey said, nearly yanking off my arm.

We scrambled up the hill, opting for a quick plan of action over a slow, unsuspicious one. That was generally how Mickey operated. Miraculously, we made it to the infirmary undiscovered. And, of course, the door was locked.

"So now what?" I asked. "We throw a rock through the window? Let's just go, before we're busted."

"Keep your panties on, Nosebleed." Mickey dug into his pockets, and fished something out. Inside his small hands was nothing else but a silver key.

"You have the key to the infirmary?" I asked. "Of course you do."

He paused, smiled, and said, "Like I'm going to tell you all my secrets." He grinned, then plunged the key into the lock.

We slipped inside and shut the door. The last time I was inside the infirmary, Miss Little had opened her heart to me, and broken my own. I felt tainted, sneaking around inside with her gone. "I don't feel good about this."

"You want to know or not?" Mickey asked.

"Yeah," I said. "I want to know."

Mickey knew just where to go, heading straight for the back window of the living room, where we had seen her before, holding a manila folder.

Above the window was a single bookshelf, stuffed with various notebooks and tattered novels. In the middle was a set of cream-colored folders. Mickey looked up to them, then back at me. "Okay, this is what I really brought you along for," he said.

I grabbed the chair from behind her desk, and pushed it up to the window. I grabbed them all, then handed them down to him. Mickey immediately started to riffle through each one.

"Why do you think she keeps some of them up here like this?" I asked.

"Maybe to keep guys like me from finding them?" He stopped. "Look." He held one up in the air like a prize. "John Church."

"No way!"

"We'll save it for later. This is what we really came for." Mickey tossed one folder on the rug between us the way he'd throw down a queen of spades. There, in front of me, was Silas Green's file.

"I heard one time he tried to hold up a gas station and killed the poor guy working the register," Mickey said, opening the file. "But you know how guys talk."

We read the contents of the folder together, skimming line by line. Just like with any file, we didn't know the whole story, only the abbreviated information on the pages before us. That said, what we read left little room for his side of things.

Silas Green. Born in Albany, New York. Sent to live with his aunt and uncle in New York City when he was ten. Midtown East. Hell's

Kitchen. At thirteen, held the title of War Counselor in one of the neighborhood's most notorious and dangerous gangs.

"What's that?" I asked. "War Counselor."

"They're the ones who meet up before two gangs go at it. Decide what kind of weapons to use, which kind can't be. Brass knuckles, pieces of pipe, belts with sharp buckles. Car antennas. You know."

"Guns, too?"

Mickey shook his head. "Hell, no! Most guys don't want to go to jail! You just want to maim the other guy, not kill him."

I looked on my small friend with suspicious eyes. "How do you know so much about all this?"

"Why do you think?" he said.

We went back to the opened folder.

Silas Green graduated to upper management of the gang by age fifteen. His police record by that time included petty theft, assault, and arson. Then, the incident occurred. Silas and two others attacked another guy in their own gang. A guy named Darrell Dugan. They beat him to within an inch of his life, then gagged and tied him to the rails of an oil heater, and stripped off his pants. Silas had an electric curling rod, maybe from his aunt, I guessed, and inserted it into Darrell Dugan's anus. It was plugged in, and instantly cauterized the guy's lower colon.

"Damn. Sounds like some sort of story," Mickey said. "Like something guys make up."

Only it wasn't made up. It was real. It happened.

Leaving the curling rod in place, they took Dugan, and wrapped him inside a living room rug. Silas, with one other, placed him inside the trunk of a stolen car, and drove to a landfill, where they threw the poor guy out. According to authorities, Dugan died sometime during the night. The official cause was asphyxiation. To top off the night, Silas drove to the nearest liquor store to steal a bottle of bourbon. The next day, he was identified by both the store clerk as well as a neighbor, who saw him carry the rolled-up rug down the hallway.

❖ ❖ ❖

"Want to see Church's?" Mickey asked. It wasn't as much a question as it was a statement. He'd already flipped open the other folder, and began pulling out papers.

We hunched together, and started at the top. Charge: MURDER, THIRD DEGREE.

"Shit!" Mickey said.

"Third degree—what's that?" I asked.

"It's where you don't mean to kill someone, but they're dead all the same."

We kept reading.

John Church. Born, raised—Alpine, Texas. And that's about as far as we got.

"I guess my apple pie wasn't enough to keep you boys from sneaking around behind my back." Miss Little stood in the doorway; we hadn't even heard her open it. The look in her eyes wasn't angry, the way I expected. It was nothing more than disappointment. It instantly broke my heart.

She stepped aside. "I think you both have somewhere else to be."

"I'm sorry," I started, but stopped when she just held up her hands. It would have made me feel better had she gotten angry instead, and just called the guard. But she just stood there, like a shadow, and waited for us to leave.

CHAPTER

thirty-nine

WE WEREN'T TOLD THAT THE HORSES WERE MISSING UNTIL WE filed out of the mess hall the next morning. The breakers, along with Benny, were called out to the stable, where the warden was yelling at Frank Kroft like there'd be no tomorrow.

How he took it! Barrow's face was as purple as an eggplant; he looked like he was on the verge of having a heart attack. I kept waiting for him to loosen that necktie of his, which appeared to be cutting off his circulation. Frank just stood there, looking like he wanted to strangle the life out of the nearest thing to walk by.

"You do the math, Frank! You realize how much God-loving money that is to me?"

Frank was still, and growing a darker shade with each passing second.

"And I'd like to know just how the happy fuck it happened! Tell me, Frank. How did eight of my horses just slip out of the fence and sashay off into the wild blue ever-fucking yonder? Was it a miracle? Maybe they just sprouted wings and took to the skies, was that it?"

"We'll find them," Frank said.

"You're fucking A right you'll find them! You'll bust the hell out of here this morning and you'll find them! And don't you pissing come back without them, I can tell you that right here and right now!"

As mad as he was at Barrow, I'm sure it didn't help that Kroft was getting it all in front of us. That worried me because I knew Frank was the type to take things out on whomever he could shake a piss at.

"SHIT!" The warden stormed back toward the office, several guards in tow. All except Frank, Joe Addison, and Elmore Holling. The three of them stood huddled up that way looking like three infielders on the mound, strategizing the next out. The rest of us listened as best we could.

At some point during the night or maybe early morning, eight mustangs had gone through the pasture fence and up into the mountains. It was common enough for them to be in the pasture overnight; new herds were usually rotated between the stables and the fields to help them calm. But how had they gotten through?

That's exactly what Kroft wanted to know, and I was the first one his sadistic eyes landed on. "You," he said.

I looked to my left, hoping to sweet God maybe he hadn't spoken to me after all.

"You were out there just days ago with Benny Retard! What the hell did you two assholes do?"

I was speechless. I just stood there with my mouth open.

He backhanded me across the head, and it felt like lightning. And then he did the same to Benny. The strike knocked me to the ground, but Benny didn't even flinch. I felt my lower lip balloon, and blood trickled out of my mouth. Frank Kroft twisted his hands into the front of my coat and yanked me to my feet.

"What did he do? You were with him the whole time."

"We didn't do anything," I said. "We fixed the fence in the places you told us. Our work was inspected."

"I don't give a squatting shit if it was inspected," Frank said. "It had to be something the retard did. We're lucky the whole goddamned bunch didn't skate out."

He was right about that, too. Eighteen horses were still in the pasture. Why hadn't they followed the others to freedom? Maybe God's animals are more like us than we think. If there was an opportunity for us to escape, would we each take it?

Frank was so convinced Benny was responsible, he personally escorted the both of us out to the pasture to eyeball each area of the fence where we'd worked. He shook each section, testing its durability. The last fence rail we set was where they'd gone out. It was separated where we nailed it, leaning over and allowing a three-foot-wide gap near the top. An easy enough space for any horse with a willful attitude.

Frank demanded an explanation. Benny only stood there and stammered, trying to find the words.

"I . . . I j-just set the f-f-fence the way I was t-t-told. I . . . I just . . ."

Frank slapped Benny across the head.

"Just the way you were told?" Frank said. "J-J-J-Just the way you were t-t-t-told? Shit! You missed two nails and the damned post isn't set plumb. Maybe the two of you were out here yanking on your cocks instead!"

I stared at the fence. We addressed it just as well as the other sections. It couldn't have just budged. It looked to me like someone took a swing at it with a sledgehammer.

Kroft was very quiet as he looked off into the stretch of the valley, and then up into the mountains. Somewhere, up in the thick blanket of pines and aspens, the horses were waiting. A gust rolled down into the valley and through the ranch, bringing a chill with it. It was nearing late September, and fall was fast approaching.

"We'll just have to get them," Frank said. He nodded, agreeing with his own statement. "We'll take a team. We'll take some breakers and some guards. Maybe we'll even take Church. He was raised on a ranch, for God's sake. We'll just bring them back."

I thought about the chance to head off on horseback, maybe even with Mickey. Up in the mountains on a hunt. I was dumbstruck.

"I can . . . help," Benny said.

Frank looked at Benny. For a second, I thought he might go at him once more, just for smiles. But the expression on his face changed, softened into one of curiosity. He looked at Benny as if the kid was a circus freak, and the curtain had just been pulled aside. He opened his mouth to say something, then turned back to the fence instead. "What do you think?" He carried his gaze up the mountain, as if following a pack of ghosts. "You know the retard best."

I didn't want to see Benny on any excursion. Too many things were coming together now, and not in a good way. But honestly, I did think he could help. I'd seen the magic Benny worked with the horses.

"They don't run from him," I said. And then, knowing I'd regret it: "Yeah, he can help."

I suddenly hated myself for saying that, for offering Benny's help to a man who had already broken his spirit and body. But it was too late.

Frank Kroft gave Benny a final look, then turned back to the ranch. "Then you're responsible for him."

CHAPTER

forty

"If you stray from your group at any time without permission . . . you will be shot on sight." Kroft's voice was commanding, but not nearly as commanding as the rifle in his hands. Behind him, Joe Addison and Elmore Holling stood at attention, a rifle in their arms as well.

"Is that clear to everyone standing here?" he yelled.

We all shouted that it was. Our ragtag search party consisted of eleven people, each on horseback. Three guards and seven breakers handpicked by Kroft. And, of course, there was Benny.

Standing next to me was Mickey, with John Church opposite him. I wasn't surprised he'd chosen John, what with his ranch experience, but my balls crept up into my stomach when I saw Frank had chosen Silas Green, too. It was all wrong. Everything was screwed up enough already without Silas taking part. But he was the most seasoned breaker, a fact no one could dispute. Rounding out the group were Eddie Tokus, Bobby Pettigrew, and Aaron Gumm.

Each horse was packed with only the basic requirements: a heavy wool sleeping roll, two canteens, some food—peanuts, crackers, beef jerky—and our ropes. We weren't expected to be away for more than two nights.

After a quick lunch, we met at the stables and prepared to head out. Reaper was there, right next to the other horses. With a white body and brown face, she easily stood out from the others, but in a beautiful way. When I approached, she swung her copper face to me, and swished her tail. And I'm not kidding, God as my witness, that horse was smiling at me. Grinning, a little mischievously, as if thinking, Can you believe they fucking picked me? She'd come a long way from the night she half bit my shoulder off. Someone else had even saddled and packed her.

Mickey rode on Coop's last successful break, Hemingway. She had a deep chestnut coat and black mane. And given her height, Mickey looked almost out of place up in the saddle.

Addison took the lead with Elmore Holling in the middle, and Frank brought up the end of our line. It started to rain as we passed through the livestock gates of Swope Ranch. Trotting out, I noticed the other guys around the ranch doing their chores and work details. They looked at us with envious eyes, knowing we were leaving the choking perimeters of the prison boundary. Benny rode in front of me and as we headed out and away, he turned to look back. Not at me, but at Swope, the place he had called home for so many months. I didn't want to ask what was on his mind, afraid he would say something as dark as the look in his eyes.

For two hours, we rode into the mountains, following the most accessible trail, figuring—but mostly hoping—the escaped horses had done the same. Our plan was relatively simple: we had that day, the next, and part of the third to find the eight runaways. When, or if (for the more pessimistic), we found any of them, we would try our best to surround and rope them, and bring them back to the ranch. Personally, I thought it should be considered a success if we captured even one of them.

Riding through the trees with the scent of spruce and juniper in my nose, feeling the give and tug of the saddle beneath me, I felt something I hadn't known in a long time. It wasn't freedom, although for some guys it could have been. It was excitement.

Before we left Swope, they gave us heavy coats and wide-brimmed hats, and I found myself thinking we looked like a group of honest-to-God cowboys setting out on an excursion into the wild.

"Hey," Silas said, pointing his finger to the ground below. Passing by, I saw a grouping of hoof marks punched into the mud. We'd picked the right trail after all.

"Let's go, keep moving," Frank said, edging us on. I wondered if the warden had told him anything else. Something like "Don't come back without them or you'll have no job to come back to." I would bet he'd said something like that.

The rain only picked up, not helping matters, and the temperature took a nosedive. I was glad to be wearing my coat, and pulled it tighter. Higher we went. For the first hour, I was able to look back and, through the clearing, still make out the ranch below. It was amazing how small it already looked.

After riding for hours through the trees, we came to a small clearing between two peaks where the trees thinned and the tall grass ran rampant. In the moist earth, we found a few more tracks and were encouraged to know we were on the right path. It was already growing dark, and even though more clouds were building in the west, the worst of the rain looked to be over.

Kroft shouted from the back, "Bring it in! We're making camp."

They told some of us to sweep aside the patches of pine needles on the forest floor, exposing drier earth beneath. Others collected firewood, though nearly all of it was soaked. But Kroft had brought a canteen of kerosene from the ranch, and doused some over the larger branches; the evening's fire was soon established. The stench of gas was overwhelming, but it was warm and would dry us out.

After a quiet meal, Kroft and the guards experienced a rare slip of compassion, and gave us a half hour of downtime. We sat around the fire while they kept watch with guns in hand.

The talk floated in and out over the fire. We wondered about the day ahead, whether we'd find anything at all. What the hell we'd even do if we *did* find a horse. Mickey didn't talk much at all, only a few times.

"Wish he wouldn't have picked me, Shep."

"Come on," I said, trying to pull something positive out of the air. "It's because you're one of the best. You know that."

"Well, yeah. Of course I'm the best. Still . . . I wish he wouldn't have. I'd kill him if I had the chance."

I knew he meant it. Can't say that I blamed him. "How long until you get out of here, Mick?"

He rolled his eyes and nodded. "Eight months. You know that."

"Yeah," I said. "Just wanted to hear you say it."

"Okay, yeah. How about you?" he asked.

I smirked. "Like you don't know. Just twelve more months to go. That'll make two." Two years. It seemed so long.

The fire dwindled, and even though the rain let up, fat clouds still choked the stars and moonlight from the sky. We had no shelter besides the cottonwoods and pines overhead, and I crossed my fingers that we'd stay dry through the night.

"Okay, ladies. This is lights-out," Frank said, walking up. There was something in his hands. Elmore Holling followed, kicking through the dead needles, opening a leather pouch.

"Line up with your bedding under the trees," Frank said. He and Holling tossed something to each of us. They were clunky and heavy.

Handcuffs.

"What the hell?" Eddie Tokus asked.

"You're not staying out here all night without them. So put them on," Frank said. "I ain't kidding."

Joe Addison stepped close, rifle against his shoulder.

"I don't believe this," Mickey said, picked his cuffs off the ground. The moans and groans were collective, but after we each lined our bedding, as Frank had called it—this was more of a joke as the bedding consisted of a single wool blanket—underneath the trees, we reluctantly latched the steel cuffs around our wrists.

Addison walked the line of us, inspecting each set to make sure they weren't loose. He stopped when he came to Benny. "Frank."

"What is it?" Frank grumbled.

Benny held his arms in the air. "Don't quite fit," he said, diverting his eyes and looking to the ground. "I'm too big—I guess."

"Well, how the happy fuck did they fit on Church?" Frank asked.

John Church smiled. "I got little wrists, sir."

"You've got little wrists and my mamma was a virgin," Frank said.

Joe Addison walked over to John Church, as though genuinely

interested in the scenario. "I'll be goddamned, Frank, son of a bitch does have little wrists."

There was a release of laughter from the other guys. Frank barked, "All of you shut the fuck up!" He looked back down to Benny.

The cuffs looked like a gag on his thick wrists. Surely Kroft would figure Benny to be the last to cause any trouble without them.

"I don't see a problem," he said. He took Benny's hand and mashed the clamp deep into his skin. Benny winced immediately in pain, and did so again when Kroft forced the other one shut. "You'll be fine for the night, so stop your whining, dumbass."

Addison started to protest. "Frank . . ."

"Got something to say, Joe?" Frank said. "Something to add to the conversation? So he wakes up tomorrow with purple hands. Not the end of my world."

Addison shook his head and turned away. Benny drew his hands to his chest and lay down on his quilt. Down the line, someone whispered, "Asshole."

Kroft didn't notice. Or maybe he just didn't care.

"Benny," I whispered. He was on my right. Mickey, on the other side of him. "You okay?"

He shook his head. "I'll be . . . okey-dokey in the morning, right?" He smiled, with pain in his eyes.

There was a look of complete disgust in Mickey's face. "Just hang in there, Lunch," he said. "Just get through the night."

I had a hard time finding sleep. It wasn't the handcuffs, as uncomfortable as they were. My mind kept going back to what Mickey said. How he'd kill Frank Kroft if just given the opportunity. I guess what kept me up was how I wanted to kill him, too. For my friends' sake more than my own. I thought how I wouldn't even think twice, shooting him, stabbing him. I started to think the same things about Silas Green, too. If you really want to know the truth, it was how I felt myself changing that scared me the most. Changing into somebody else. Somebody exactly like my father.

CHAPTER
forty-one

IT WAS THE BOOM OF THE RIFLE THAT WOKE ME, NOT THE YELLing—I'm almost positive of that. The shot came from somewhere to my far left, the yelling from my right. The report only added to my disorientation, and I wondered if the roof had been peeled off of the bunkhouse. Then, reality washed over me in a single, heavy wave.

When it happened, everyone else hunched and jerked their arms above their heads in synchronicity; I was the only one stupid enough to raise my head.

Another shot ripped through the air, and this time I heard something flick past my ear like a fat bug. I whirled to see who was firing.

"What—" Mickey started, then followed my eyes and said, "Oh, Gawd! Oh, man!"

Benny did his best to cover his ears with one hand and the opposite shoulder. John Church was on his stomach, silently eyeballing the world.

At the end of the clearing, kneeling on one knee with rifle poised and aimed, was Silas Green. Behind him, Eddie Tokus and Bobby Pettigrew were mounting their horses. Each of them had a rifle slung on their back.

The shouting coming from my right was Joe Addison. It took just a glance to see Elmore Holling was already dead. Addison was on his stomach, doing a G.I. Joe crawl. He'd been shot through the leg and blood was spurting up and out in perfect water fountain style.

I didn't see Frank.

Silas fired again, this time hitting Addison in the upper back. He stopped with the army crawl and slumped to the ground. His ruined back started convulsing in jerky spasms, and he looked almost like he was sobbing into the dirt.

"Let's go!" Bobby yelled from his horse.

"No! I don't see him!" Silas screamed. "Where'd he go?"

"Forget him, let's—"

Bobby Pettigrew's high-pitched voice was cut off by resonating gunfire. During midsentence, he lost half of his face. It was that sudden. His body did a slow, wavering hunch before sliding off the horse and onto the needle-dusted ground. One of his feet was still caught in the stirrup.

"Shit!" Eddie Tokus screamed, his one ear stuck out like an opened door. He yanked hard on his reins and dug his heels into the horse. It broke into full gallop, carrying the bouncing, overweight, bushy-haired boy on its back.

Silas fired his rifle a fourth time. This time, it was followed by a wet gurgle that came from thirty yards away from me. It was the sound a dying animal makes.

"Got him," Silas said. As he pulled himself on his horse, I realized he wasn't wearing handcuffs. They hadn't been broken apart at the chain—they had been unlocked. Somehow, the son of a bitch had got a key.

Silas Green pulled the rifle back over his shoulder, and turned it on us. But before he even had the chance to draw a bead, a deafening shot tore into the tree just above his head.

"Get down!" Frank Kroft half shouted, out of sight.

Silas kicked his feet into the horse's side, and tore away.

❖ ❖ ❖

A deep cough filtered out from where Kroft had taken cover. I stumbled to my feet, nearly falling twice without the use of my hands. Everyone tried to follow.

"Check on Addison and Holling," I told Mickey. "We need to make sure." I jogged to where I'd heard the coughing, and tripped over a tangle of wiry branches. It was still early in the morning, and the world was underneath a veil of dew.

Frank Kroft was lying on a patch of bloody leaves and branches, but it was something else that yanked me to a stop. On the ground at my feet was a gun. Frank's .45 semiautomatic.

My feet were glued to the forest floor, and I saw myself suddenly acting out a macabre scene. I was taking the gun, putting it to his head. Squeezing the trigger. The image faded, and I looked at him with opportunistic eyes. There he was, this monster who dominated our lives, breathing shallow, his blood everywhere.

But even then, I did not hold the strength. Somehow, he still held control over me. Sometimes I feel he still does. How in the hell does that happen? I've yet to figure it out. It's eaten at my core and made me feel hollow, and spent. Like a rotting pumpkin, forgotten, weeks after Halloween. Only I've been left to stew for over forty years.

Frank opened his eyes and stared through me. "Pull . . ." A series of strewn coughs stumbled out of his mouth, dappling dots of blood on his shirt. "Pull me up." He held out an arm. I looked back at the gun, and bit my lip until I tasted blood. Reluctantly, I reached down, and helped him to a sitting position. He leaned over and fumbled the .45 from the ground and let it rest in his lap.

"Who's left?" he asked.

I closed my eyes and released the held breath in my lungs. "Me, Mickey. Benny, John, Aaron."

"Guards?"

I paused. "I don't think either of them . . ."

He settled into another round of coughing. He'd been shot in the upper right side of his chest. Blood soaked the entire half of his shirt, creating an odd mix of crimson and cream.

"What about the horses?" he asked.

Reaper was still roped. So was Hemingway. Maybe some others. "A few are tied up. But some are dead, I think. Some might be just gone."

"Help me up."

"Maybe you should stay still," I said.

"Now, dammit, help me up!" This was followed by more heaves, some of which dotted blood onto my own shirt and arm.

I half yanked him from under his left arm, and he staggered to his feet. I thought he was going to crumple right back to the ground, but he surprised me, and braced himself on the nearest tree. He took a slow, forced step, then another, making his way to the camp like Frankenstein's monster staggering through the trees.

Elmore Holling had been rolled over onto his stomach. I guessed the guys didn't need to look at his dead face staring up into nothingness. The hole that flayed the center of his back might have been worse, though. Most of the others were huddled around Joe Addison. Mickey already snagged the keys to the handcuffs from Joe's belt, and unlocked Benny's and John's, too. I held my own cuffs out to Mickey, and Frank nodded an approval as best he could.

"Let me see him," Frank mumbled, shoving the .45 into the back waist of his jeans. The guys made a clearing and in the center lay a blood-smeared mess. Addison's left leg was drenched, as was his shirt. His body had quit as he'd reached for a fistful of nettle growing up the slope. John Church was hunched over him.

"Why are you staring at him?" I whispered to John. The way he looked at Addison seemed less like genuine interest, and more a sordid, amused curiosity.

John didn't answer me. He didn't have to.

Joe Addison blinked. He was alive. I couldn't even see his chest rise or fall, but there he was, blinking his eyes. Frank dropped to his knees, putting his head to Joe's chest. "Heart's still got a strong beat," he said. "But he's losing blood."

"So are you," I said.

"Don't worry about me," he said. "Joe. Joey!"

Joe Addison's lips appeared to move long before any voice came.

When it did, it was barely there. "Can't . . . feel leg. Jeezis . . . don't wan die."

"Easy now. Easy. Just breathe, Joe, that's all you need to do." Frank snapped his head to John Church. "Go peel the shirt off Pettigrew."

John stared as if he didn't hear a word Frank said.

"Now!" More coughs, and more blood. Some of it flew into John's face, and he stood, wiping an arm across his face. He only shook his head, the way a parent might do to a child.

"I'll do it," I said, standing up. I crossed the camp to where the dead kid lay, preparing myself for the sight of a guy missing half his face. A bird cackled nearby, and it was the only thing that seemed real.

Bobby Pettigrew was worse than I imagined. His horse had dragged him in a few circles before it loosened the caught foot. I turned him over to unbutton the shirt, and worked as quickly as my clumsy fingers allowed. I tried not to look above the poor guy's neck. The smell was obscene, and my gut wavered momentarily on the edge of a full and immediate release. A slab of what I guessed to be his cheek and ear hung loosely to one side like a slice of shaved deli meat, and that was really the most recognizable part of him; everything else was carved inside out. I clenched my jaw until I thought my teeth were going to crack, and focused on what I came for. Bobby Pettigrew wore two shirts, an outty and an inny, and I figured what the hell, might as well get them both. I tore at the sleeves and then the neck of the undershirt all the way down so I could yank it cleanly away. The ripping of the fabric caused his ruined neck to gulp more blood onto the needle-scattered floor. I finished the job with eyes closed, then stumbled back to the group, ripping the shirts into pieces as I walked.

We wrapped the self-made tourniquets tightly around Addison's thigh, just above the gunshot wound. That seemed to slow the bleeding from his leg. His chest was another matter. After pulling away his shirt, we saw the shot had entered high, hopefully missing his lung. It wasn't bleeding as hard as his leg; maybe, by dumb luck, the bullet had gone through without hitting an artery. Mickey wrapped a long strip around Joe's neck, over the wound and below the arm. We wadded up another bundle of cloth to stuff underneath the tourniquet, and put pressure on it. He'd already lost a lot of blood, and his skin felt cold and waxy.

"Need to get him out of here," Frank said, visibly putting more effort into his weakening voice. "We'll put him on a horse; somebody's got to ride with him. You can all make it back before night if you leave now." He broke into another hacking fit that didn't want to taper off.

Aaron Gumm said, "You mean all of us are going, right?"

Frank found Addison's pack and pulled out the holstered .45. It must have been what Joe was going for when doing the army crawl. Why he wasn't already wearing it was a mystery. Frank picked himself off of the ground and fumbled with the gun, checking the rounds. He limped toward his own satchel and retrieved a fistful of shells.

"You boys are going back without me," he said. "I've got business with those others."

"You won't last the day," I told him.

"Maybe not, but I'm still not leaving them. Those assholes are coming back to the ranch, probably the same way Holling'll be." At that he stopped and stared at the lifeless Elmore Holling. He hobbled to the body and rolled it back over. Holling's stout face stared upward with empty eyes and an open mouth. Frank reached inside Holling's jacket and fished around. He came out with an empty holster.

"Where's his sidearm?" Frank asked. "Don't make me even try to say it twice!" he said, flinging more blood onto his shirt.

Frank beaded each of us with an accusing glare.

Finally, John Church said, "They must have gotten it when they took his rifle."

"Is that the God's honest, boys?" Frank asked, gripping his own gun tight and looking too exhausted to search us himself. "That it?"

"I th-think I seen it," Benny said. "Think I seen it in Silas's belt." We stood in silence as Frank sized us up.

He finally accepted this as truth. "Fine. I'll collect it once he's on the ground." He staggered to his horse, almost falling twice.

We all helped to get Addison up in the saddle behind Aaron Gumm, which was a job in itself. He had little strength left at all and depended solely on us. We tied a section of rope around Aaron and

Joe Addison, to keep Joe in the saddle should he pass out. The rest of us pulled ourselves up onto the remaining horses, ready to make the journey back.

"If you don't show up, you'll be hunted down," Frank said. "I'm sure you all know that."

We said we did, and I'm sure each of us believed it, too.

Frank mounted his horse after only a few efforts, amazing us all. As he settled into the saddle, the convulsions came again, throwing blood and phlegm onto the neck of his horse. His own tourniquet slowed his bleeding, but it wouldn't last. There was a hatred in Frank's face that made it hard for any of us to feel much compassion for the man. I looked at Mickey and saw a cold look of pleasure. The chance to kill Kroft had come for us, and we didn't take it. I guess I'm glad for that, now. It was a redeeming fact in a morning filled with violence.

Frank muffed a "Hyah" to his horse, and broke up into the woods, leaving behind two dead, one nearly there, five prisoners, and four horses. The sky was growing dark, and just as Frank left us, the rain began to fall again.

CHAPTER
forty-two

We'd made our way through the thick trees and narrow trail for maybe a couple hours when the lightning came. The sky was the color of charcoal, giving the illusion that nightfall was just around the corner of our morning world.

We decided to get off the trail—what little trail there was—and take shelter under the trees. Thunder boomed closer and closer to us as we tied off the horses and huddled together, pulling our coats tight and our hats low. Mickey put his head up to Addison's chest, just to make sure he wasn't dead. It surprised me when Mickey gave the thumbs-up.

A crack of lightning split across the sky, pulling a rip of thunder behind. Another followed just seconds after.

Only, the second didn't sound right. We looked at each other, cold and drenched, our faces blank. In the distance, barely audible in the beating rain, came another sound. It was a happy kind of scream, like a cowboy screaming, "Yee-haw." Reaper jerked beneath me, and circled. "It's okay, girl," I whispered. "Gonna be okay, you'll see."

"That was him," Aaron said.

"Could have been the storm," I said. "You know, playing tricks on us."

"No way, Shep. I heard it, too," Mickey said, squinting through the rain. "It was him. I think he just got Frank."

Another bolt of lightning. This time we were sure it was lightning, but all the same, it only pressed the fear deeper that Silas was now coming after us.

John Church looked up the mountain, into the trees. "It was him."

"We gotta move," I said, gathering my courage as best I could. "Come on," I reached for Addison. "We have to get him up again."

"Shep. We don't have to run," Mickey said.

"What do you mean? You heard—" I stopped, seeing for the first time what Mickey had pulled out: Elmore Holling's M1911 pistol. It looked obnoxiously large in his little hands, but Mickey held it with a stillness that made him look dangerous nonetheless.

"Holeee shiiit," I said slowly, mesmerized by the weapon. "You did lift it." And of course he had; Mickey, once again pulling the stars from the sky. He looked older somehow, with it in his hands.

"You got shells?" John asked.

"In Addison's pack," Mickey said. "The clip only holds seven at a time, though."

Aaron Gumm looked nervous. "Hey, you guys, we've still gotta get this guy down to the ranch. He don't look so good. Dontcha think?"

To accentuate his point, another gunshot was fired, closer than the first. This time, it sounded like it came from ahead of us, down the trail.

"He's in front of us now!" Benny shouted.

"I ain't staying on the damn trail," Mickey said. "One big group o' gypsies? Screw you and no thanks. It'll be a duck hunt for them."

"Well, I ain't getting off it," Aaron said. "You all can go to hell, but I'm sticking. You'll lose yourselves up here and then he'll find you for sure."

"I'm with Mickey," I said. "They'll be looking for us to go back the same way we came. And even if the rain's covering us, it's covering them, too."

"If we go off-trail," Church said, "it'll be a slower trip. That guard won't make it."

John was right. I said, "If you want to stick to it, Aaron, you're taking Addison with you. Maybe you'll make it. Maybe he will, too."

"Fine. Who's coming with me?" Aaron asked as he hoisted himself onto his horse.

"Not me, kid," John said. "Not with those gunshots down there."

Mickey crossed his arms. "Me neither. But I can't make Benny's decision for him."

Benny shook his head up and down. "I'm staying!"

"Send help when you get there," I said. We fastened Joe Addison once more onto the horse, tying the rope twice around him and Aaron. He came out of consciousness just enough to murmur something incoherent before passing out again.

"You're all either stupid or crazy," Aaron said.

He kicked his horse into a trot, and disappeared into the trees with a dying man strapped behind.

I DIDN'T THINK IT WAS POSSIBLE, BUT THE CLOTTED SKY GREW darker, and the rain fell even harder. We were soaked cold, and hungry.

"We should put some more ground between us and that gunfire," I said. They all agreed.

"Silas is coming," Mickey said. "Man, I can just feel it."

We moved east along the mountain. I think it was east. It was difficult to see in the storm, but we kept quiet and listened. I thought I heard another series of shouts some twenty minutes later, but they were distant compared to the ones we'd heard before.

"Hey, W-Will," Benny said, his voice low. "We only have one . . . gun, right?"

"Yeah. That's right," I said. "And they have at least two, maybe three now." But they lost one of their rifles when Bobby Pettigrew got his face blown off. Frank took it with him.

"Okay, then," Benny said. "Maybe we won't have to . . . use it, you know?"

"I hope not," I said, but I had a gnawing fear we might have to use the hell out of it.

As we pressed on into the thick, I heard my stomach groan. Of all things, I suddenly thought of Miss Little's apple pie. That memory felt like home to me, and because of that I tried to drive it from my mind. It was replaced with an uglier memory; the story she'd disclosed that afternoon.

Until that day in the mountains, I'd kept Miss Little's tragedy to myself. With the news of my mother, I was just never able to invest much thought in Miss Little's loss. How her two little boys slipped out of her life. How everyone blamed her. I never stopped to think how it must have hurt to share something so fragile. She watched over us, she'd said. *Over us all.* In our closed-off world, stripped of our childhoods, Miss Little became a mother figure, even if we weren't aware of it.

I decided to share her story. Both Mickey's and Benny's attention was immediately focused as I found the words. I saw a mild comfort in their eyes, and thought maybe it was just what they needed to hear.

Sometime later, in the midst of the static rainfall, there was another gunshot. This time, it was barely audible. It could have come from miles away.

For the rest of the day, we continued to ride under the rain and lightning, in the direction we thought would lead us back to the ranch. None of us wanted to admit, or even suggest, the uncertainty of our bearing.

Nature was not working with us; the darkness and the storm made everything confusing, casting dim light and shadows everywhere, making any path we chose seem like the wrong one.

Time dragged, and through our growing doubt, everything started to seem wrong and backward—our direction, our situation, hope that we'd be okay. We were on the brink of exhaustion and feeling more helpless with each passing minute.

"Okay, so maybe we're hosed," Mickey said, after riding for an hour.

"You think so, genius?" I said.

"I don't guess you have any brilliant ideas, do you, Magellan?"

Up ahead, alone on his horse, John Church let out a long breath.

We pressed on with heavy hearts and dampening spirits. When the day finally began to fade, the storm showed glimpses of surrender. The intervals of lightning lagged and stretched, and the rain turned into a fine, cold mist that stung my face like pinpricks. Doubt was everywhere. For the first time since leaving the ranch, it began to sink in that, just maybe, we might not make it back. The pregnant sky all but masked what little sunlight there was, and we didn't know which direction to head.

"We're gonna have to make camp," John said. It sounded as if he was saying it more to himself.

"Agreed," Mickey said.

We found a narrow clearing after a somewhat lengthy search; Mickey and I believed the night's campsite should meet a certain set of criteria. Not that we were being particular, at least not overly so. We were just procrastinating, scared to finally stop and wait for Silas to come looking.

The clearing featured a rotting, overturned mountain maple lying at the feet of other, surrounding maples and pines. It would be more than adequate for the night. We dismounted, and then roped the horses to the nearest branches. They immediately planted their noses in the ground, licking at the brackish rain puddles on the forest floor. Reaper looked up at me and snorted.

"No fire, guys," I said. "Even if we could get one lit, can't risk being seen."

"That's okay," Mickey said. "I just hope the rain's done for the night." He rummaged through the packs and found the last of the food. Some beef jerky strips and hard bread. The crackers were soaked, and I dropped what was left of them to the horses.

So we sat, side by side in the growing darkness, and ate. We hadn't heard anything suspicious in over four or five hours, and figured—with our luck—we probably got so turned around that we accidentally separated ourselves from Silas to a safe enough distance. None of us talked about him, or Frank, though there was no doubt it was in the forefront of our minds.

In time, the clouds broke, and through the treetops I caught the moon. It was winking at me, masked behind swaying branches and bushy needles. I saw the stars for the first time in nearly a week.

"I think we're okay . . . for the night." Benny's voice was so incredibly smooth and comforting that I instantly believed him.

We settled in, and as we talked in hushed voices, Mickey performed another miracle when he fished into the worn leather pack at his feet and removed Cal Jenkins's AM radio. Both Benny and I had the same taken-aback reaction: disbelieving laughter.

"Nice," John said. An ever-so-slight smile crept onto his face.

With a click of the dial, a hushed and synthesized static eased out of the radio's single speaker. Mickey thumbed the dial, searching for the station, the only station we cared about and had the privilege of hearing on select Saturday mornings. A tinny whine droned up and down and up again as the tuner's orange bar traveled east to west.

"Not too loud, Mickee," Benny murmured, looking all around like he was waiting on something in the shadows to just reach out and grab him.

The static crackled, then cleared, and the connection was made. KGUC, out of Gunnison. Where the favorites always lived. Like a starburst, our makeshift camp was filled with the harmony of the Platters singing "The Great Pretender." Only this time, I didn't think of Anthony Curio popping Suzy Micheli's cherry in the backseat of a Dodge. I couldn't help but remember what Benny had told me just days ago as we mended a fence. A fence that would soon be knocked apart.

Sometimes . . . I hear that song. In my dreams.

"Hey, maybe we oughtta cut it." I was flooded with paranoia. I remember thinking (and I sometimes still do) that if we'd never turned on that radio . . . if we'd just never heard that song, the cycle of events already set into motion could have been busted apart like a hammer through a window. I guess it was just another way of bullshitting myself, but later I was desperate enough to believe that.

But I was obviously in the minority. Even Benny, who'd told me the vision to begin with, already seemed to have forgotten, and was smiling with the rest of them.

"Sshh," Mickey hissed, his eyes closed. "Oh, man, we just need a can of beer and some smokes, am I right?" Hearing him say that was funny, even though he didn't mean it as a joke. And that's just the way I always seem to remember Mickey. Don't really know why. There are plenty of other times I can recall him goofing it up at the mess hall table, or laying down a fat hand of cards on my cot, calling me a douche. But when I now think of Mickey Baines, the first image to sink in my mind is of him leaning against that rotten tree, eyes closed, listening to the Platters.

The stars blinked in and out of view as the treetops wavered and the clouds rolled across the sky, and the Platters gave way to Chuck Berry's "No Particular Place to Go." And it couldn't have been any more accurate. Still, to let my mind escape our reality, just for a moment, was to almost imagine the four of us camping at the state park outside Chicago, free as birds in the wind. I've found that if you really want to, letting your mind escape isn't all that hard. Sometimes it's just human reaction.

Next to me, Benny palmed his brother's box of jacks in his hands, turning it over, and over, and over. I'd be willing to bet not one day went by that he regretted taking Todd's place, no matter what had happened since. You could see it in his eyes whenever he spoke. It was how he almost cried, or sometimes did, whenever a letter would come from home. Benny's father, and once or twice it was his mom, wrote down whatever it was Todd had to say to his hero, his big brother. After Benny's accident, he could still read, of course. It just took him twice as long to hack out the words and sentences.

Benny followed my eyes to the tin, and read my mind. "S-Someday . . . I'm going to give these back to him, r-right?" he said.

"I know you will." It made me wish for my mother's picture, or any memento from home, to hold on to and feel its familiarity, its existence, in my hands.

Benny dropped a jack back into the box, snapped shut the lid, and gave it a quick shake. He smiled as it rattled. "Someday."

As the night went on, we made small talk, trying to keep positive thoughts in our minds and on our lips. Until I finally said, "I wish Coop were here. He'd tell us some crazy story and we'd all end up ragging on him."

The horses stood roped nearby, facing us and the music. Except Reaper. She just watched the darkness of the forest. I didn't like that, the way she seemed to be waiting on something to happen.

"I'll tell you a story," John Church said.

CHAPTER

forty-three

BENNY FRITCH CAME TO THE RANCH OUT OF LOYALTY. MICKEY Baines, by way of revenge. For Cooper Kingston, it was through accident, and me—well, I like to think it was a little of each. But it was John Church who came out of a raging violence.

As John began to tell us how he came to the ranch, I glanced at Mickey. (We'd almost read the story ourselves—the ranch's version—but only had time enough to see the most important words: *Murder. Third degree.* I'm sure Mickey was also thinking about that as he turned down the radio's volume.)

"You've probably heard by now," he said, "maybe you haven't. I came from a horse ranch, doing all the same shit. Never knew anything but this."

He's going to do it, I thought. He's going to tell us what happened, explain how the murder label got pushed on him. He's going to justify everything. I sat next to him that night, next to the legend of Swope Ranch, in absolute awe that he was sharing with us. I remember wishing he was my big brother. Sounds funny to say that now. But then, on that night . . . yeah, I wished for it. I was too young and stupid to know any better.

"My dad was really my stepdad," he said. "But I never knew any difference. My mom married him when I was little. I grew up on his ranch, in Texas. Outside Alpine." John stopped and let out a long breath, as if he'd already grown tired. Then he went on. "Lots of people worked the place; Dad always kept it going at full staff since he was on the road a lot.

"Anyway. Few years back, a new kid's hired on. Tim Holly. Tall, skinny guy. He had crazy, bushy red hair and a mouth packed full of crooked teeth. I saw those teeth all the time because he never shut his mouth. Talked, bragged—*all* the time. Everyone called him 'T,' and, shit, I guess I hated him from the start."

A gust of chilled wind rolled through the trees, and over our bodies. I pulled my coat tighter, and looked into the dark shadows of the timber as John spoke. His hushed, raspy voice cut through the air like a razor across a carpet.

"He was seventeen, just a couple years older. But I was still bigger. Maybe he hated me, too, because he started this game, trying to best me at everything. Who could chore fastest, rope better, bale the most hay. Shit like that. Sometimes we tangled, swapping black eyes and bloody lips. You know, goofing around.

"So a few months roll along; Dad hit the road again. Dallas. I was pretty much running the ranch when Dad wasn't there, even though I was only fifteen. And these rumors started going around about my mother. Hell, they were probably all true.

"I was in the barn one morning, watering troughs. Through the split-open doors, I could see my house. Back of it, anyway. I saw the back door open, and T was stepping out. Behind him was my mother. She was wearin' some kinda see-through thing, and he kissed her. Right there, on the mouth. She smiled, and he laughed about something, then turned to the barn to come help me out."

Mickey and I were hardly even breathing. I looked at Benny. He had his mouth open, and was just rocking back and forth, his eyes glued to Church.

"I don't know how long he was fucking around with her, off and on like that. But he saw the look in my eyes that morning, and he knew I'd seen them. And you know what he did? He laughed at me. Laughed, with those fucking yellow teeth. 'Hell, John,' he said. 'Looks like you got something on your mind! Bet it'll make you feel better if you tell me.' He started giggling. Like a kid.

"I was carrying a salt lick, and I hurled it like a shot put at the wall. And he just laughed. He said, 'Can you smell her on me? You ought to—her pussy was *wet.*'"

I heard Mickey draw in a breath at that. I tried to imagine what I would have done if someone talked about my mom that way. Maybe I was more like John Church than I thought.

"And then . . . well, everything just kind of blurred together then. Like one o' them runaway trains. I didn't much care what I did next." John paused there, lifting his face up into the breeze as if it were cleansing. Sometimes, he didn't just look a year or two older, but like a grown man instead.

"What *did* you do?" I asked.

"Drove my fist straight into his mouth. Before T could fall to the ground, I caught him. Pulled him inside the nearest horse pen and plunged his head into the water trough. His feet started thrashing around, this way and that, like a catfish picked on a hook."

I thought of Silas Green, and the way he twisted and contorted as John held his head in the commode. A chill crawled up my neck like an insect.

"I drove his head down into the bottom of that trough again. Then again. Then again. It made a funny kind of sound that was soft and quiet. Like—*whump, whump, whump.* He screamed, I guess, under the water, because all at once a thousand air bubbles raced to the top. Then his fucking legs slowed down a little, stopped kicking out like they were. After a while, they just kind of stopped. But I didn't. Nah, I kept going. I liked hearing that *whump* sound each time I rammed his head down into the bottom of that old thing.

"Y-you just . . . killed him?" Benny asked. My heart sank, seeing the shock and the revulsion in his innocent eyes. Neither Mickey nor I had ever told him what we'd seen in Church's file that day in the infirmary. The label of MURDER. We had no reason to. "Killed him, j-just like that?"

Church looked at Benny, then into the trees behind. "Yup. I guess so. The only reason I ended up in this place and not somewhere worse was because my mother pleaded what I'd done was self-defendin'."

"Do you regret it?" Mickey asked. "Regret what you did to him?" It sounded so much like Cal to me, I actually turned to make sure it *was* Mickey. His knees were drawn in, and I saw him shiver in the moonlight.

"Sure," Church said. "I kind of feel cheated I can't go back and do it again."

A hush fell over each of us as we struggled to digest what he'd just said. He wasn't joking. He wasn't pretending. John Church killed a guy, and he simply didn't care.

"That's not . . . right," Benny stammered out. "You're a b-bad person."

John Church considered this carefully, at least that's the impression he gave. Finally, he eased into us, and furled his brow. "You know what? I never tried to pretend I *was* good. Sometimes, I think all of you are waiting on something. Waiting for me to, I dunno, come around. Be a fucking pal, or . . . some shit like that. Have you ever thought some people are . . . just who they are? Good or bad, you know, and that's okay? Will's fucked up inside because he tried to kill his dad and doesn't know what to make of it. Mickey's out to prove to the goddamn world he's not small. And Benny . . . Well, Benny's head's so stuffed with straw, he probably don't even know who he is anymore. And all that's okay if you wouldn't give so much of a shit how the world sees you, much less what it thinks of you." He eased and slouched further onto the ground, resting his head on the overturned stump. "Anyway. That's what I think."

Even then, even after hearing the coldness of his words, I listened to him the way a kid might hear his big brother. I tried to sympathize with what he'd done. After all, was my crime, my intended crime, any worse? I didn't attack my father with a clear and conscious thought that I wanted to kill him, at least I didn't think so. Would I have, if Mr. Francello hadn't pulled me? I still don't know the answer to that, even now.

It's amazing that any of us slept at all that night, but we did. Maybe it was sheer physical exhaustion from riding all day, or just what we'd been through emotionally. Most likely, it was both. That, and the hypnotic way that the wind lulled in between the pines, rustling the needles and the limbs like a primitive lullaby. We slept so soundly, in fact, that none of us heard John Church rise, untether his horse, and slip away into the early morning.

CHAPTER
forty-four

DISORIENTATION. PANIC. "WHAT DO YOU MEAN, 'HE'S GONE'?" I ASKED.

"He's gone!" Mickey shouted it louder. "He's totally GONE! He rode out, and we never even heard him."

Benny was up on one elbow, swiveling his head from me to Mickey, obviously confused. Mickey was livid. His small body seemed to pulse with anger and frustration as he wrung his hands together like they were wet dishrags.

"No," I said. "No, he'll be back. He just . . ." But I had nothing to say.

"He just what, Shep? He just fucking *what*?"

I looked in the direction we'd come the day before, squinting my eyes and leering into the timber. I turned and scanned the opposite way. The trees blended together and everything looked the same, no matter how desperately I searched for the streak of brown that was his coat, or the copper color of his horse. The forest was waking up around us; birds called. I strained my ears, cocked my head, and I grew more frantic. "How could he just leave us? How could he fucking leave us while Silas is out here, too?"

In the midst of confusion, Benny had the most simple and correct answer.

"He didn't . . . care."

Reaper snorted, almost as in agreement, then I dropped to my butt on the soggy ground. I covered my face with my hands and whispered, "I thought we were his friends."

Mickey snorted, a little too much like Reaper. "Least we still have the damn gun."

I felt there had to be an explanation, some sort of reasoning for what he did. People don't just leave like that, I thought. He talked to us, *opened up* the night before. Hadn't he? Could that have just been my own naïve misconception?

Sitting there in the dirt and the dead needles with the morning scent of wet pine draped over me, I finally realized what I'd been too blind to see. What Benny saw from the very beginning. John Church wasn't our friend. Some people *do* just leave like that. He didn't want to ride with us, and didn't care what happened as a result.

My face flushed with humiliation as I remembered arguing with Benny. How I told him I wished I was more like John Church. I should have been looking up to the one I was shouting at that day in the stable before he got his head kicked apart. All along, I should have been more like Benny.

WE RODE THROUGH OUTSTRETCHED COTTONWOOD TREES AND PINES, each one painting us with wet, prickly branches. Reaper slowed, and dipped her head to the ground. We didn't know for certain which way we were going, or if we were getting any closer to the ranch. The morning sky was already overcast, obscuring the sun. It gave us only a vague sense of direction. We were taking the horses downhill, but just ahead were more slopes and inclines.

After riding for almost an hour, I heard a rustle off to one side, close enough to make me jump. There, underneath a stretch of loose rocks, I saw the source. A fat raccoon poked his head through a cropping of needles and leaves. It nosed through the brush outside a shallow cave formed between the deep ruts of open mountainside. He ducked, then scampered along with no agenda whatsoever.

"More rain's on the way," Mickey said, squinting up to the open patches of sky above us. "It's getting dark again."

"We'll get there," I said.

There was an air of uncertainty hanging over those words. I think we were all beginning to feel it creeping up behind us, around us, as much as no one wanted to admit such a thing.

A steady rain did come, and again we were drenched and cold and losing confidence. Nothing looked familiar, and I couldn't see the surrounding mountaintops due to the congestion of trees. I started to wonder if we weren't traveling in the opposite direction. The sky was painted charcoal, and the slashing rain made it impossible to tell if we were traveling north or south. East or west. Overhead, thunder cannoned through the peaks.

"I've never been with a girl," Mickey said.

It came out of the blue, just like that. Normally, we would have laughed, but no one made a sound. Mickey wasn't joking around. He looked as if he might cry.

"I know I told you guys I had," he said. "But . . . I never did. Never even felt a tit before."

It was quiet for a moment, until Benny broke the lull. "S-Sometimes . . . I'm mad at Todd. That I'm here."

The sound of Reaper's and Hemingway's hoofs on the damp earth and muck was like hearing a clock; it was almost hypnotizing. I said, "My mom's dead because I wasn't there to save her."

Mickey nodded, as if understanding exactly what I meant. Maybe even Benny understood. I watched them on their horse, and thought that if Coop were here, he'd be on Reaper, with me. We stopped talking after that, content to let the rain be all we needed to hear.

The bolt of lightning stopped the world for us all. Reaper crow-hopped, and I swung her around, expecting to find a smoldering tree. Benny cried out in surprise, and by the time I realized it wasn't lightning at all, the chaos had already begun.

Hemingway collapsed to the ground with a hideous half snort, half cry, sending Mickey and Benny flying over his head. I saw blood spurt out of the horse's rib cage, and was about to yell something, anything, when I heard another crack of gunfire. This time, something whizzed past my neck. My instincts immediately kicked in and I threw myself from the saddle onto the forest floor.

"Where is he?" Mickey screamed, holding out the pistol and shaking it the way a child might whip around a squirt gun. *"Oh, man! Where is he?"* He squeezed down on the trigger of the .45, and sent three blind shots into the woods. Each one with a resounding *BOOM.*

From somewhere up the slope, behind the thick blanket of pines, Silas Green said, "I want the dummy. Hand him over and the rest of you can go to hell."

I scanned the trees, trying to pinpoint his location. Eddie Tokus was out there, too. Somewhere. That meant two guns against our one.

It was quiet. Just the leaves, just the far-off sound of birds. Then, a barrage of cackled gunfire pierced the air. "I want the fucking dummy!"

"Why don't you eat me!" Mickey yelled into the forest.

My gaze danced from the timber to Mickey, the heavy pistol now steady in his hand. Benny and I lay close to the ground behind a mess of brush. Out of the corner of my eye, something large flashed by. It was Reaper, trotting back the way we'd come, away from the danger.

"That how it's gonna be then?" Silas screamed. His voice bounced off the trees, making him sound like a ghost in the woods. He could have been forty yards away, or he could have been a hundred. "That it? You two homos willing to die instead of handing him over? You sure about that? Cause you better be."

Somewhere in the distance, I heard Eddie. It was soft, barely a whisper in the air, but there was no mistaking. He sounded scared. "I ain't killing no one, man. Ain't gonna do it."

My best guess was that they were forty or fifty yards to my right. Beside me, Benny was breathing like he'd just run a mile. He whispered, "I c-can go, Will. Maybe I'm supposed to go. It's okay." He actually started to rise.

It was the most pissed off I'd ever been at Benny. I was mad at him for being stupid, and at the time, I thought he was being selfish, too.

I slapped him across the face. "Shut up! You're not going anywhere!" I hissed, and I slapped him again. The confusion and hurt in his face instantly killed me.

Mickey screamed, "You're not getting anyone, you crazy shit-faced basta—"

The resonant sound of rifle fire cut him off.

Silas's warbled voice floated through the trees. "Get back here, Eddie, you son-of-a-*whore*!"

So. Eddie had run. Silas was shooting after *him* now, not us.

"You're dead!" Silas screamed. "You better run fast because you're dead!"

Did Eddie keep his rifle? I was betting so. Over a rise, I suddenly made out a blur of red. Eddie's coat. He was taking Silas's advice, bouncing and grunting his way through the dense trees and out of sight.

It was then that Silas made his first mistake. He leaned out, just ever so slightly, from behind a tree.

"There," I said, matter-of-factly, pointing with a shaky hand in his direction. I directed the statement to Mickey, who was gripping the .45. He understood seamlessly.

In all of one second, Mickey aimed and squeezed the trigger with the coolest of ease. The report was commanding; its effect, immediate.

The shot clipped Silas in the upper leg. There was a piglike grunt, then, "Fuck you! *Fuck you!*" He screamed more out of rage, I thought, than pain.

"Stay down!" Mickey hissed at us, which was a good thing because Benny started to get up again, maybe thinking we were going to rush Silas now that he was hurt.

Phantom shots rang. I heard a bullet zip into the ground just feet from my head, another into the trees behind us, two more into the dead horse just feet away. Then, Silas began to retreat. He fired, and fired again, all the while, screaming, "You're all dead! All of you!"

I could see him now. He looked like a monster lurching from tree to tree, and even at over fifty yards, I saw the crazy in his eyes. Mickey fired twice in his direction, and in just moments, an eerie quiet settled upon us. We waited.

Silas was gone.

❖ ❖ ❖

MICKEY WAS SWEATING THE WAY MY FATHER USED TO AFTER A DAY at the factory. Wet strands of his brown curls were smeared across his narrow forehead like they were pasted there. And the blood looked to have leaked right out of his short frame.

"Everyone okay?" I asked, already knowing they were. Shaken, scared to death, but okay.

"Think so," Benny said.

Mickey just nodded, not taking his eyes out of the trees. Shadows were everywhere.

We gathered around the dead horse. The mouth was still open, like it tried to scream with its dying breath.

"Man," Mickey said, taking more bullets from his pocket and reloading the .45's clip. He did it just as cool as an outlaw in a Western. "Fucking Hemingway."

"Could've been one of us," I said, staring at the ruined horse. Cold pinpricks of rain slashed across my face, and then fell even harder. I scanned the sky above, but there was no hint of it letting up.

"You know something?" Mickey said, casting his own eyes upward. "I really hate rain."

"We're l-lost, right?" Benny asked.

"We'll be fine," I said. "But it's not going to do us any good wandering around in this shit with it getting darker."

Mickey said, "He'll be coming back. We need to move."

"What do we do?" Benny asked.

I remembered that fat raccoon, from earlier in the morning. "The cave," I said. "You know, the one we passed earlier? We could head back there, ride all this out. It'll keep us dry and out of the woods where we're moving targets."

"Sounds like a plan to me," Mickey said.

"Yeah," Benny started, "That sounds—"

Another gunshot ripped from down the slope, from behind us, and it suddenly felt like someone had swung a Louisville Slugger into me.

I'd been shot.

"No!" Mickey screamed, instantly down at my side. He clawed his hand over the wound, but blood seeped and ran between his fingers anyway, as if in spite.

"Oh, *shit,* man!" I cried out, finding Mickey's eyes. "Oh, *shit,* Mickey, it hurts!"

Benny nudged Mickey out of the way, and planted his mammoth hand on me. Wrapped his steel fingers around my shoulder and held me firm, like a damn vise. His actions were cool, and calm. But the look he gave told the exact opposite. I thought his eyes were going to drop right out of their sockets. There was something on his face, and it took me a second before I realized he was wearing a splattered pattern of my blood.

"I th-thought he l-left!" Benny stammered. "Thought he left!"

Another shot screamed over our heads from the timber shadows.

"He did," Mickey said. "That's not him shooting at us. It's fucking Eddie Tokus. We fell for it like a couple of damn kids!"

I lay there bleeding, and wanted to say that we *were* just kids.

"Eddie?" Benny asked.

"He never ran away," Mickey hissed. "He only circled around behind us, waiting for a chance." He grabbed Benny's hand, which was still locked onto my shoulder, and looked at the wound. "Son of a bitch. Lunch, listen man. Can you help him to the cave?"

Benny nodded furiously, and whispered, "Yes!"

I don't know why I remember this, but Benny's hard blue eyes frightened me. It was how serious they suddenly turned, how determined. It was just a shoulder shot, and I still had the sense to know I wasn't dying. But those dead-shot eyes of Benny's were so ominous. Seeing it written down this way sounds foretelling, but I don't mean it to be.

"Okay," Mickey said, and slapped my cheek like we were fucking gangsters or something. "Then do it. Go." He dug his feet into the mud and the dead pine needles, and took off like a track sprinter into the trees, toward where the shots had come from. All the while, he fired his gun and screamed. It was the screaming that sounded the most disturbing, not the gunshots.

What else could we do? I reached over to Hemingway with my good arm, and tore at the saddle pack's buckle. "Help me," I gasped, and Benny was finally able to yank it free.

I started to rise, was about to ask for a hand when the forest suddenly turned upside down.

"Come on," Benny said. In all of one second, he scooped me up and threw me over his shoulder. He did it as easily as a seasoned farmer heaving a bag of grain.

"Gots to hurry," he said, grabbing the saddle pack out of my hand, too. "Gots to go!"

My shoulder hurt like it was going to fall off, and I half gurgled an acknowledgment. He was already running, and all the jostling and bumpiness of the venture made any speech almost impossible. Oddly enough, I remember feeling very much like I was again riding Reaper.

I was amazed, even with my added weight, how fast Benny ran on that day. If I hadn't witnessed it from my own front-row seat, I never would have believed it.

Somewhere behind us, there were more exchanges of gunfire, and more shouts. I cursed Mickey under my breath for leaving us. And something else crept up. A cold knowledge that Silas might be watching us, ready to shoot us down at any second.

Benny clumped ahead even faster. Through trees and up and down the inclines of the mountain he ran. But Silas never came. By some miracle of God, we somehow escaped him. Maybe he'd stayed to fight alongside Eddie when Mickey charged into the trees like Eliot Ness. Maybe not.

Benny started to slow, and then, finally, he stopped. Very gently, he dropped me to the ground. I was dizzy from being bounced on his shoulder like a baby, and when I was able to look down at my blood-soaked shirt, I was surprised I hadn't yet passed out. He pulled off his coat and tore away the Swope-issued button-up, tying it around my shoulder and under my arm as tight as he could to stop the bleeding.

"W-Why did he do that?" Benny asked.

"He tried to save us," I managed, not very coherently.

"He's gonna be . . . okay, right? You think he m-made it, right?"

I didn't want to answer him truthfully. "Yeah, he'll be okay. The stupid bastard." We caught our breath, or at least Benny did. His makeshift tourniquet could have passed Boy Scout inspection, but I still felt weak. From someplace we couldn't see, the echo of a rifle rumbled.

"He'll try and meet us at the cave," I said. "I think I can run, you don't have to carry me anymore."

Benny looked offended, but just nodded his head. "Okay. Let's go."

The rain came harder, faster, and colder. The minutes stretched into well over an hour. The clouds grew thicker, daylight faded into dark, and like animals we ran. I jogged on my own, but soon grew too tired. Benny once again picked me up, and hoisted me like we were marines. Like we were brothers.

He stopped once, and vomited. As soon as he finished, he dragged an arm across his face, and picked me back up. There was no way to tell for sure which direction we were heading, and no way to guess at the time. Through the rain and the deep bruises of storm clouds in the afternoon sky, it looked as if nightfall had landed early. It only heightened our panic to find the cave and take shelter.

We must have covered three miles. I guess that doesn't sound like much. Certainly no marathon. But three miles can be an eternity if it's dark and storming, and you have to run up and down steep, thatchy slopes and across rocky creek beds, trying your best to not trip and break a leg.

Would you believe it? By sheer luck, we found it. From a distance, the cave looked ancient, and dark, and like it had been just waiting for us to return all along.

The inside of it didn't go too far into the mountainside, maybe just ten or twelve feet. And all around the entrance were cracked and crumbling rocks, perfect for small animals or even snakes to hide. We didn't care. It was hidden, and we'd be protected. Wind screamed across the mouth of the cave, creating an eerie, low howl.

We climbed up and burrowed inside; Benny slung me in like I was a doll. Once inside, we collapsed, physically and emotionally exhausted. Neither of us spoke. I didn't know if Mickey was alive or dead, although the optimism in Benny's eyes should have been enough to convince me our missing friend was okay.

"Why'd he d-do it?" Benny asked again. "Why'd he l-leave?"

I stared out the mouth of the cave at the brackish mixture of browns and greens. The day was all but gone; just the hint of light remained. Lightning flashed, and filled the outside world with a white brilliance. "He gave us a chance to run. Maybe he thought we'd be surrounded and outgunned if we all stuck together. He left us unarmed. But he gave us a chance to run."

Benny furrowed his brow, as if trying to digest this information. After a while, he settled on staring out the cave alongside me.

We waited for the rain to stop, and for Mickey to appear. Benny sat hunched over, Indian style. The cave was shallow and claustrophobic inside, leaving only enough room to either sit or lie down.

I stopped bleeding, thank God, and the color began to come back into my face. At least that's what Benny told me. I pulled back my shirt, and craned my head as best I could to get a look at my shoulder. What I saw made me want to throw up. Even Benny made a face.

"Oh! Doesn't look g-good, right? Oh, m-man."

It was nearly black. I was unprepared for that. Even though it was bled out, the wound itself was already inflamed. There was no exit wound on the back, and I guessed the bullet hit my collarbone and got stuck inside. That's how it felt.

Benny stretched out his legs, and went to pull something from his front pocket. He stopped. "Will! You s-seen my . . . jacks?"

I shook my head no.

He flipped over onto his stomach, then felt at his back pockets. They were empty, too. "Oh, man! Th-They're gone, Will! Oh, sh-shit!"

"It's cool, Lunch, it's okay."

But he shook his head, violently, the way a wet dog shakes off water. "You don't . . . understand! I n-need them. Oh, shit, right? Sure . . . you d-don't got them?" He looked at me with huge, pleading eyes.

"No, look." I checked my pockets just for his peace of mind.

He grabbed the saddle pack we'd brought along and dumped it, rummaging through the gear and what food remained with cold, clumsy hands. "They're not . . . here!" In the midst of his search he froze, and looked up at me. His eyes cut into mine, but he was somewhere else entirely. "Oh, n-no! They're in . . . Reaper's bag! Where is she, W-Will?"

"I don't know. She could be anywhere now." But I knew wherever she was, she was cold, and getting soaked. Just like Mickey.

Benny jerked away, and actually tried to shuffle out of the cave that very instant. His head was outside when I somehow caught him by the ankle with my good arm. The reach stretched every nerve and tendon in my body, sending needles of fire from my neck down to my left hand. "Benny, man! You'll just get yourself killed!"

"L-Let me go!" he screamed.

"You're not going to find the damn horse in the middle of the night!"

"You ain't my f-father, let me . . . go, right!" He struggled with me, kicked at me twice.

"They will *kill* you, man! You think I want to see you die? What would Mickey tell you? Huh, Benny? What would Mickey fucking say?"

Finally, he stopped. I pulled on him, and he rolled back into the cave beside me with one last heave. He was crying. His fists were balled up into huge knots and he crossed his arms on his chest, knees drawn up, like a newborn.

"Wh-Where is he! Why'd he . . . leave us like th-that? I d-don't want him to die! I wanna g-go home! I just wanna . . . *go home*!"

I put my arm around him. "It's okay. You'll see. Mickey will be okay."

Hours dragged and the wind and the rain fell as if in spite of us both. I tried to keep watch, but it was too dark to see anything through the narrow opening, and the only time it wasn't was during the erratic flashes of lightning. And those were becoming few and far between.

I didn't need to see it to know the world outside was drowned and blended into a static noise of rain and wind. Nothing ever came that night except the passing storm. Benny fell asleep, still crying. I stayed awake as long as I could.

CHAPTER

forty-five

"WILL. WILL, WAKE UP."

Benny shook me.

It was still raining, only it sounded different, and strange.

"Come on, w-wake up," Benny called again.

I lifted my head from a bed of pine needles. My shoulder looked worse than it had the night before. The tourniquet Benny had made from his shirt was dyed in blood, and my wound now looked in danger of becoming infected.

"It's . . . hailing."

Tiny hailstones dropped and bounced against the ground. Tiny, not even the size of a pea.

I sat up, still groggy, and flinched from pain with every movement. "We'll have to wait until it stops. Then we'll go. Maybe we'll find Mickey."

"Yeah. Okay," Benny said, watching the small stones of ice bounce off the trees and ground.

"You think . . . those guys . . . are still out there?" Benny asked.

I nodded. "Somewhere, yeah. But maybe we'll luck out. Maybe we'll find help." I was then struck with an image that bore itself into my head with no invitation whatsoever. I remembered Coop telling us the story of Alferd Packer that day in the mess hall. About how his group got snowbound in the mountains, only miles away from where we sat in that cave. Packer killed the men he was with, then ate from the dead. We made fun of Coop that day. My fourteen-year-old mind told me being stuck in the mountains was some kind of payback.

"Will?" Benny whispered. He pointed a finger in the air. There was a kick of earth, a rustle of branches from above the cave.

My body tightened; every hair stood on end as we waited for what might come. If only we had the gun. I held a finger to my lips and Benny nodded.

The intensity of the hailstorm grew, as did the size of the ice falling. The ground began to disappear beneath it all. Then, above us, was a low grunt, and more rustling.

In the clearing, just outside the cave's mouth, the source of the sound emerged in a flash of white, snorting as she trotted toward a large white-barked aspen, hunting shelter of her own.

"Reaper!" Benny shouted. "Oh, m-man!"

"Easy, easy. Just wait, all right? Wait for the hail to die off. Look, even she has enough sense to stay out of this stuff."

And she did. Reaper hugged the base of the aspen, getting as much shelter as the hovering limbs could afford in the storm.

The ticktack sound of ice bouncing off ice filled the world, and the temperature plummeted even lower. I could even see my own breath. Reaper whinnied, unable to completely protect herself from the stings and pelts of the hailstones.

"She's going to . . . run, right? Any s-second, she's . . . going to run," Benny said. His eyes were anxious, and darted from the horse to the ice all around. "I'll n-never get them b-back."

"She's not going anywhere. Just cool it!" But I knew he was right. I could just feel it. She was here now, but any second that window would close, and she'd spook.

I thought about how Benny had carried me over his shoulder. Taking my burden, and delivering me to safety. He'd saved my life.

"I'm getting them," I said.

"Will?"

But I was already inch-worming out of the cave, hurt shoulder and all. He peered out after me with a mixed look of shock and horror on his face.

"Be . . . careful!"

I got to my knees, then my feet, and scurried out like an ambushed rabbit. I ran in crazy zigzag lines with one hand held over my head, as if that would lessen my chances of being struck. I felt like I was playing dodge-em in the streets back home. I have to give Reaper credit. It was a miracle she didn't fly away at the oncoming sight of me. I know I probably would have.

"Go!" Benny yelled, somewhere behind. And I could have sworn I heard the sound of clapping hands.

In less than twenty seconds, I reached her. "Hey there," I said. "You found me, huh? How'd you do it? How'd you know?" I fumbled with the straps of the pack, still tightly fastened behind the saddle. She jumped twice and I thought for sure she would rear up, but she never did. She only swung her large head and sniffed at me, and that was it. "Don't worry, it's okay now. Everything's okay, we're going back." Down at the bottom of the drenched leather pack was a little tin box.

"I got 'em!" I yelled. "I got 'em, Benny!"

"Hurry!"

I reached my good arm around Reaper's neck and planted a kiss into her wet hair. "Sit tight." The hailstones poured down as if angels above were firing bullets of ice onto the world. It was that quick and that hard.

I stuffed the Sucrets tin into my jeans pocket, and ran back up the slope. Halfway up, halfway toward safety, I caught Benny's eye. For only a brief moment, I saw a joy and excitement in those eyes that I had never seen before. For just that instant, nothing bad had ever happened in his life. No handicap, no Frank Kroft, nothing. Only the radiant smile, the wide eyes. Pelted by sheets of hail, I smiled back at him.

I stumbled at the entrance, and python arms snapped outward, and yanked me inside. I started laughing, in spite of everything else, and threw the box of jacks at him.

"Thanks . . . Will," he said. "You're my friend."

"I'm your friend." I fought to catch my breath.

Outside, the ice covered the forest floor. Loud snaps accompanied the coming-from-everywhere ripping noise as tree branches were broken from their trunks.

I thought I heard my name, somewhere, out in the wind, in the ice. I picked up my head, but never heard it again. Only the storm, I thought. Only the ice.

I didn't even notice the storm was over until Benny said something. I looked out and saw he was right. It had finally run its course, but not before completely covering the world in a frozen layer of slush.

"What do we do now, Will?"

"I don't know." I tried to give an optimistic smile, but succeeded only in a half effort. "I don't know."

Outside the cave and down the slope, Reaper let out a low grunt.

"Just us now . . . Will. Just you and me. Not right. M-Mickey should be here."

"Yeah. I know." We crawled out from the cave, and I felt the world drip over me. It already felt hopeless.

"Wasn't . . . supposed to be this way," Benny said.

I tried to ignore the shooting pain in my shoulder as I sloughed my way through the ice toward Reaper. "Nothing was supposed to be this way, Benny. But I'm glad you're here with me right now."

"Yuh. Glad, too . . . Will. And h-her." He looked to the horse—the one that had changed his life forever. "Glad she's here." I felt a lump in my stomach at that.

I unwound Reaper's reins from the branches. "Ready to go home, girl? You know the way, don't you? You can take us back." She nudged me with her snout, air whooshing out of her nostrils. It was the first time I had ever referred to the ranch as home, and I almost took it back, but I didn't. "Come on, Lunch. We have a long way to go."

❖ ❖ ❖

THE WOODS WERE SILENT EXCEPT FOR THE SOUND OF CRUNCHING hailstones underneath Reaper's hoofs. Nothing around us felt alive. There were no birds, no insects, no animals. There was no breeze, only cold, stale air. It was like the inside of a funeral home.

Benny sat behind me on Reaper. In the silence of our surroundings, I heard his breathing very distinctly. Reaper slowed more and more often. I felt the muscles in her back twitch, felt the rub of the slipping saddle with each hoof step.

Benny's breathing turned sharply into a low whisper. "Will. I don't feel good."

"You going to be sick? Want me to stop?"

"No. It's s-something else. Will. Something here . . . making me not feel g-good." His voice was choppier.

"What is it?" I trusted Benny's instincts. Maybe more than I did my own. There was something about him, after his accident. Something different besides the way he looked or how his mind worked now. Whatever it was, it was special. "Are we going right?" I asked. "Should we turn around?" I looked back, and saw empty eyes. Sad eyes, as if he'd just been told an awful secret, but he only shook his head.

"D-Don't know," he said. "Guess keep going . . . the way you think. Be caref . . . careful."

I could have turned around then. Could have gone in any direction. But we rode on.

We ate hailstones before leaving the cave, for water, but I was still thirsty. And I was hungrier than I could ever remember; with each hundred yards, my stomach rumbled, taking my mind off my shoulder.

The woods were so still and frozen they made me feel paranoid. It felt like the trees watched our every move. I was about to tell Benny this very thing, when I noticed a clearing up ahead, filled with speckled sunlight and surrounded by reaching pines. Something was in one of the trees.

"Oh, shit," I said.

"T-Turn ar . . . around. Will, t-turn around."

It was a body. It dangled from the end of a rope fastened ridiculously high in a giant ponderosa. And I knew I couldn't just turn around and leave because in my mind it was Mickey.

"*Wiiiill,*" Benny whispered.

"I've gotta see," I said. "I gotta see him."

I felt like someone was squeezing my heart as we neared the tree, and the body. Slowly, it became more distinguishable. And then, it wasn't Mickey. Why had I thought that? It wasn't a boy at all. It was a man, hanging dead and upside down by his legs and feet.

"Oh . . . no," Benny whispered again, as Reaper took us into the clearing. She stopped just below the pine.

It was Frank Kroft. He'd been shot in two places—the chest, the crotch—and hung grotesquely at the end of a rope that looped above even higher branches. A new breeze drifted through and began to sway the body, and I felt close to being sick.

"How did they hang him so high?" I asked.

Benny looked away. "C-Can't look at him!"

"How's anybody going to even get him down?" I whispered.

"We should go, Will. Sh-Should go."

Benny was right; we needed to go. There was nothing we could do, anyway. The clearing itself felt haunted, and dead, and not just because of the body hanging in the tree.

Silas Green's voice cut both through the air and my heart at the same moment.

"Hello, William Sheppard."

The cocking of the .45's hammer was loud and pronounced; I swear the noise bounced off the tree bark around us. How did he know we'd find the clearing? How did they plan it? And there was only one answer: they didn't know. They couldn't have. It was fate, or dumb luck. Either way, it didn't matter.

"Where's Church?" Silas asked. "I wanted to say hi to him personally."

"We split up," I said. "He's probably back at the ranch by now, sending help."

Silas's sarcastic eyes skated around the woods. "Yeah, sure," he said, securing a coil of rope to his belt. "Doesn't matter. Don't give a shit."

He motioned his head to Frank Kroft, hanging in the branches. "What do you think? Eddie didn't really like it, but I think it's fine work."

At the mention of his name, Eddie Tokus dropped his eyes to the ground. He looked ashamed, and I wondered if something had happened between them, an argument, maybe. I was amazed at the constant control Silas held over Eddie. Here he was, taking orders from a guy who had ripped his ear clean off. He looked like an obedient dog, one that had been kicked into submission since birth. Even so, Eddie was in over his head, and I think he knew it.

Maybe I can get to him, I thought. It was worth a shot. "Okay, Silas. You got us. Now what?"

Silas Green lowered his rifle and grinned. "Now, we play."

"ALL RIGHT, DUMMY," SILAS SAID WITH A TOOTHY GRIN. "YEAH, YOU know I'm talking to you, don't you? How're you at climbing trees?"

Benny looked up, confused. "I—I d-d . . . don't know."

"You duh duh duh don't know?" Silas laughed. Eddie joined in, but in a softer way. "I want you to go let that motherfucker down. You go up and let him loose. He's ready to come down, I think."

Benny turned to the tree and his eyes doubled.

"Why are you doing this?" I asked.

His voice boomed. "All you need to do is keep your mouth shut! Think you can handle that, Sheppard?"

Benny swung his head left to right. "I c-can't do that. Can't, no sir, I can't!"

Silas pushed the rifle's muzzle into Benny's neck. "Go on, Lunch. Climb that bastard. Climb it before I shoot you dead."

Benny looked back to the tree, then back to us. I could only watch with sympathetic eyes. He nodded, and faced the pine. It had heavy branches that hung low and would make for an easy climb if he were careful. I was sure Benny was scared of heights, though, and his climb would be anything but easy.

"You're a real asshole," I said.

Silas winked at me, and held his gun steady.

I stood in the shadows of the trees, next to Eddie and Silas. We watched Benny struggle his way up the pine. The thick branches bowed and gave way as Benny Fritch began his slow ascent. Fifteen feet off the ground, his foot slipped, causing him to grasp at random branches in utter panic.

"What are you doing, man?" I spoke softly, not masking my disappointment.

Silas turned and started to open his mouth when he saw I hadn't spoken to him. Eddie couldn't look me in the eye, and instead faced Benny, who recovered from his slip and proceeded another five feet.

I asked again. "What the hell are you even doing here?"

"Shut up," Silas said, turning his eyes and his gun back to Benny.

Eddie was quiet, but he bit his lip, and shook his head back and forth. Then, he glanced at me, but only for a moment.

"You don't have to do this, Eddie. It doesn't have to be this way. You can—"

Silas rammed the rifle's butt into the side of my head, and I staggered backward. "I said close your mouth!"

The tree limbs above shivered; Benny was nearing Frank's body. A rope was bound around the body's ankles, and stretched taut to the even higher limbs above. The rope's limp end dangled to the ground below. Silas must have used a horse to accomplish the hanging. Either he or Eddie must have climbed to the top, to loop the rope, and then it was just a matter of pulling back on the reins to hoist Frank up. Where was the horse now?

Benny reached the body. It turned listlessly, as though touched by invisible hands. High as it hung, its horror was still plainly visible below. It couldn't be real. I closed my eyes, and realized I could smell the bloody mess.

Silas must have shot Kroft at close range. The damage was obscene, but the chest looked the worst. His body rotated, and I saw that his back was reduced to only a flayed, collapsed mess where the shot exited. Fragments of flesh, bone, and shirt flapped and hung widemouthed. Silas hadn't stopped there. He'd fired what looked to be repeated blasts into the crotch.

I hated Frank Kroft more than I'd ever hated anybody, or anything. And yet I still couldn't look at what was left of him without a sense of pity in my gut. To that point, it was the most horrible thing I'd ever seen.

Benny lurched at the sight and the stench; the body must have been hanging for a considerable time, I guessed, as blood had stained most of the clothing and mixed with the rain in large, brackish puddles below.

"Go on, now," Silas said. "Untie him." He kept the rifle steady.

Benny reached out, grabbed, missed, then grabbed again at Frank's bound legs. He hoisted the lifeless body with a thick arm while reaching for the rope's knot with the other. Benny fumbled with it for moments on end.

"Oh, oh, G-God!" Benny retched, then released the knot. The tree's limbs snapped, and Frank's body fell. It slumped and snagged its way to the ground, bending at incredible extreme angles as it clapped into thick branch after branch. With a final, disturbing thump, the body collapsed to the forest floor. The legs were bent horribly askew and his neck was left twisted too far around. I heard Benny crying high above, repeating one word in the midst of his sobs: *home*.

"NOW IT'S YOUR TURN, WILL," SILAS SAID. "YOUR TURN TO DO ONE thing for me. Then we'll be cool. You do this, you and the idiot can go." He lowered his rifle, wearing an absolutely honest expression on his long, pallid face.

With my eyes still stuck on Benny, who was clearly now having his greatest difficulty climbing down, I said, "What do you want?"

Silas pulled out Frank Kroft's .45. He stretched his arm toward me and for a second, I was sure he would squeeze it off, ending everything right there. Instead, he said, "Take this."

I didn't move a muscle. I couldn't.

"Take this," he said, "and put the one shell that's in it inside the head of that white bitch over there."

It took a second before I understood what he wanted. "No. Why would you want me to do that?"

"Because you care about her so damn much," he said. "That's it, baby."

"She's just a stupid horse, man. What's that going to prove? You already ended it with Frank. I know the things he did. He got you, too, didn't he? But you took care of it and we can all go now. Come on, man."

I guess I struck a nerve, mentioning Frank that way, and he flinched. "You don't know a damn thing about it," he said. "The hell do you know? He never went to you! So shut your fucking mouth and take the gun. Then we'll be square, Hopalong."

Benny cried out, again almost losing his footing. He was still twenty-five feet up, and his descent slowed to a conservative crawl.

"How do you know I won't put the shell in your head instead?" I asked.

Silas smiled at that, laughed even. "I guess I don't, do I? But think about this. I've got my gun trained on you the whole time. Eddie has his looking at Lunch Meat up in the tree. Now, you'll only have one bullet in your chamber. You'll have to turn it on me quick. Plus, what if you miss?"

Eddie raised his rifle to Benny.

Silas tossed the .45 to where I stood, and clicked the safety off his rifle, pointing it at my head.

I bent, and took the gun in my hand. Just yards away, Reaper was roped to a tree. She looked at me and swished her tail.

The situation was surreal. I felt absurd even thinking about trusting Silas, but in the end, what else could I do? I said, "I do this . . . and we can go?"

"I promise. Just be smart, Will."

Holding the gun was like holding on to a brick, and it hung limp at my side. I looked from Benny to Eddie, with his rifle aimed. Silas stood like a slab of marble, his rifle trained on my head. I walked to Reaper. She let me reach out and pet her mane, then turned and nudged me. My arm blazed at her touch, but I ignored it. I focused, tried to accept what I was about to do, but every nerve in my body screamed in protest.

Benny. I said his name again and again in silence, justifying my actions. Benny dies . . . I probably die, too. Or this. This one single act, this brutal execution. This animal who has trusted me, and me alone, for so long now.

"I'm sorry, girl. I'm so sorry. I . . . I love you." Then I couldn't talk; the words became thick and lodged in the back of my throat as tears welled.

I looked back, my eyes searching for any other way, any possible escape. Silas's rifle was pointed steady at my head, Eddie's up toward Benny. Lunch, who was carefully finding his way down to join me. Then we would go. Then we would go home.

Hot breath flashed against my palm and I rubbed her nose, stroked her snout. "I'm so sorry." I was crying as I closed my eyes, I can remember that very clearly. I held the gun to her head. She regarded it as of no threat, nudging it as she might a silly plaything. "So sorry." The trigger eased back, back, back and I clinched my jaw, waiting for the blasting violence.

The clap of gunfire burned my ears, my hand flung in response. There was a single cry from her, and it sounded so awfully *human.* Tears fell quietly, but I didn't lose control. Reaper fell to the ground and died. The shot had entered her brain, and she simply was no more.

I still remember how silent everything suddenly became. In a place of abundant life, there was nothing. Only the ringing in my ears, and the way her body sounded as it crumpled to the ground. I heard it again, and again; my mind refused to let it go. I threw the gun to Silas's feet in disgust. My heart hammered and my ears rang. Eddie scampered to retrieve the pistol and shoved it into his tight pant waist.

The smile that broadened on Silas's face was what nearly got me killed. I fought every urge to run at him in a blind frenzy, tearing his eyes out, biting off his ears, any savage thing I could humanly think of.

"Thank you, Will," he said, and swung his rifle up to the trees and fired a single shot.

CHAPTER

forty-six

"WI—" WAS ALL BENNY SAID BEFORE HE FELL INTO THE ARMS OF the pine. Strength all but left my body as I watched him plummet to the ground in jerks and twists, knocking and tearing against the sharp branches of the tree.

"You bastard! Oh, you fucking bastard!!" I stumbled in crazed disbelief to Benny's side. He was still alive, struggling to draw breath in unbearable fits. I turned him on his back. Cuts and scratches lined his face, neck, and arms. His shirt was torn. A gash raked across his forehead, a piece of skin dangled over his left eye.

But his chest. Dark red seeped wider and wider from the single bullet hole. Benny lurched, clawed at his throat. In the time it took for him to fall, both shoes were ripped from his feet by the grasping branches.

"No! Oh, God, Jesus. Oh, please." I cradled his head in my arms as he kicked out again and again with his feet.

"You know what they say. The bigger they are . . ." Silas grinned, resting the stock of his rifle against his shoulder. "Man, you should see your face right now! It's like you really believed me!"

"Will . . ." Benny whispered in jagged, shallow breaths. "I'm sorry, Will."

"No no no. Don't talk, Benny. Just be quiet, okay? Just be quiet, stay still."

"You're my friend, Will. Right? Benny's friend?"

Before I could answer, I felt a cold hand grasp my neck, pinching around my collar, yanking my body backward so hard that my jaw jerked into my chest. My shoulder exploded in pain, and the trees spun above me. Trees, and Eddie's rifle, pointed directly at me.

"Hey," Silas said. "Hey, you knew I took your mom's picture all along. You knew it, right?" He lowered his voice and leaned into me. "You wanna know what I did with it?"

I could hear Benny dying. I could hear his fingers digging into the dirt.

"I jerked off to it," Silas said. "Every night! Jerked off *on* it! Ha! What a douche you are, Sheppard. Truly."

He turned to Benny and sent a deep kick into his side. Then another to his head. "Did you know I used to have a gang, in New York? Man, I've known a Frank Kroft all my life. Different versions of him. And I grew up with a Frank Kroft in my gang. He took me in, taught me lots of things."

I was watching Benny, in horror, but saw Silas's history file in my head. A guy named Darrell Dugan. Silas, with a curling iron.

He went on. "One day I got tired of DD coming at me. So I got revenge. But still, that guy taught me lots of shit. Hell, when I was seven, he taught me to throw down my bike and dislodge the chain. I could take it off and wrap it around my fist in all of ten seconds. But that tree just bested me because Benny's fall only took seven by my count." He turned back to Benny.

"You shot him," I stammered, tears falling down my cheeks.

"Yeah." Silas shrugged. "And look at you now, Lunch."

He hunched over Benny, and placed his hands onto his bleeding chest. "Guess I'm just finishing what that horse should have done long ago." Silas wrapped his smeared hands in an almost motherly way around Benny's cut face. "This is your blood, Benny. You should wear it proudly."

Benny only shook, struggling to gasp at each measure of air. His mouth opened, closed, and opened again.

"Now. It's finished." Silas took out a pocketknife, opened the blade from the sheath, and with focus, punched it into Benny's side, leaving its stock jutting crudely out of his body like a broken rib. "You lay here and think about them apples," he said. Benny screamed out with what breath he had left.

They held me there. Held me, and made me watch my friend die. I was on my knees. I put my face into the ground, weeping, screaming, grabbing fistfuls of pine needles. My face was red, and soaked with tears.

They finally released me, and I fell forward, onto Benny. My beautiful friend who never should have been there in the first place. "Benny, Benny, oh, God, Benny."

His eyes—those icy blue eyes—remained fixed on the tree branches above, and I reached out to close them. In the movies, dead eyes always close when another person rubs their palm over them. But in the real world they just creep back up. Not in a quick way, but slowly, and they stare at you in a way that makes you wonder if they're really dead at all.

A thin whine pursed through the air, and I realized it was coming from me as I continued to both weep and be strong at the same time. My lower lip trembled and snot hung from my nose.

The jacks. I reached and removed the Sucrets box from Benny's pocket before Silas took even that away from me. Whoever found him—whoever took him back to the ranch, would find the box and just throw it away. I couldn't let that happen. I wouldn't. It's hard for me to explain why, but that little box of jacks deserved better than that. I knew I might not make it either, but I was still alive and, dammit, I'd hold on to those jacks as long as I could. They were *Benny's* jacks. No. I guess that wasn't quite true, was it? Before that, they were once Todd's. Maybe I recognized that, too. And thought if I ever made it out, I'd return them, someday, to their original owner.

Somewhere, through the trees and across the sloping ridges, a gunshot ripped. It was close, maybe a mile or two away, and followed by a faint shout. There was no doubt it was directed toward us. It was a search party. Guards, from the ranch.

"Get up, faggot," Silas said, kicking me in the ribs. "Let's go."

"No. Please, man. Just leave me here." I couldn't look away from Benny.

"Not your decision to make." He pulled me to my feet and shoved me ahead. "Can't stay here anymore, now can we?"

As he and Eddie led me away, I cast a final look to my friend. He deserved better than to be that broken body before me. I had no choice but to feel responsible. "Benny! Benny, I'm sorry!"

"Open your mouth again and I'll shut it for you," Silas said.

"Oh, God! Help me!" I screamed.

Something crashed into my head and streaks of white fire filled my vision, but I did not fall. Behind me, I heard a bolt snap and felt the muzzle of a rifle between my shoulder blades.

"Once more, Will. Damn, that would be fine, just once more!"

I turned away from Benny Fritch, and I stumbled on.

WE WALKED FOR WHAT SEEMED LIKE AGES, OVER STEEP RIDGES AND through a wardrobe of outstretched branches. My entire arm burned now, not just my hurt shoulder. Inside, I already felt dead. I just wanted to go home, then remembered there was nothing for me there, either. I was nearing the point where thoughts drowned in my mind, suggesting maybe it wouldn't be so bad to just let Silas Green shoot me. But I walked. One foot, then the next.

"Where're we going, man?" Eddie asked, breaking the silence. "What's next? You said you had a plan."

Silas said nothing.

Eddie picked up his pace. "Hey, I don't want no more part of this, man. I think I'm done."

"You can leave when I tell you to leave," Silas said. His face was long, his expression smug. His shirt clung to his chest and one long, pale arm hung heavy at his side. The other was wrapped tight around the rifle. "We're not done."

I pressed. "He's going to kill me, Eddie. And you know what? After that, he's not just going to rip off another ear, he's going to kill you. That's what guys like him do. They stab you in the back."

Eddie looked at me with a shroud of disbelief. There was something in his eyes, though. I had him thinking. Had him worried.

"Sheppard, I'll tell you something. It's not going to bother me one shit to put you in the ground."

"So what's stopping you, then?"

He stopped, and raised the rifle to my head. "You have no idea how it angered me to know Church wasn't with you yesterday. That was so damned frustrating, Will. I wanted him there so badly."

"What about Eddie?" I asked, grasping at anything to stall him. My nerves fired, my adrenaline pumped. And, just like that, I didn't want to die. Maybe Mickey was alive, maybe I'd see Miss Little again. High above, a songbird called out from the treetops. The sweet smell of pine was rampant, and the breeze blew it into my nose and into my soul.

"Eddie isn't any of your concern," Silas said. "One-eared Eddie isn't anyone's concern." He seemed to take pleasure in the act of drawing a slow-motion aim.

I winced. My body shrieked for me to run. Dodge left. Dodge right. Rush Silas. But my feet wouldn't budge. There was nowhere to go. I waited for the shot, even as my eyes tried to find hope.

Behind him, Eddie flipped his rifle around so that he held its barrel firmly in both hands, the way a guy might grip a baseball bat. He lifted it high, and as the songbird in the trees called once more, Eddie swung. The rifle's stock blasted into Silas's head, making a solid connection.

Silas fell, dropped his gun, and writhed in pain. Eddie was quick. Damn, he was quick, faster than me. Before I even had the thought, he swiped at the loose rifle with a pudgy hand, snapping it up and pinning it underneath one meaty arm as he took aim again with the other gun.

"Mickey's out there, Will," Eddie said. "Somewhere. He got hit, but he's okay. I only aimed for his shoulder. Silas thinks I killed him, but I didn't." He stepped back. He was white as a bleached sheet. "I may be a lot of things, but I ain't like him. I ain't no murderer." With that, he turned away, and trounced clumsily through the trees with a rifle tucked underneath each sweaty armpit and a pistol in his pants waist.

"Son of a bitch!" Silas tried to rise to one knee, still groggy.

I wasted no time, rounding a kick into Silas's chest with all my strength. Something snapped as I did, and his agony brought a smile to my face.

Another kick. As my foot connected once more into his chest, he darted an arm around my shin and yanked backward, flinging my body down toward him.

"You want yours? Tell me how it feels," he said.

Pain blazed from my head to my feet. My spine lurched upward, my back hyperextending. Something was wrong with my back, my side. My flesh felt like it was on fire. A knife. He had a knife, and he'd sliced me with it.

"No." I pushed off, my hands flinging back, searching for the wound. I couldn't tell how bad it was, I could only see my hands come away with lots of blood.

He stood up, but not easily. I *had* broken one of his ribs, maybe even two.

I was defenseless. I backed into a tree and pain flared at the touch. I couldn't fight him with that knife in his hand. He probably grew up fighting with one. I'd lose my life. My instincts told me, yelled at me, to take flight. I could outrun him. As much as I was hurting and bleeding—I could still outrun him. The new wound on my back was bad, but not bad enough to make me pass out. These thoughts left my mind entirely after what he did next.

"I'm finished dicking with you," Silas said. He flung the knife to the ground, sticking the blade near his shoe, and pulled out an item that had been lodged in the waist of his pants behind his back. It was another pistol.

"No! How'd you get that?" I knew, though, even as I said it. It was the one Mickey ran off with. Eddie must have gone to retrieve it, then given it to Silas. He cocked back the hammer, and I threw my arms up in front of my face.

The more I think about that moment with Silas, the fuzzier it gets.

I shouted to myself, silently, inside my head. But it wasn't my voice that I heard; it was Benny's. The memory of that voice hasn't faded; it has remained a constant. The voice screamed my name.

Click.

It should have been the sound of a bullet firing into my head, and even so, a deep shiver pulsed up my spine and into my brain. My stomach turned, and bile seeped up the back of my throat.

Silas slapped at the .45 with his open palm.

That was all I needed before instincts took over. I ran. I ran so fast that I nearly ended my escape before it began, almost colliding face-first into the bark of a maple. I flung my hands out, pushed away from the tree, and hauled ass.

Behind me came another collection of curses. The mountain was not sympathetic to my cause. I left in a direction that forced me to scale a high slope. Pine needles flew from underneath my worn sneakers with each clumsy, racing step. Cresting the slope's peak, I saw nothing but downhill on the other side.

He was on the run, now, chasing me. I heard him scream, "What are you gonna do? Night's coming, you gonna run in the dark, bleeding all over the place?"

I knew he still had the knife. The semiautomatic, though, I didn't know. Maybe it was useless and he'd thrown it away. I could only hope. I ran to the brink of collapse. The back of my shirt, now mostly blood soaked, was growing cool in the early evening air.

There was no chance he could have kept up, not with busted ribs. I shifted direction four times, and after what felt like an hour of running, jogging, and just trying not to collapse, I finally stopped at the brink of a dry creek bed. Silas was right about one thing. Night was coming. The sun dipped behind the trees and the shadows of the woods grew longer. Night was coming.

The last time I stopped, I nearly took a nosedive on an overturned tree. It was thick, and a crisp scorch ran the length of the bark. I heard nothing in the fading evening but my own pulled gasps. The creek bed just ahead contained large, jutting rocks that would provide a moment's shelter. I hobbled toward them and made up my frantic mind to pause only long enough to catch my breath and drink from the creek.

Lying there, images flashed across my eyes until they burned. Closing them made no difference, and I saw John Church anyway. I saw Coop, holding a full house and laughing, laughing. And before I realized I was slipping away, I even saw Benny hanging from the wrong end of a rope, just dangling in the night breeze. Blood pooled at his feet, and was the color of fresh ink. Exhaustion has a way of creeping up on you, no matter how you try and fend it off.

CHAPTER
forty-seven

I'VE NO IDEA HOW LONG I SLEPT. ONLY THAT I AWOKE CONFUSED, and in searing pain. It was dark now, and in the patches of sky between the trees were stars that shone so bright, it looked as though they'd just been freshly placed in the heavens.

Paranoia gripped my thoughts, and I turned in all directions. What had woken me? A wind rolled down the mountainside and across the creek bed. Maybe it was only the swaying branches of the surrounding trees. A thin voice whispered a different reason, though. Not the wind. Even while sleeping, I had heard something.

It was him. He was up to the embankment, hiding somewhere, his gun was working and now pointed directly at me. I fought to stay collected among these thoughts, but felt close to panic. Crouching behind one of the larger rocks, I felt safer, and tried to harbor any confidence left in myself.

There was a low noise. A crack of wood.

If I scrambled across the creek bed, I ran the risk of twisting an ankle on the floor of rocks. If I ran the other way, toward the embankment, I'd just give my enemy a closer target.

I decided to take my chances over the rocks. On the other side of the bed was a shallower rise in elevation that ran upward into a blanket of trees, too thick to see past with only the light of the moon and the stars above. If I could make it to the trees, I had a chance. If he had the gun, and if it worked, then I only had a prayer.

With breath held, I pushed off, and bounded into the rushing creek. Nerves tightened and my body flushed as I tried to be both quick and graceful. Then, something broke through the brush and trees behind me, and looking back through the moonlight, I saw him.

I guessed the pistol didn't work, or he would have used it. I suddenly wondered if he'd tried to fire it while I lay there asleep. Still running, I turned once more and saw the buck knife, its blade gleaming in the moonlight.

He made no noise, barreling toward the creek. No yells, no screams. He just ran. I saw him favor his side, saw he had a distinct limp, and took what little hope I could from that.

Almost across the creek bed, my foot slipped and my ankle buckled. I cried out, but not because of the pain. I was furious at myself for not being more careful. Adrenaline coursed through my body and I buried the pain, running on the foot in spite of it. There would be time to nurse it later.

I cleared the rocks and ran to the cover of the trees. Most of the moonlight died in the crisscross of needles above my head. Under this cover, I ran with arms outstretched to keep from slamming into the indifferent trunks.

I heard Silas breathing, somewhere behind. He was gaining. I tried to push faster, but it was just a matter of time before my leg went out. In my mind, Benny's voice whispered, *"Hurry! Don't stop."*

The trees thinned suddenly at the base of another incline. There was nowhere to go but up. I grabbed at tree limbs, pulling myself to the top of the hill. I was halfway there when I looked back and saw him.

"There you are," he yelled. "You're dead, you know? Hope you know that." Knife in hand, Silas started up the incline behind me.

I fell. My fucking foot slipped, and I fell. I bit my tongue when I landed, and blood filled my mouth. This time I heard my own voice: *"Get up! Move your ass!"*

I forced myself to my feet and somehow reached the top of the ridge—more trees, more darkness. I ran into the gloom with no hope left at all.

My ears throbbed and I was sucking air, each gasp more painful than the last. My ankle and leg flared and the cut across my back was bleeding again. But I ran for my life.

Something happened at that point that made me believe there is a God in this great universe. You can play off certain things, but sometimes, there's simply no other explanation. Luck can only be so blind.

I tripped. Over something heavy and thick, I tripped, and planted a nosedive immediately into the ground. I rolled hard over my busted ankle, and heard something snap. I either broke the bone or tore apart the tendon.

Then someone called out my name. It was a hushed, weak voice. And it was filled with excitement.

I tripped over Mickey Baines. Mickey, who was still alive, if barely.

"He's coming!" I hissed. "I can't run!"

He nodded, like he understood exactly. Reaching out with weary hands, he grabbed a stone and flung it to me with a grunt. "Stay still!" he said, and put his head back to the ground.

I reached and grabbed the rock. It was damn heavy, and I wondered how he'd had the strength to throw it.

Branches rustled and heavy footsteps crunched. Silas Green crested the ridge. Through the thin darkness, he saw me, and ran faster. Knife in hand, prey in sight.

Just as I did, Silas tripped over Mickey Baines. Only this time, Mickey sat up and wrapped both arms around Silas's legs.

"The *fuck*?" was all he had time to yell as he came to a tumbling halt just before me.

I've read there are times in a person's life when bare instincts can consume you, forcing you to do things you'd otherwise never do. That's a true statement; I can testify. Without thinking, I struck. The rock came down easily into Silas's face. It came down again, and again. With each blow, there was a distinct crunching sound, and I knew it was his face—his nose, his jaw—breaking. He pulled back his lips to scream, and there were no teeth; there was only blood.

He screamed. At first in rage, then in pain, and then he stopped screaming altogether. With the rock in my trembling hands, ready to come down again, I stopped. I looked at it, saw that it was coated and smeared with Silas's blood, as were my hands. His eye was cut, mashed in, and pointed in a skewed direction, unlike the other, that was fixed on me behind a gloss of red. But all of that wasn't why I stopped.

I stopped because I noticed he was still breathing. I remember thinking that with one more strike, I could stop that breathing, take it away for good. But as much as I wanted to, in the end, I couldn't do it. I heard the voice again, in my head. Benny's voice: *"Enough."*

"Enough. It's over." The rock slipped out of my hand and hit the ground with a weighted thump. Silas Green slumped into unconsciousness. I should have had the balls to kill him. I was absolutely disgusted that I hadn't been able to.

"He has rope," Mickey said, looking more worn out than ever. "Tie him to a tree, leave him for the others to find."

"Mickey . . . I—" Tears began to well, and I couldn't even think of the words.

He looked from Silas to me. "Where is he? Where's Benny!"

When I said nothing, the painful horror of what he already suspected began to sink in.

"No," Mickey said. "Oh, no." He lowered his head into his hands. "Oh, God, oh, no. Not Benny." Tears fell down the sides of his flushed face.

He grieved, while the monster who took our friend lay bleeding at our sides. Mickey rubbed his palms into his eyes, and sniffed.

He said, "I've . . . lost some blood. That bastard, Eddie, caught me in the shoulder. Think I even . . . passed out for a while. Been stumbling and resting my way from tree to tree. It's hard to breathe, Will. But I'm here. I found this lake, it was my saving grace. Would 'a died of thirst if I hadn't found it."

I looked past him and saw ripples of moonlight not far from where we were. I hadn't noticed until just that moment. The darkness and the trees clouded it away from me. "You don't know how good it is to see you, Mickey."

"Good . . . to be seen. Just wish . . ."

"Yeah."

We took the coil of rope from Silas's belt, then dragged him to the nearest tree. As we threw him against the rough trunk bark, he groaned, but only once. The rope was long enough to wrap across his chest, under his arms, and around the trunk more than three times. We also bound his wrists and feet. Mickey used the buck knife, the one intended to cut my throat, to cut the rope instead.

Mickey dropped to the forest floor, breathing deeply. He looked so pale and tired, and yet he persisted. He looked at me with small, stony eyes.

"I need water. From the lake. Help a guy out?" He pulled a work-boot from his left foot, and held it out with a trembling hand. I took it, then he dropped to one elbow, and then flat on his back the way one might casually gaze at the stars and heavens above. That's when it hit me. *Nothing* would be the way it was before. The blood on Benny's face—his upturned eyes—tortured my soul. But I still had Mickey. Through it all, I still had him.

"You bet. Just take it easy. Everything's . . ." I was going to say *"Everything's cool,"* just as an expression, but nothing was cool. Nothing would be all right. God, how had I almost said it aloud?

Mickey understood. He understood perfectly, and just nodded, closing his eyes. I turned and left.

CHAPTER
forty-eight

THE CRISP WIND SWEPT THROUGH THE TIMBER AND INTO MY FACE; it felt cleansing. I lost sight of the water as I dipped into the trees, hobbling on one good foot, a twisted or even broken ankle, a cut back, and a gunshot wound in my shoulder. But for Mickey I would have walked a mile.

There were shadows, rocks, and fallen branches everywhere, but I finally arrived at the lake's edge. The water was cold, and I drank until my stomach felt bloated and heavy.

I don't know how long the thing was standing there, back in the trees. I sensed it watching me, like the cliché, but it's true. It felt like someone dragged a shaving razor up the back of my neck, and I just knew. It was hidden, and still, the way a predator crouches and waits for the right moment. When it came forward, long, scratchy juniper branches bent and dragged across its body. From the depths of my mind, bloody and impossible images thrust themselves forward: Mickey was dead. Silas had risen, was coming for me yet again. I felt my bladder release and the flow of urine stung the open scratches on my legs. My heart nearly stopped.

What emerged was giant, and black, all over. So clean and dark that even to this day I promise you that it *shined.* I was just a kid, only fourteen, but my next thought was that it was a ghost, or demon, come to claim me. For bringing Benny into the woods.

I told myself, whispered it aloud, that it was just one of the horses we set out to find. After all I'd been through, here she was. A solid black mare. The prize we all hoped to find together, just days ago. An insatiable anger welled inside of me. Anger at Silas, for being who he was, for breaking the fence, letting the horses escape. Anger at myself, for taking responsibility for Benny. Anger at John Church for deserting us. Even anger at the horses, for leaving, making us follow them in the first place.

I kneeled to the lake's shore, and came up with small stones in my hands. The first one missed, and went into the trees. The second one struck her in the neck. The third, in her ribs. "Get out!" I screamed. "Get out of here!" I began crying. "Why did you have to leave! Why the hell did you leave us?" I bent to pluck more rocks from the ground, but by the time I was up again, the horse was gone. I never saw it again. I think there is a certain peace in that.

I DIPPED MICKEY'S BOOT INTO THE LAKE, AND LET THE COLD WATER fill to the leather brim before I limped back into the trees. As I neared the clearing, I saw him, outlined by the pale light of the moon. He sat still, near the tree, arms propped on bent knees.

"Mickey," I said, out of breath, giving in to my pain and exhaustion. I bent over, sure I was going to be sick, but nothing came. I reached out and put a hand on his shoulder.

He was crying.

Then I saw the buck knife, lying on the ground next to him. Its blade no longer shined in the moonlight, no longer reflected a clean surface. It was smeared in a dark coat of . . . something. It matched the color of Mickey's hands.

"I had to, Will," Mickey sobbed, shoulders bucking up and down in fits. "I had to do it. He killed Benny. So I fucking had to."

"What did you do?" I whispered, but Mickey didn't answer. He just sat there, and wept. Silas Green was exactly where I'd left him, bound to the tree trunk. His head still down, chin to chest. Only now there was blood.

I reached out with a shaking hand and wrapped my fingers into Silas's wavy hair. His head was hot, and sweaty, and though I already knew what I would see, I brought his face up into my own. I knew because of how easy his head pulled back.

Mickey had cut his throat.

From jaw to jaw, his neck was opened in a single dark thread. Blood trickled down his opened neck, and I caught my breath when I saw his dead eyes staring into mine. I let go, and his head once again lolled forward onto his soaked chest.

Mickey broke down, harder than before, head in his hands. "Why did he die, Will? Oh, shit! Why did Benny have to fucking *die*?"

I crumbled to the ground beside him, and held Mickey with what remaining strength I had. In a selfish way I was glad. Mickey had finished what I could not.

CHAPTER
forty-nine

THE VOICES CAME JUST HOURS LATER; THEY GREW UNTIL WE WERE certain they weren't only in our minds—ghosts in the night, coming to claim us. They were the voices of a search party. We called out, yelling with thin shouts through the trees until at long last they found us.

The group came across Joe Addison first, still strapped to Aaron Gumm's horse. He was on that mare for two days and, miraculously, was still alive. Aaron Gumm never made it. Almost a hundred yards from where they found Addison and the horse, they found Aaron, lying facedown at the base of a tree. There was a hole the size of a football in his back. I can only guess that Silas got to them the night Aaron left us. I don't know why they didn't finish off Joe Addison; they probably thought he was already dead.

We told the men about John Church abandoning us in the mountains on horseback. We told them that Eddie Tokus was still out there, somewhere, maybe still running with his gut bouncing up and down. That was the last thing I remember saying before waking up in a new day, in a new place, and feeling waves of loneliness all over again.

❖ ❖ ❖

I AWOKE THINKING I WAS STILL ON THE MOUNTAIN. MICKEY WAS SOBbing, repeatedly wiping his hands on the white sheets of his bed, and all of a sudden I found myself wishing Silas's gun hadn't misfired. I didn't want any of the memories of what happened. I closed my eyes in the darkness of the infirmary, hoping to sink into the depths of the night, sink down and away from everything I knew.

Next to my bed, on the counter, was the Sucrets box. Miss Little must have found it in my clothes. I opened the tin. Inside were five jacks. I took one out and ran it between my fingers, selfishly taking a strange, hollow comfort from it. I tried to block the images that kept returning. Benny—lying broken and cut underneath a giant tree, his body shot, and his eyes stuck wide open. Silas—tied to a tree with his neck sliced open like a grinning red mouth.

I opened my eyes and focused instead on Mickey. He had taken a bullet in the lower shoulder, just missing an artery as well as his left lung. As much as I detested him, I was thankful Eddie Tokus was at least a good aim if nothing else. Besides the infected gunshot wound, I'd only broken my ankle and sustained a pretty good laceration along my back.

Throughout those few days, Miss Little did the only thing she could do for us, besides her duties—she grieved. With us, and for us. She held our hands and sat with us, not saying anything because there was nothing to say. Sometimes she only mouthed the words, her glassy eyes staring into a place that was somewhere else entirely. Other times flat, low whispers escaped her mouth. "My boys. My boys. My beautiful, precious boys."

She could have been thinking of her dead children, but I don't think so. She meant us, all of us. I know that.

WARDEN BARROW CAME, WITH A GUARD, AND MEN IN SUITS I DIDN'T recognize. They wanted to know, word for word, detail by detail, what happened. I'm sure they recorded Joe Addison's own account, but that was only part of the tale. They questioned Mickey and me separately, probably to see if our versions matched up, or whether we were frying up some sort of grand fucking conspiracy. And so I told them. I sounded like I was on autopilot, but I didn't care.

They asked me a lot of questions about John Church. Turns out he never returned to the ranch. Neither I nor anyone else there ever saw him again. Did he die, somehow, up in the mountains? I don't think so. All I can say is this: some people *do* just disappear in this world.

I would never again see Benny, and as it turned out, after only four days back at the infirmary, Mickey was gone, too. First to a hospital, and then to a juvenile ward back east. I never even got to say good-bye. No one ever told me where, exactly, he went. Not even Miss Little knew. So there was no way for us to ever get in touch; the ranch took even that away from both of us. We were left to pick up pieces of ourselves that I felt weren't meant to ever be picked up. Better days were not guaranteed. Only fragments of a hope I'd already given up on.

They took me to a different hospital. The one in nearby Gunnison, the same place they had rushed Benny to after his accident. I wasn't there long, only time enough for them to take plenty of X rays and tell me I was going to be fine. After that, I stayed on the ranch. Alone. And alone was how I felt most of the time.

I visited Miss Little from time to time, but never knew what to say. I resorted to sitting at her table, usually sipping tea, and staring into my cup. Sometimes I just listened to her talk. Usually, that was enough. It became sad for me to see her. I sometimes felt she missed Mickey more than I did. Mostly, I had the feeling she just didn't know how to fix me.

My time passed in a smothered daze, and a storm of depression hung over me for the remaining months I was at the ranch. When my time was up, it was up early. Parole. I'm sure because of everything that had already happened. I was never implicated in any wrongdoings during the ordeal in the mountains, and was told that I no longer represented a threat to society. I wanted to laugh at that, sitting in front of the warden. I don't know why, but I had to stifle giggles like a four-year-old.

When it was time to say good-bye, Miss Little said she wasn't going to cry. She said she'd already shed too many tears, for all of us. She was true to her word, and hugged me in her firm arms. When I made to pull away, she pulled me closer, tighter, and held me until I began to cry into her shoulder. "Do anything you have to do. Just *survive,* child. And remember I love you. If you lock away everything else, never forget I was here and that I loved you."

Warden Barrow gave me a bus ticket bound for Cleveland, Ohio. To Grandpa Jack's. The warden said my grandfather would take me in, be my guardian until I turned eighteen and could go out into the great world on my own. I bawled as the bus carried me away. Does that sound pussy? It's true. I don't care how it sounds. When I came to the ranch, I carried a small picture of my mother in my shirt pocket. Leaving, I took only one thing: Benny's tin box of jacks. I held it tight in my palms as the bus rose and fell into the mountains.

The friends I made at Swope Reformatory are always kept in my heart of hearts, unlocked only at the most private of moments. I'm constantly afraid that just by conjuring them up, those memories might fly away as easily as a flock of blackbirds. And I could never fly after them. I could never bring them back. Then, I'd be left alone. Lost, and never knowing why it is I feel as broken as I do. Can you understand now why I never chose to tell my wife?

CHAPTER *fifty*

MAKING FRIENDS WAS ALWAYS DIFFICULT FOR ME AFTER THAT. A great many things were difficult for me after my time spent on the ranch. For the longest time, I'd wake up at odd times during the night, wondering where all the guys were; or worse, wake up smelling the scent of pine trees.

Grandpa Jack took me in, and I think he suspected I'd been through something traumatic, just because he never asked me about it. Only once did he even touch on the subject. We were sitting in his living room watching *The Andy Griffith Show* when out of nowhere he said, "I did a little time, once. Up in the state reformatory outside Columbus."

I looked at him, not quite knowing what to say, and so I settled on, "I didn't know that."

"I guess it's not something people like to talk about."

I watched Opie Taylor pause on the steps long enough to hug his father, and the two walked arm in arm inside. "Yeah."

I often spent my time in quiet places, thinking. I wondered where Mickey had gone. What he was doing. I can't say why, but there was never any peace in my heart when I thought about him. I hoped and prayed to find him someday, and that he would be well. I hoped he was making it.

I actually wrote a letter and mailed it out to Swope—can you believe that? It's true. I addressed it to Miss Little, and asked about Mickey, if there was anyone there who could help me find him. I waited for months, checking the mailbox each day. But in the end, nothing ever came, and I guess I finally just stopped checking at some point.

I went through school, did just enough to keep from failing out. Largely, I just didn't care. I went into the army after graduating, and immediately wished I hadn't. But I stuck it out and, by the grace of God, eventually fell into a decent line of work.

Before I knew it, I took a piss one morning and stood in awe at the middle-aged person in the bathroom mirror. I guess that's something most folks do at some point in their lives. I was fifty-one.

Not long after, I received a call one night. It was snowing outside, yet again, and I thought about having to shovel the walk the next morning as I put the receiver up to my ear. I almost threw the phone at the wall when I realized who it was: a ghost.

But instead of flinging the phone, I simply whispered, "Is it you?"

There was a pause, and I was so afraid he had hung up.

"I just needed to hear your voice . . ." His own voice was deeper, but the same. It was familiar.

"Mickey . . . It's been so long. We never even got to say good-bye."

"Yeah," he said. "We never did."

"I looked for you, for a while. Always wondered. How'd you find me?"

"I can get anything, Will. Remember that?" His voice was both like a stranger's and a brother's, but hearing it took me back. It was a voice that knew all my secrets.

"Most days," I said, "I try hard not to remember anything. You know?"

"I know."

I closed my eyes and imagined we were at Swope, sitting on a cot. It felt like ages ago, probably because it was.

"Do you ever dream about it, Will? Do you ever wake up from that place?"

A tear welled and slid down my cheek. "Yes. More than I care to say. It eats at me. In a way I can't even explain."

"Yeah. You don't have to," he said, in a quiet, faraway voice.

"What happened to you, Mickey?"

There was nothing on the line, and I had a sickening thought that he never called in the first place. That I was imagining the entire thing. But then, he was there.

He ignored my question. "I saw Benny two months ago. In a jail cell in Boston. He was sitting on the floor between a needle addict and a homeless drunk. He looked just the same, Will. He was the same little boy we knew . . . and he was there, looking at me with that hair in his eyes." He sniffed, and his voice cracked.

"Mickey—"

"And I've seen Coop. I feel like I'm losing my mind, but I've seen him. Swear to God. Only he never stays. Not like Benny. He always flashes, in and out of a crowd like trout in a river. But it's that red hair, the same eyes. Same smile. He told us we could be kings. You remember that?"

He let out a long flash of air. "My life . . . it was always on a bad path, Will. It was just bound to happen, I think. I fell into trouble, into worse things. I'm trying to get past it, to turn it around. I'm trying so hard.

"Seeing Benny, and Coop—I don't know. It put things in line. But when I saw the other one, that's when I knew. I'd just shot up, hadn't even taken off the rubber band when I saw him walk from the hallway into the bathroom. It was *me.* As a kid. From straight out of that . . . place. And I knew I was going to die. I don't think it's far off now. I think it's coming if I can't turn my life around. So I just . . . I just wanted to hear your voice."

"You remember how Miss Little held our hands that night in the infirmary?" I asked. "After?"

He didn't answer, but somehow I saw him nodding with closed eyes.

"Sometimes," I said, "when I'm sleeping, and my wife takes my hand, I dream that it's Miss Little. With her long brown hands, holding us. Those are the good dreams, but they don't come as much as the bad ones."

"The best parts of us now are the things we left behind. Have you ever thought of that?" he asked.

"Every day, Mickey. Every single day."

"I still don't know how to deal with that. It's been years. And I still don't know how."

"Come see me," I said. "Or maybe I could come there."

He waited, and then whispered into the telephone. "You all feel like ghosts to me. I keep trying to forget, but you keep coming back." His voice was more distant, I felt him slipping. "I loved you like a brother, Will."

Then he was gone. The barely there click on the line sounded like ice cracking. I couldn't hang up. I sat on the kitchen chair, holding the telephone to my ear. A beep began to sound, followed by a monotonous, recorded voice. And I was a thousand miles away. I was in Colorado.

ALMOST A MONTH TO THE DAY AFTER RECEIVING MICKEY'S PHONE call, I crawled out of bed earlier than usual. I was careful not to wake Mina, who looked all too comfortable, hair disheveled and face plowed deep into her pillow.

I'd tossed for most of the night, and gotten up three times for bathroom calls. I think I'd dreamed of the woods again, as I'd been doing ever since Mickey's call. I might have even dreamt of a large wet stone I once held in my hands in the Colorado mountains.

Sometimes, when I'm having those nightmares, Mina tries to wake me by brushing her fingers through my hair. Other times, she lets me ride them out, mumbling in my sleep, shaking my head. She says sometimes I kick my legs underneath the sheets. Once, she even found me standing halfway in the closet before she led me back to bed. That was where I kept Benny's jacks, but I never told her that.

On only the rarest of occasions, I'd secretly take down the jacks, to see if they really existed and were not just something I imagined. I'd give them a shake, the way Benny had all those years ago.

Quietly, I headed out to our small, detached one-car garage in the back. I no longer parked there. Years ago it had become a sort of makeshift workspace. Boxes, tools, and sawhorses took up most of the area.

Another Thanksgiving had come and gone, and Mina was asking for the Christmas junk. We kept most of it in cardboard boxes that proudly displayed HERDY'S MARKET on the side in big, fading red letters. Finding them, let alone getting to them, was always a chore.

I rummaged my way to the back of the garage, sorting through items that should have been thrown out years ago. This holiday hunt became a tradition for many years to follow, and finding everything always came with a thrill of victory. It was a conquest of sorts.

I was knee-deep in clutter and nearly finished when Mina called from the kitchen that breakfast was ready. And as I sat down to the table with my coffee and the morning paper, I found myself thumbing through the obituaries. I've always held a morbid habit of reading through them, never sure what I'm looking for, not looking for anything, really. But I stopped when my eyes caught the name. *Time* stopped. I stared at it, reading it again, and again, running my finger over the print. The picture was unmistakable. One ear. He'd aged, as we all had. Judging from his face, the years looked to have been hard, but his eyes . . . A person's eyes never change.

Edward Tokus. Died Thursday. He was fifty-three. Survivors include . . . of Chicago, of Akron, of St. Louis. Funeral to be held in St. Louis on Sunday.

I had told Mina very little—bits and pieces, really—about my time in Colorado. But once, I went into detail about the friends I made there. She knew there were parts too extreme and too painful to share, so she just let me talk; she didn't ask any questions. I think I might have told her if she ever pressed me, but I thank God she never did.

We left Chicago for St. Louis the day before the funeral. I still don't know why I went. It wasn't to pay respect to Eddie, I know that. Maybe I was holding on to some thin hope that Mickey might be there.

It was cold at the burial, and snow covered the ground and the tops of the grave markers. At the memorial service, we sat at the back of a small Presbyterian church, alone on the pew. There was a large photograph of Eddie, propped beside the casket and the flowers. I gazed at that portrait during the entire service, remembering things like how I'd once punched him in the throat while the madness of youth swarmed around us.

Mickey was neither at the church nor at the cemetery, and before the burial service even finished, I squeezed Mina's hand, and we quietly slipped away. That was when I saw Benny Fritch, running behind a copse of barren hackberry trees. He was still thirteen, and his floppy hair was as yellow as I could ever remember, and he was happy. He opened his mouth to laugh, and then fell away through the branches and leaves. Behind him, chasing, was a streak of red. A thin boy who disappeared as soon as I saw him.

I stood there in the snow, staring into the bony, white-barked trees beyond the graves, not able to move, not able to breathe, until Mina kissed me on the cheek and wrapped an arm around me.

"You're still here," she said.

CHAPTER

fifty-one

THE MORE TIME PASSED ME BY, THE MORE I LEARNED TO STOP looking in the bathroom mirror. It was just too damned depressing. I grew old. My life slipped away in a blur of brief moments of agony and happiness until one morning I awoke thinking Mina was still lying in bed next to me, face plowed into her pillow. I never get over that—realizing she's not there at all. That's usually how I begin my days.

Somewhere along the way, my hair has turned white and my face has wrinkled. And the odd thing, if I ever do stop to see what I've become, is how my eyes haven't changed at all. They still look like the eyes of a fourteen-year-old, searching for peace.

I still think of my friends at times. Of the wisdom we had, even at that age. And how blind we were at the same time.

There was once a boy who said we could be kings if we wanted. I think what still hurts so much was that we all believed him.

I'VE SEEN BENNY, AND COOP, AT ODD TIMES HERE AND THERE, EVER since that day at the cemetery in St. Louis. They come in and out of my world like coins on a sidewalk. But oddly, I haven't seen them since

Mina died. Maybe they realize I've suffered enough. Or perhaps I've just gotten too good at shutting myself off.

Tonight, I look out my bedroom window at the oak. It has withstood the storm and will likely see and survive far worse in the decades to come. I've spent two days writing all of this down, stopping to eat only occasionally, stopping to sleep even less. Writing it has been much like popping a few aspirin in an attempt to kill a chronic migraine. It doesn't take away the pain, but it helps a little.

I don't know what will become of this journal, or who will read it. It was for me, really. That's what's important. Now there's just one thing left to do. In the closet, next to where Benny's Sucrets box used to lie hidden away, is the handgun.

Thanksgiving has again come and gone, and if Mina were still here she would be pestering me to dig out several aged cardboard boxes. But she isn't here. I haven't celebrated Christmas since the year she died, four years ago. I honestly can't see the point in it.

And so, I draw these memories to an end. Tears are falling down my face, even as I write this. But I don't feel sad. I have loved during my life, and I have been loved, and I think that is the greatest thing anyone can accomplish.

I thought I was a good kid, but then I tried to kill my father. I know now it's okay to suffer that, to feel the regret and the guilt. But I'm most sorry I wasn't able to save you, Mom.

I WILL BIND THESE PAGES WITH A RUBBER BAND, AND LEAVE THEM lying on the pillow where my wife used to lay her sweet head. I love you, Angel. I love you, Coop, and Mickey. I love you, Benny. I'm sorry I took you into the woods.

CHAPTER
fifty-two

"YOU'RE STILL HERE," SHE ONCE SAID.

In my oddest dreams, or nightmares, I never would have believed I'd return to these pages. Yet, here I am, writing. I want to hurry, to land these thoughts on paper because just seeing them written might make them more real to me.

The gun. I took the thing down from the closet shelf and loaded it with two shells. I spent a considerable amount of time thinking about that one, too. I decided on two bullets in case I muffed the first shot. I've read too many times in the news about botched suicides, leaving people to stew in their own shit for the rest of their lives. If the first bullet didn't do the job . . . I don't know, maybe I'd have enough control to fire the second.

I also took the box of jacks from the bedside table. As an afterthought, I realized I wanted to leave the tin on top of the journal. It felt heavier, somehow, as I gave it a final shake. A pang of guilt washed quietly over my heart.

I opened the lid. Inside, four tarnished jacks lay still and silent, as if frightened by the sudden intrusion. There used to be five of them, but I left one on top of Mina's coffin before she was buried. I know how that sounds, but it just felt right. It still does.

The last person to really possess the jacks was Benny. He said he was going to take them back and surprise his brother, Todd, with them. That was the night John Church told us his story, the last night we were all together. That memory, along with so many others, was a scar on my soul that never fully healed.

No man has ever wept like one who has done so with a pistol shoved upside down in his mouth. I must have sounded like a three-year-old, wailing alone in my little yellow house. The muzzle was cold against the roof of my mouth, in stark contrast to the tears that filled my eyes and ran down my cheeks.

The hammer click-clacked back and I slipped my finger around the trigger. The barrel clattered against the top of my teeth as all strength threatened to leave my arm. Animal-like moans and grunts floated up through my throat and muffled mouth as I tried to work myself up to it.

And then I was running blindly, in the dark, in and out of the trees while Silas Green chased me like a bloodied rabbit. The branches scratched at my face and my feet slid into the leaves and needles of the forest floor. Benny's voice, deep and broken, echoed my own thoughts while I ran.

This kicked a door open in my mind, and his calm, whispered voice was suddenly there, all over again. In the fucking room.

"Had a dream . . . I saved your life somehow."

The gun fell into my lap and I screamed. I took it with both hands and fired into the ceiling, and then fired again. It felt like a dead thing in my hand after that, and I flung it across the room and fell to my knees sobbing.

CHAPTER
fifty-three

FOUR DAYS LATER, I WAS IN THE GARAGE, WONDERING WHY I WAS there with each passing minute. Christmas was two weeks away, and I'd gone to search for old cardboard boxes. I still didn't fully trust my reasoning, but after the failed attempt with the gun, I made a decision. To just play each day by ear. To just . . . stop, and to stop thinking.

I thought about the tree, and the ornaments, and decided that I wouldn't really be celebrating, but just setting them up more as a tribute to Mina. I was half covered in junk and boards and boxes when, in the distance, I heard the kitchen phone ring. I was too trapped to try and catch it, so I let it be. I had a machine, but had permanently turned it off a few years back. There was never really a need for one, anyway. I didn't even have a listed number. Then, finally, on what could have been the twentieth ring, it stopped.

I was in the farthest corner of the mess when it started to ring again.

"Son of a bitch. All right! All right!" I fell, fell again, then stumbled out of the garage and toward the back door. Inside the kitchen, fully expecting each ring to be the last, I picked up the phone.

There was silence. "Hello?" I said again.

The voice I finally heard was female, and sounded tired. "Hello? Oh,

I'm . . . Hi. Sorry, didn't think anyone was going to answer. My name is Rose Timmons. I'm looking for someone, was wondering if you could help me out."

"Probably can't," I sighed.

"I'm looking for a William Sheppard. I think he used to live at this residence about ten years ago."

"Guess you've got a bingo. I'm William Sheppard."

She was quiet.

"Hello? Still there?" I asked.

"Is this the William Sheppard who was in Colorado when he was fourteen?"

I didn't say anything. I couldn't.

". . . Will? Is it you?"

My words were so thin, even I barely heard them. "Yes. It's me."

Now she was quiet. "I can't believe I've found you."

Confusion's a funny thing. It can lead to childish, nonsensical fears. I suddenly had a thought—that there was some mistake, and after all these years the ranch had found me. To bring me back to serve another year or two, or ten, even though the place had long since been shut down.

"Exactly who has found me?" I asked.

"Let me introduce myself again, Mr. Sheppard. I'm Rose Timmons. I work at a retirement home in Grand Junction, Colorado. I'm a nurse and a caregiver for Doreen Little."

I had to sit down, but really, I more so fell into the chair than anything, hearing that name. It's odd how you just can't bury the past deep enough that it won't claw its way back up. "Miss Little . . ."

"Miss Little. And she has been looking for you, Will."

"Looking for me? She's still *alive*?" I asked.

This was met with warm laughter from the other end of the phone.

"Oh, yes. And kicking. Eighty-three years old, but she's still sharp as a knife, has all her wits about her, that's no lie. Let me try and explain. I've gotten to know her over the years, Will, and she has told me more than I'd have ever believed."

Rose Timmons went on to tell me how Miss Little had turned in her resignation the day after I left the ranch. Warden Barrow refused it, and told her she'd leave only after a replacement could be found, even if that took a year. So she stole the keys to a pickup truck and left during the middle of the night.

Miss Little went to Denver, and found work at a hospital. After only a few years, she was head director of nurses. She enjoyed a successful career, and was later offered a lucrative job at the largest hospital in Grand Junction, where she worked until retiring in her early seventies. She remained independent in her own house until breaking a leg, which brought about her move into the retirement home. She never married, and never had anyone but those in the home to care for her.

"She's talked about you and your friends so much to me, Will. She only really opened up about it all around a year ago. That's when I began to suggest she look you up. I guess the idea sort of stuck, and she started to grow excited with thoughts of you coming out here. She talks about you and Michael as her boys, and joked that you just need to bring your wife, if you have one, and move."

"I . . . I don't have a wife. She passed away, four years ago." It still hurt to say that out loud. I suppose it always will, but that's not such a bad thing, really.

"Oh. I'm sorry, Will. I truly am."

"You said 'you and Michael.' Did you mean . . . Mickey?"

"Michael Baines. Yes. That was the miracle, actually. He sort of dropped off the radar fifteen years back. But I have a talent for finding things. I searched for a long time, but we finally found him. Just a week ago, in Eugene, Oregon. He's a prominent resident there, and owns a couple of successful printing shops. To tell the truth, that's how we finally found you. He faxed me your number this morning. And now, he's already on his way. Should be here tomorrow, in fact. What do you say, Will? What about you, now?"

My heart was at the bottom of my stomach, kicking and flipping like a gasping fish. Michael Baines. Mickey. Business owner. Oregon. "You mean, to live there?" I asked.

Rose laughed. "For now, just come, Will. And don't worry about anything. Miss Little said so herself. She'd literally be telling you right now, but she's out with a couple of the other nurses buying new outfits. You should have seen her face when Mickey told her he was coming."

"He *talked* to her?" Everything felt like it was happening, and not happening, at the same time. I looked over at the small black-and-white picture of Mina that I still kept on the ledge over the kitchen sink. I'd taken it one Thanksgiving morning, sneaking up on her. She was dusted in flour from head to waist, and the happiness in her face was mesmerizing. After she died, it always hurt to look at that picture, and so I didn't. But now I felt something else deep in my soul when I looked at it. I felt a forgiveness for who I had become these past four years.

"Yes, of course they've talked!" Rose said. "Come on, Will. What do you say? Come see her before she gets any older."

Mina would have loved a trip to Colorado. Mickey would be there. And shockingly, Miss Little. A new feeling seeped into my body, one that at first I could not identify. It had been too long since I experienced anything of the sort. Excitement.

What I said was more of a broken whisper. "Okay."

"Will?"

"Okay. Tell them I'm coming." My excitement rose, and the tears came again, only this time they were ones of an immeasurable joy.

She screamed into the phone, laughed and cried, all at the same time. We talked for a little while longer. We spoke of arrangements, and I told her I would leave Chicago by bus. I could have flown, but it wouldn't have felt right. No, leaving by bus, as I had years ago, was fitting, and it would give me time. Time to contemplate and to reminisce. To try to find that boy I used to be and to try and find my way back to him. At least time to prepare.

After I said good-bye and hung up the phone, I walked to the ledge and picked up the small picture frame. I removed the photo, kissed it, and dropped it into my shirt pocket, where it would remain close to my heart.

I went to the bedroom closet, pulled down a shoebox. Inside was the gun. The next day, I took it to a local pawn shop and received a hundred and forty dollars, which I put toward the bus ticket.

The tin box. I still knew what I had to do, and it scared me. I was frightened of the person I might find, the person to whom that box rightfully belonged. Was he still alive? In Colorado, I'd get Rose and Mickey to help me find Todd Fritch.

And this thick manual of pages, filled with my messy handwriting? I'm going to take them with me. They are my thoughts and experiences, and I realize now I can't just leave them behind. I've created my own invaluable possession. Terrible, but cathartic.

My nervousness was becoming outweighed by my excitement, and that was good. For an aging man, it was better than good. It was fucking A.

CHAPTER

fifty-four

Once again, I found myself on a Greyhound bus traveling to Colorado. It was cold, and the seat was cramped, but I didn't care. I was excited and anxious and too happy to be bothered by much of anything. I packed only one bag, which was down below, and inside my jacket pocket was my flour-dusted Mina. I felt alive, *really* alive, for the first time in a long time, and people had to wonder just what could make an old man smile so often while sitting on a crowded and cold bus. I told myself I was just going for a visit. Nothing drastic.

I told myself that.

It was a surreal thing to travel the same path into the mountains that I took as a thirteen-year-old boy. The feelings inside me were so different, yet the scenery was exactly as I remembered. There was no hailstorm this time, and I said a prayer of thanks for that. I'm not sure how I would've handled it; I probably would have taken it as some sort of omen. I cracked my window as we ventured higher and higher into the rugged peaks, and, for the first time in decades, was comforted by the sweet aroma of the mountain pines that seeped into the bus.

Six seats ahead of me, I saw a crop of red hair, and when Coop turned around and looked at me through those thick glasses, I wasn't afraid like the previous times I'd seen him. And I could have sworn he was holding a book. Cooper Kingston. He liked magic tricks, and worshipped literature. He was smart, and caring. Sometimes he had thin skin, but Coop had such a good heart. He was our older brother and he was my friend, but as soon as I saw him, Coop was gone, replaced by a brunette listening to an iPod.

Across the aisle from me was Benny Fritch. When I saw him, I caught my breath, and wanted to reach out. He was *there,* as real as I was. Benny, with his floppy blond hair, and his razor-sharp blue eyes. Sometimes we called him Lunch Meat. He was his heart, and his heart was him. He trusted me. He was a genius with horses. He would have done anything for us, would have died for us. Without question, he was the best of us all. "You were my friend," I mouthed.

He smiled at me, and the next time I looked back, he, too, was gone. But not really. I felt him. I felt both of them, and the peace that filled me was just as great as the sadness. I can live with that.

The bus arrived in Grand Junction early, and I decided to wait for my welcoming party across the street at a small neighborhood park. I was glad to have just a little more time to think about where I was, and why I was there. I was nervous, and had no idea what to expect. I sat on a bench and kept watch for Rose Timmons pushing a frail, elderly woman along in a wheelchair.

When a silver Cadillac pulled up, I was shocked to see the woman who stepped out of the passenger's seat. I'd imagined a crippled, age-riddled Miss Little, shrunk into a chair. But instead, Doreen Little was the very definition of vitality. At eighty-three, she looked more like she was in her late sixties.

And then, Mickey was there. He was unmistakable. Just shorter than Miss Little, but filled out. His face was lined, as my own was, from a hard life, but he looked so healthy. His hair was now silver. And when he saw me, and smiled, his eyes squinted, and were lost within a sea of freckles. In that moment, he looked so much like the boy I'd known a lifetime ago that I had to catch my breath.

I ran to them. We all embraced, and laughed, and cried, out of such an unbelievable happiness. The moment was something too good to really be happening. We must have looked ridiculous, but we didn't care. I will keep that afternoon forever with the perfect clarity of a snapshot.

"My boys!" Miss Little said. "My boys have come home to me."

In that instant, I had a family.

In that moment, I was home.

WE STAYED AT THAT PARK FOR WELL OVER AN HOUR. WE WERE ALL too excited and too filled with happiness to do anything but sit at a picnic table. I often became lost underneath much of the talk, staring at the way Mickey's eyes still squinted behind the wash of freckles. My God, I felt like we were still kids. Could all of these aching years really have passed? Miss Little's voice and laugh were just as I remembered. I almost told her how Mickey and I watched her that night, through her window. Watched her sing to Etta James, but in the end that was the one thing we each kept to ourselves.

"Life do come around," she said. "Don't it? Don't life just come around! Lord, I dreamed of you boys for years. *So* many years. Dreamed I could . . . hold your hands, like that night I sat with you."

She looked from Mickey to me, but . . . that's not right. She looked through us, as if seeing a long-lost memory, or maybe the ghost of an old friend. She knows, I thought. She knows I put a gun to my face just weeks before. I could be wrong about that, but I don't think so.

I looked down, into the splitting wood of the table, and she said, "You're not haunted anymore, are you, child?" She smiled, the way someone might when they already know the answer.

"No, ma'am. Not anymore," I said.

"No more," she said. "None of us. No more."

I pulled the blue tin box from my pocket, and placed it on the table between myself and Mickey. He stopped talking in midsentence, and his words lost their strength, like a water spigot slowly being twisted off. He picked it up, felt its weight, the *realness* of it, and examined it with wet eyes.

"I want to give them back," I said.

He nodded, opening the box. "We'll find him. If he's alive, we'll find him. We'll take them back."

Did I know then, or at least suspect, that I was going to stay? There, in Colorado? Probably. Really, there was nothing to return to in Chicago except an empty house. And an empty life.

A hand covered my own. It was soft, and motherly. Miss Little pushed her glasses higher on her nose, and smiled a triumphant smile.

She said, "My boys."

CHAPTER
fifty-five

MOUNTAIN VIEW CEMETERY, RAPID CITY, SOUTH DAKOTA. THE winds softened, and the early spring morning showed promise of a breaking sun. That was good. Tall groupings of trees hung still around us, a quiet backdrop to the small, colorless headstones all around. We sat beside one of them—an ordinary, pale granite block that had a small crack weathered across one side. But to me, and to Mickey, the grave was anything but ordinary.

We sat that way for a long time, not saying much. Not saying anything at all. At one point, Mickey cried, quietly. I had no more tears to give. I reached up, and ran my knobby fingers along the etching. Along the name and the date. There were two headstones next to it with identical surnames, although they didn't look as old, or worn.

"Did he hate me, for leaving the way I did?" Mickey asked, his eyes lost in the marker next to us. "Charging off into the woods with my gun, leaving you two behind?"

"He never hated you," I said. "He was confused. But he knew you tried to save us. He was just sad, and worried. But he never hated you."

Mickey nodded, thinking on this.

"I've tried to stop replaying those days in my head," I said. "Doing that only makes them less clear to me. I used to feel responsible for him. For taking him up into the mountains."

Mickey said, "You shouldn't."

"I don't, anymore. I've recently made peace with that. We were only children. It's the ones who were in charge who made the mistakes. We were only left to pick up what was left."

"He should have never been there," Mickey said.

"We'd have never met him if he weren't."

He nodded. "I'd have rather not met him than be sitting here right now."

I reached into my coat's breast pocket, and brought out the blue Sucrets box. The coloring had faded over the years, and it squeaked when I opened it. Inside, there were now three tarnished jacks.

Just one month earlier, we'd been at a different cemetery, in a different state. And just as I had then for Cooper Kingston, I took one jack, and I placed it on top of Benny's headstone.

"We miss you, Benny." Somewhere in the Black Hills sky above us, a hawk screeched. I closed the tin box and slipped it back into my pocket. I rose to leave, and waited on Mickey. I gave the headstone one final look. It simply read:

BENJAMIN FRITCH
FEB 19, 1950—SEP 29, 1964

Mickey said, "Good-bye, Lunch," and gave the headstone a single pat. "I love you, man. We all did." He wiped his face, and stood. The sun broke through the clouds for the first time that morning, and shone bright on his upturned face. He smiled.

I patted the folded map in my pocket, and felt my heart jump at the thought of meeting Todd Fritch, not even ten miles from where we now stood. It would be hard, and emotional, recounting the days that we knew his brother. But it would also be necessary. I'd have to stop, first, and purchase some new jacks, to fill the tin box. I remembered Benny once telling me how he had done the same.

We walked together through the cemetery, back to the car.

Mickey talked, I listened. We made such plans in Colorado and we were already making new ones. Listening to Mickey talk now—it still sounded like a dream. We were going to buy some land, of course. Start a small horse ranch outside Grand Junction. Just why the hell not, was Mickey's reasoning. We were going to take care of Miss Little, not that she really needed much help. In our vision, in our greatest dream of dreams, we could see it all: horses, sunny days, laughter. Cards at night. Maybe Todd would even come. Whenever he wanted, for as long as he wanted.

And as Mickey talked, I couldn't help but suddenly notice two young boys, sitting cross-legged beneath a ponderosa in the far corner of the cemetery. They didn't notice us. They didn't seem to have a care in the world.

"Did you say something, Will?" Mickey asked.

It still makes me sad to see them. But I hope they never truly leave.

Acknowledgments

I'D LIKE TO TAKE JUST A MOMENT TO GIVE CREDIT WHERE CREDIT IS due. You hear all the time that no novel is really written alone, and while I'd like to think the first draft does indeed roll out of my mind unassisted, there's that whole rewriting and revising part. That's where a good deal of the magic is made, and also where much assistance is usually given.

I'd like to thank Amy and the boys, of course. Amy read many of the pages first and promptly informed me which ones stunk and which ones did not. My parents, Robert and Evelyn Hilton. When I was a child, my mother instilled in me a love of art—drawing, painting, and creating stories. But the most important thing I ever learned from them was to believe in myself. Thanks, Mom and Dad. Then there are my friends, Denny Vitola, Lyse Salpeter, Bob Nailor, and Mitch Whitington—these guys offered as much support and advice about endurance as they did about writing, not to mention some great recipes here and there.

Now, if a writer has a halfway decent agent, he should most certainly be grateful. I, however, believe I landed one of the best in the game, hands down, when I took the call from Laney Katz Becker. She drew my manuscript straight from the slush pile, and neither of us has looked back since. I feel truly blessed to be under your wing, Laney. My deepest appreciation goes out to my editor, Kerri Kolen, who championed this novel in the first place at Simon & Schuster. She did a crackerjack job on each and every page, making it a better book than I ever hoped it could be. There are always hard decisions to make when revising—pages to slash and characters to downsize, but Kerri never once strayed from the heart of the story. Thanks also to Kate Ankofski for her dedicated assistance and hard work. I'm forever grateful to everyone on the Simon & Schuster team who pitched in and worked on this project. Thank you.

And to whoever has read along this far, I am humbled and most gracious. I truly hope you enjoyed the show.

—DEH (2011)

About the Author

DAVID E. HILTON earned a bachelor's degree from Howard Payne University in 1998. He wrote *Kings of Colorado* mostly in his apartment's stairwell just after the birth of his first son. He spends his spare time either writing or training his miniature dachshund to run in the annual Budda Weiner Dog Races. He lives just outside Austin.